WARPED DESIRE

"It has to be this way every weekend," Laura said as we lay side by side.

"How can it be? My father will be home."

"After he has gone to sleep I can come to you."

"What if he should catch us?"

"He won't catch us. We'll be smart. He's a sound sleeper but if that doesn't work out we can always take a ride into the country."

I sighed and closed my eyes.

This was my father's wife.

And my lover....

THE STRANGEST SIN

"Sharon Doyle felt dirty when she woke up in Jimmy Slade's bed, but that wasn't unusual. She always felt dirty after a night of passion in Jimmy's cheap room..."

Sharon owns a bar and too often ends up blotto at the end of the evening, letting Jimmy take her back to his place. Her neighbor Carl Evans is a nicer guy, but he won't make a move. Between them is Bert Robinson, the local racketeer who wants Sharon all to himself, no matter what it takes. But Sharon is tired of them. She finds herself more attracted to her bartender, Lucy, who keeps the local guys satisfied in a room upstairs. It's a lit-fuse situation, and all it takes is a single act of violence to set it off.

WARPED DESIRE

·

THE STRANGEST SIN

·

TWO NOVELS BY

Orrie Hitt

WRITING AS KAY ADDAMS

INTRODUCTION BY

James Reasoner

Stark House Press · Eureka California

WARPED DESIRE / THE STRANGEST SIN

Published by Stark House Press
1315 H Street
Eureka, CA 95501, USA
griffinskye3@sbcglobal.net
www.starkhousepress.com

ISBN: 978-1-944520-95-3

Book design by *jcaliente/design*, Austin, Texas
Original cover art by Paul Rader from Midwood Books
edition of *Strange Breed* (1960)

PUBLISHER'S NOTE

First Stark House Press Edition: November 2019

A PRO, START TO FINISH
by James Reasoner

Look around on-line and you can find plenty of scholarly articles about the sociological significance of the rise of what's come to be known as Lesbian Pulp Fiction during the 1950s and '60s. There are also numerous essays written by lesbians about how important those quickly produced, luridly packaged paperback novels were to them. Especially for women in smaller, more isolated communities, the books were proof that other people like them really did exist in the world, when much of the time it must have seemed like they were utterly alone. This is yet another way in which popular fiction demonstrates its true worth. Most of these articles and essays are excellent, and if you're interested in the subject, I recommend you do some searching on-line and read them.

This introduction isn't one of those scholarly articles or personal essays. I'm neither an academic nor a lesbian, so while I can read, appreciate, and enjoy those other approaches to the subject, they don't really resonate down inside my gut.

No, this is about a guy sitting at the kitchen table in his house in a small town in New York, sitting there with a typewriter in front of him while the hectic lives of his wife and kids (and sometimes the neighborhood kids) swirl around him as he pounds out reams and reams of fiction between drags on a cigarette and sips from a cup of iced coffee, making a living for himself and his family with the words that flow from his brain to his fingers and onto the page.

Now, *that* guy I can identify with. His name was Orrie Hitt.

•

But before we talk about Orrie (and yeah, I feel enough of a kinship with him to call him by his first name, just like when I talk about Robert E. Howard I often refer to him as Bob, even though we never met, either), a little background is in order. During the first half of the Twentieth Century, novels appeared occasionally in which lesbian characters were either the protagonists or played supporting roles in the story, but it wasn't until 1950, the first year of an explosion in original paperback fiction, that lesbian novels began to be recognized as a separate, potentially lucrative genre. That "potentially lucrative" angle was what mattered to the publishers, and when Tereska Torres' novel *Women's Barracks* sold four million copies for Gold Medal, editors and writers sat up and took notice.

Torres' novel about female soldiers during World War II had a lot more to its plot than a lesbian storyline, but that was part of it and the part that people in the business seized on as the reason for its popularity. *Spring Fire* by Vin Packer (Marijane Meaker) soon followed from Gold Medal, along with novels by Ann Bannon, who also wrote non-fiction volumes about lesbians under the name Ann Aldrich.

Other publishers jumped on the bandwagon, as publishers will, and during the next two decades, scores of lesbian-themed novels appeared from lower-rung houses such as Beacon, Softcover Library (a later incarnation of Beacon), Midwood, and Nightstand (and its associated imprints). Some of the more prestigious paperback publishers put out lesbian novels, too, but the genre was a mainstay of the "Adult Reading" outfits. And this doesn't even take into account all the outright pornography featuring lesbians published during that era, especially during the later Sixties as the books became more graphic and more about the sex, rather the combination of sex and surprisingly compelling human storylines from the Fifties and early Sixties.

Experts on the genre estimate that only a few dozen out of these hundreds of books were written by actual lesbians, and they're the ones that get the most attention these days. Most of the others were written by veteran paperbackers, guys (yes, nearly all male) who were literary chameleons, capable of writing about suburban swingers this week, seductive coeds next week, and lesbians the week after that. Or suburban lesbians or lesbian coeds, if that's what the editor wanted. Whatever they had to do to get the next manuscript in the mail and the next check making its way to them.

Many of these writers had enough talent to string together enough words in a readable fashion, on the right subjects, to keep the publishers' printing presses working, but that was all they had going for them and their books are largely forgotten. Some possessed that extra spark that raised their efforts to a higher level. They never turned out a really bad book, and when they were on their game, their novels were excellent and still hold up well today as fine examples of storytelling and craftsmanship. A few were good enough that they went on to much better things and their careers soared. We know their names: Block, Westlake, Silverberg, Hunter, Ellison, and more.

Which brings us to Orrie Hitt.

•

Nobody ever poured their heart into their books more than Orrie. And Orrie's heart was with the little guy. "Guy" being a non-gender-specific word in this case, because it included all the gals who were down on their luck, too. The ones who struggled to escape their upbringing by slipshod parents, the ones who fell for the wrong man, the ones trapped by circumstances. In fact, "trapped" may be the best word to describe all of Orrie Hitt's protagonists, male and female. They struggle mightily to defeat the overwhelming odds against them, but they just can't quite do it. And so they turn to other things for solace: sex, drink, drugs, violence . . . The game of life is rigged against them, they decide, and so for a time they give up.

But deep inside them, a defiant spark still burns, a desire to do the right thing, to live as decent human beings, and if they just keep trying hard enough, long enough, eventually those efforts will be rewarded.

In Orrie Hitt's world, they usually are, but man, he puts his people through the wringer first. Because people is what they are, not just characters. Not to Orrie. He believes in them, and he doesn't want to let them down.

With this enormous amount of empathy that Hitt brought to his work, it's no surprise that he would feature lesbian characters frequently in his books. Not only do they have the same worries as his other female characters—getting mixed up with lousy guys, bad jobs, cruel bosses, the fear of getting pregnant—but they have to struggle with their sexuality as well, along with the knowledge that if they give in to their "warped desires" (hmm, that sounds like a good title), they'll be ostracized by the society around them. There's not much sense of empowerment in Hitt's treatment of lesbians, but such a concept didn't really exist in that era—and let's face it, not many of Hitt's characters are empowered to start with.

But he was always a canny pro, and he knew that lesbian scenes helped sell manuscripts. Even in his books where the female protagonists are straight, there will often be a scene or two of lesbian experimentation. And in some of his novels, the lesbian relationships are at the center of the plot. For these novels, he sometimes used a female pseudonym: Kay Addams.

•

Beacon Books published *Warped Desires* in 1960, under the Kay Addams name and with a cover that leaves no doubt what sort of book it is. Unlike many of Hitt's novels that center around the lower financial class, the narrator/protagonist of this one is a wealthy young woman named Doris Foster. Her father, a former actor, is now a lumber yard tycoon in the small city of Benton. Her mother died trying to give birth to the child that would have been Doris's little brother, and she blames her father for that tragedy. She also hates him because he's taken a mistress, a gorgeous brunette who's only four years older than Doris herself.

Doris, who's a beautiful blonde, has graduated from high school and, as the novel opens, is about to go off to college at Cedarcliff, an exclusive, all-girls school that's about eighty miles away. For the first time in her life, she'll be out on her own.

Before that can happen, her boyfriend, the manager of her father's lumber yard, proposes to her, and Doris accepts his ring even though she really doesn't believe they'll ever get married. This feeling is reinforced when the guy pressures her into giving up her virginity to him before she leaves for college. She hates and fears the experience. Most of the women in Hitt's novels fear becoming pregnant, and this feeling is heightened even more than usual in Doris because she's convinced that if she does, she'll die, too, just like her mother did.

So she hates sex with men, worries that she's not a real woman, goes off to an all-girls school, and winds up with a beautiful roommate in the dorm. What do *you* think is going to happen?

Well, of course she gives in to her warped desires (there's that phrase again), with more than one partner, and along the way Doris gets some more experience with men, too. In fact, she learns a lot about sex and life and herself, and Hitt spins this fairly sordid yarn in such smooth, readable prose that the pages race by. I understand that books such as this, written by male authors under female pseudonyms and aimed at a primarily male readership, aren't the lesbian novels from that era that are the subject of academic articles and personal essays, but as an example of a sort of genre that sold a lot of books for Hitt and other authors, you won't find a better one.

•

The Strangest Sin, published by Beacon in 1961, is somewhat different. It qualifies as lesbian fiction, but that relationship is only part of a much larger plot that winds up almost epic in scope. *The Strangest Sin* is really about the disintegration of a small town when the manufacturing plant that is its major employer closes down. In order to tell this story, Hitt splits up the action among three roughly equal protagonists: Sharon Doyle, a lovely 22-year-old blonde who has inherited a working class bar from her parents; Lucy Forbes, who works for Sharon in the bar but turns a few tricks on the side as an amateur prostitute, despite feeling a longing for Sharon; and ne'er-do-well reform school graduate Jimmy Slade, who has an affair with Sharon, lusts after Lucy, and whose main ambition in life is to go to work for Bert Robinson, the sleazy gangster who runs the criminal underworld in the small city where they all live.

Lucy has had a lesbian relationship in the past, and Sharon is drawn to her, too, so inevitably they wind up in bed together. But while all this is going on, Sharon also has to cope with the bar's economic downturn as a result of the factory closing, as well as breaking off her affair with Jimmy, which has come to disgust her. Jimmy is torn between fully embracing the world of crime and gangsters or trying to better himself, something that has always seemed impossible to him. A lucky break appears to put him on the right path, but then his luck turns bad. So does Lucy's, when she finds herself hiding out from the law because she's blamed for a crime she didn't commit, and her only way out of trouble seems to be a bizarre stranger who lives in a shack by the river. Meanwhile, like an evil spider, Bert Robinson pulls the strings behind the scenes to manipulate the three of them, willing to go to any lengths to get what he wants.

Hitt keeps all these plot elements swirling in masterful

fashion, and his storytelling abilities and sympathy for his downtrodden characters are at their heights. I don't know if he intended for this to be a Kay Addams book when he wrote it or if the editors at Beacon put that pseudonym and the lesbian-sounding title on it, but it doesn't really matter. Either way, *The Strangest Sin* is a grand story, a noir epic that's one of Orrie Hitt's best books.

•

Together, *Warped Desires* and *The Strangest Sin* are a potent combination, a one-two punch of solid storytelling and characterization and heart. Earlier, I mentioned some of the writers who toiled in the same literary vineyard as Orrie Hitt but went on to bigger and better things. Orrie never did. He continued sitting in his kitchen turning out books, plagued by shady publishers and worsening health. His last novel was published in 1970. He passed away from cancer in 1975, spending his last days in a VA hospital. During his life, he achieved a certain amount of fame (or notoriety) in his hometown as an author, but he never made a fortune. By all accounts, though, he was a happy man, a good husband and father who was devoted to his family, and I suspect he enjoyed his writing and liked knowing that there were readers out there being entertained by his work . . . and, if they stopped and thought about it, maybe learning a little about human nature, too. Once he was gone, though, his books and his name slipped into obscurity for many years.

During the past decade, there's been a revival of interest in Orrie and his work, and I'm proud to have played a small part in that. Many of his books are available again, in both print and ebook editions, and a new generation of readers has discovered the novels of this talented, big-hearted wordsmith. I think it's safe to say that Orrie Hitt is one of my heroes, not only because of the books he wrote but also because of the way he conducted his life and his career. The man was a pro, start to finish.

He was also enormously entertaining to read. Check out these two novels and you'll see what I mean.

—Azle, TX
August 2019

James Reasoner is the author of more than 350 novels and many short stories in a career spanning more than thirty years. He married his wife Livia Washburn in 1976, and they had two daughters. Reasoner has used at least nineteen pseudonyms, in addition to his own name, including several co-written with his wife. Early in his career, Reasoner did freelance work for newspapers. For several years, he and his wife owned two local bookstores. His first novel, a mystery called *Texas Wind*, was published in 1980, but Reasoner's primary focus over the years has been writing stories of the old west.

WARPED
DESIRE

I had been given many things. A name, of course—Doris Foster, to be exact. I had been given beauty—there was no doubt in my mind about that. And I had been given intelligence and feelings. Oh, many feelings. Feelings for men, for instance. But there were some feelings in me I really wasn't sure about—feelings circling around Laura Stevens, and.... But I'm getting ahead of my story.

Let me go back to my last night at home.

I dressed carefully, trying on three dresses before I settled on a clinging blue one with a high neckline. I seldom use lipstick but I applied some and noticed in the mirror that the shade of red went very well with my long, blonde hair. As I leaned forward, biting down on a tissue, my blue eyes stared back at me. George Richards said I had the bluest eyes in Benton, population fourteen thousand, and he may have been right. But, then, George had said lots of things to me during the six months I had been going out with him.

"I love you," George had often said. "I love you so crazy that it hurts."

George worked for my father as office manager of the Foster Lumber Yard and he had been trying to date me for a long time before I had finally given in. That had been right after I had been named queen of the senior class and he had escorted me to the biggest school dance of the year. My father had been pleased that I had gone with George.

"He's a comer," my father had said. "The day will come when I'll turn the whole operation of the business over to him."

I thought that my father, only forty-four, was a little young to be thinking of retiring, but he had the biggest lumber business in the county and he had made a great deal of money from it. At one time he had been a successful actor, but after the death of my mother, when I had been twelve, he had invested his savings and all he had been able to borrow into a venture everybody had considered risky. However, my father had worked hard and it had paid off. Our big home on Central Drive was free of any debt. Dad gave me a hundred dollars a month allowance. He drove a Caddy and I drove a new Ford. But no matter how much money my father had, he could not buy the respect that I should have had for him.

I left the dresser and crossed the room. It was a wonderful room overlooking the swimming pool installed the year before. The whole house was wonderful. Nothing, my father frequently explained, was too good for us. It was funny, but whenever he said that I thought he was talking about Laura Stevens.

Laura was only twenty-two, but she owned a dress shop in town. She had dark hair and dark eyes and she often bragged that nature had more than generously endowed her breasts. When she was at our house, which was almost every night, she often wore a sweater without a bra. Her excuse was that she was tired of being confined all the time.

"Let 'em bounce," she had said to me more than once. "Everybody knows I've got them."

I didn't care much for Laura and this was one of the reasons I was glad to be going away to school. I knew that I would miss my friends in Benton—how much would I miss George?—but I had visited Cedarcliff during the summer and it had seemed a nice enough place. The school, a very expensive one, lay outside Cedarcliff itself, a town of less than two thousand people.

"No boys are allowed on the grounds," Miss Lily had told me. I hadn't learned her last name but Miss Lily was in charge of the school. "Just on Saturday nights. We put on a dance for our three hundred girls and the nice boys from town are invited."

She had said the word "nice" as though hardly any boy qualified and I had decided that most of my dancing would be done with other girls. Nina Wilbur, who was to room with me and who was in her third year, had assured me that it wasn't as bad as that, that nearly a hundred boys showed up every Saturday night.

"They're after one thing," Nina had added. "Give you one guess what it is."

I didn't need one guess. I knew. Every boy I had ever met had been after the same reward. In high school many of the girls had talked about it and some of them had said that it was fine. I hadn't believed them. Sex to me, because of what I remembered about my mother, had been an ugly, dirty thing, an act which appealed only to the animals.

"Don't," I had heard my mother say to my father many times.

"Why not?"

"You know what the doctor said. He said if I had another baby it might kill me."

I had been young then, very young, so young that I had often shared the same hotel room with them, but the desperation of my mother's pleas had been enough to make me hate him.

"What are you worried about?" he had always demanded. "We've been at it these many years and Doris is the only one who's come along."

But she had had something to worry about and it had happened. He had made her big with another child and she had died while trying to give it birth. The baby, a boy, had also died.

"There are two kinds of luck," my father had said to me. "Good and bad. We had some bad."

It had left me with a fear of what the male wanted to do to the female. Until I had gone with George I had avoided every boy who had wanted to take me out. In George, I had thought, I had found somebody different. He was older than the boys in the school, a Cornell graduate, and he was tall and rather handsome. It had been often necessary for him to come up to the house to see my father and discuss business; and despite all my fears I had been attracted to him.

"I won't hurt you," he had told me the first night we had been together. "I'll never hurt you, Doris."

We had gone for a ride that night, not a long one, and when we had returned to the house my father had been waiting for me.

"I'm glad to see that you're breaking out of your shell," my father had said after George had gone. "I haven't mentioned it before but it's had me worried. You're only young once and you're meant to enjoy life. You haven't been doing it."

Now as I put on my blue flats and checked the seams of my stockings, I wondered if my father was enjoying his life. I guessed that he was. Success had brought him money and money had brought him Laura Stevens. He was, I knew, making the most of both.

I was early for my date and I sat on the edge of my bed, remembering. On hot nights I had usually left my bedroom door open, and more than once I had heard Laura and my father in the bedroom across the hall, making love. These instances had left me in a state of moral and physical sickness. How could they treat love so lightly and cheat the decency around us? I had asked myself these questions many times but I had never been able to find the answers. What Laura and my father shared was not love or anything close to love. It was the driving, hungry need of savages.

I arose from the bed and found my pocketbook. Yes, I would be glad to get away from the house and forget them.

I opened the door and stepped into the hall.

"Doris?"

As I stopped and turned I saw Laura coming toward me from the direction of one of the bathrooms, probably the one at the end of the hall. She was stark naked, her body alive and moving, and I assumed that she had just taken a shower. This was another thing she did every night she was here. Nor did she bother to wear any clothes while she wandered around upstairs.

"I may not see you in the morning before you leave," Laura said, coming up to me. "I want to wish you all luck."

"Thank you."

I had seen her this way many times before and, regardless of what I thought of her relationship with my father, just the sight of her wondrously female body fascinated me.

"You don't like me," she said, suddenly. "Do you?"

I did not know quite what to say.

She continued. "You think I'm a slut because I keep your father happy, don't you?" She tossed her head and her dark eyes flashed.

"I don't want to argue," I said.

"It isn't an argument. It's the truth. And if I were you I'd probably feel the same. On the other side of it, you have to admit I brought him some measure of happiness and he has given me some, too. It isn't a question of age. Age has nothing to do with it. It's a question of respect and of knowing that you're doing the right thing, knowing it in your own heart. My parents are furious about this but it doesn't bother me any. I have my life to live and they have theirs. That also goes for your father and for you, as well as me."

I couldn't help staring at her, at all of the glory of her womanhood. Why was this? Even when I saw a beautiful girl on the street I was instantly attracted to her, wondering if she had ever known love, wondering if she felt about some things the way I did. Many times I had tried to decide the reason for this but I had always come up with a blank.

"You may not be wrong about living your own life," I said. "It isn't very important whether or not you are. I have never tried to change my father and I'm not going to start now. He's old enough to know what he's doing."

"That's the way to look at it."

She left me and entered one of the bedrooms. I knew how she would dress. She would put on shorts that were short-short and a halter that could only make a feeble effort at covering her.

I was ashamed of my father and Laura for what they were always doing to each other, ashamed at myself for knowing what they were doing. Some night, I thought, he would give her a baby and then they would have to be married. That was why I had decided on going away to college, on becoming a teacher, on earning my own way as soon as I could.

Now I walked to the stairs and started down. I hoped that my father wouldn't be in the living room and that I wouldn't have to talk to him. I couldn't look at him without seeing the pretty face of my mother, without remembering her pleas and her pregnancy and her death. He had, I thought, destroyed her with his bull-like need and for this I could never forgive him.

He was in the living room and he held a drink in one hand. He had been drinking a lot lately, possibly due to the influence of Laura, and there were fine lines starting to show in his otherwise handsome face.

"Hi," he said, smiling.

"Hi."

"Final date with George tonight?"

"Our goodbye date."

He asked me if I wanted a drink and I told him I didn't. It wasn't that I didn't drink. I did, once in a while. It was just that I didn't care for one at the moment.

"Laura is concerned about you," he said.

"Why?"

"Because she thinks you hate her."

"Let's not go into that." I placed my pocketbook on a chair near the front door. "What you do is your own affair."

He took a long drink from his glass.

"I'm glad to hear you say that." He paused and he was no longer smiling. "I may marry Laura. I don't know yet. We've talked about it some but we haven't decided. You think these things over before you go into them."

"Yes," I said mechanically.

"She'd make a good wife and now that you're going away I'll need somebody in the house. I don't want to go on the way I have been going. There isn't any sense to it. People talk and I've heard some of the things they've said."

I had heard the stories, too, of how he was keeping her, and the remarks had hurt. I had also heard that he had put up most of the money for her dress shop but I didn't know about that. All I knew was that I couldn't imagine him married to her. I would have a stepmother only four years my senior and I would never be comfortable in the same house with her.

"You can add two thousand dollars to your checking account," my father said, draining his glass. "I put that much in the bank for you today."

I already had more than a thousand.

"You didn't have to do that," I said.

"No, but I wanted to. You'll be away from home and there'll be things you will need." He walked to a cabinet and picked up a bottle of scotch. "I just hope you'll come home weekends. It's only eighty miles. The roads are good and you can be here in no time flat."

I had made up my mind that I would only return home during vacation periods but I didn't tell him that.

"All right," I said. "It will depend upon how much work I have to do."

"They say the school is tough."

"I guess it is."

"It ought to be pretty good though, considering the kind of money it costs. With what they charge they should make a fortune on just two hundred girls."

Cedarcliff had been his idea and not mine. He had wanted me to have the best. I would much rather have gone to a bigger school.

"George is late," I said, having nothing better to say.

"He's probably at the yard. Considering the hours he puts in, you'd think he owned the business."

Laura came down the stairs and she had on a halter not much more than a bra. Her shorts, high on her thighs, set off straight and well-formed legs. I couldn't look at her without the memory of her bare flesh coming back to me. My head began to pound.

Some day Laura would probably be my second mother.

She poured herself a drink. Right then, recalling what my father had said, I myself needed a drink. But I would have a drink or two later with George. Maybe more.

Suddenly, staring down the drive for the coming of his car, I didn't care much what happened to me.

I had to forget that pounding in my head.

2

There aren't many places to go in Benton, just a bowling alley and the movies. I had seen the movie the night before with George, and I'm no good at bowling.

"Where to?" George asked me after I got into the car.

"I don't care," I said.

"Have dinner?"

We didn't hire a cook at the house, only a maid who cleaned up during the day, and most of our meals were eaten out, unless Laura got the urge to work in the kitchen and she never did a very good job of it. She did all right with salads and things like that but when it came to a roast she was nearly helpless. I wasn't any better.

"A sandwich would be fine," I told him.

George started the car and we moved down the driveway, slowing as we approached the street.

"Guess that's enough for me, too, Doris. With you going away I don't feel very hungry."

I glanced at him, at the fine features of his face, his brown hair, and I decided that I would miss him as much as he would miss me. We had had some wonderful times together and now it was all being changed. What I would remember most about him, gratefully, was that he had never touched me unless I had given him reason to believe that I wanted to be touched. And I hadn't given George reason to think that way very often.

"What about the place at Moon Lake?" George was asking.

"It's fine with me."

Moon Lake is about five miles from Benton and is a rather large resort area. Most of the people come from New York and many of them own power boats. Moon Lake Inn is on the lake and if you stay out of the bar and in the dining room it is a quiet place. We had been there several times, and three or four years ago my father had had a cottage on the lake. We had spent our summers there and I had enjoyed myself. There had been a girl next door and we had gone around a lot together, even to sleeping together in the same bed. I had been fourteen at the time, in the early stages of physical development, but she had been a couple of years older and she had had a wonderful body. Whenever she had stayed with me I had gotten into bed first and then secretly watched her undress. She had been blonde, all blonde, and one night, in the darkness, she had kissed me. It had been a thrilling kiss, a kiss that had sent the blood pounding through my veins, but nothing had happened beyond that. The next day she had fallen from a rented horse, broken her leg and I had not seen her again.

"You're quiet," George said, turning left onto the highway.

"I was just thinking."

"About what?"

"Things."

"You worry me when you're so quiet. I have the feeling that I'm boring you."

"No, it isn't that."

He passed a truck and drew back into the right lane.

"All packed for school?"

"Just about. If I've forgotten anything I can have my father send it along."

"If he's here."

"Why wouldn't he be here?"

It was his turn to remain silent for a short time.

"I may be talking out of turn," he said finally, "but I have an idea he's going to marry Laura Stevens. And I don't think the marriage is far off." Again he paused. "I'm taking over the management of the lumber yard tomorrow morning."

"Well, fine. You've worked hard, you deserve it and he couldn't possibly get anybody better."

"He's going to pay me an extra hundred a week for it." He added, "And thanks for your confidence."

I tried to imagine my father married to Laura but the vision just wouldn't come. All I could think of was how they drank and the things they did to each other.

"She's marrying him for his money," I said, hardly realizing that I was saying it.

"Maybe. You never know. But you have to give her credit. Her parents had nothing and she started out with nothing. As soon as she was out of high school she took on a line of mail order dresses and sold them from house to house. She saved her money and that's how she opened her store."

"Or my father helped her."

"Your father didn't meet her until she already had the store. He may have helped her since then. I don't know."

A car went past us and the girl was sitting very close to the boy. Why wasn't I that way with George? Once we had been to a party and on the way home I had felt the need to love— somebody. He had put his right arm around my shoulders and his hand had hung down to cover my right breast. I had told him not to go further, that I didn't believe in it, and he had respected my wishes.

"Laura's a tramp," I said, recalling how she walked around the house in little more than her skin and how she made no attempt to conceal her reasons for doing so.

"Those are harsh words, Doris."

"They may be but that's what I believe."

"And I think your father is in love with her."

"He's in love with her because she lets him have his way— if you know what I mean."

"I know what you mean and it could be. But if he were only interested in the physical side of it, there are any number of girls he could have. Girls, I might add, who might be more appealing than Laura."

I did not believe that. Laura had a richly beautiful body. Few girls could measure up to her. But when I thought of her giving herself to my father, I became almost ill. Possibly in that moment I realized I disliked my father more than Laura Stevens.

"Well, I wish them the best of everything," I said as we neared the lake. I laughed. "It isn't every girl who has a mother almost her own age."

"It'll work out all right. The thing is not to fight it."

"I'll try not to."

At the inn we found a table near one of the windows. George sat opposite me and for a second I watched a sail boat cutting through the water.

It turned out that we ordered nothing to eat. We just drank. I wanted to forget about my father and Laura and all that had gone before.

"Another drink?" George asked.

"Why not?"

"Well, you never have more than two and then you quit. This last one was your fourth."

I reached across the table and took one of his hands.

"Fourth, fifth or sixth—what does it matter?"

George grinned and toyed with my fingers.

"I've got something for this hand," he said, reaching into his pocket. "A ring."

"George!"

He opened the small box and I saw the gleam of a diamond.

"It isn't a big one," he said. "But it's paid for. Later on I can get you a bigger one."

I had no words.

"You're crying," he said.

"I can't help it."

George squeezed my hand.

"It isn't anything to cry about. I just love you and I can't do much about it—except hope that you feel the same way about me." He removed the ring from the box. "Will you wear it?" he asked softly.

A thousand things raced through my mind. George had a bright future, and he would make a good husband and father. I had often imagined myself married to him but none of the details had ever been very clear. He would work from eight until five, sometimes later, and at night there would be love, love in a bed meant only for two. Eventually, if we were lucky, there would be a baby, perhaps more than one, and I would be a mother. It was this last which frightened me more than anything else. I would get big, my stomach swelling, and if anything went wrong, as it had with my mother, I would die. But I wanted to live and be happy.

"It's pretty," I managed to say.

"Will you wear it?"

"I've still got four years of college," I reminded him, unable to think of a better excuse.

"I can wait." He was stubborn. "I can wait four years or ten but it isn't necessary that you go to college at all. I have a good salary and we can get along. Your father told me that my income would keep going up and we wouldn't have anything to worry about."

We talked some more but in the end I accepted the ring. There was no harm in it. I would continue with my schooling, at least for the present, and if the engagement failed, it failed. I was making him happy and not hurting myself. It seemed to be the thing for me to do.

"Your father knows about this," George said.

"Does he?"

"Yes. I spoke with him about it this morning. He said for me to give it a try and he wished me luck."

We had several drinks after that and he did a great deal of talking. He was going to work hard and he was determined to make Foster Lumber Yard bigger than ever, bigger than my father had ever hoped it would be.

"Not weekends," he said. "Those I'll keep for you."

He had about a thousand dollars saved and on his new salary he would be able to save more. By the time we were married he would have the money for the furniture and the down payment on a house. There was a new development starting out of town and he thought we would enjoy living there.

"You'd have your car and I'd have mine," he said. "There wouldn't be any trouble about transportation to town."

I was feeling the drinks and I agreed with everything that he said. I could do worse, I told myself. And the drinks had helped me to forget about my father and Laura. The drinks, in fact, had helped me to forget just about everything.

We left the inn around midnight and as we walked to the car he put his arm around my waist. For the first time since I had known him I felt terribly close to him. When he kissed me before I entered the car, I returned it, feeling his lips move over mine, the strong pressure of his arms about me.

"I love you," he said.

We didn't go right home but I had expected that. On any other night I would have persuaded him not to park but on this night it seemed proper. I was wearing his ring and he was in love with me. Could there be anything more binding than this?

We parked on a road which at one time had been the highway but was now filled with holes and overgrown with small trees. After he shut off the motor I could hear the sounds of cars moving to and from Benton.

"You've made me very happy," he said.

"I'm happy, too." I wasn't sure whether I was or not. The darkness was all around us, pulling us together. "More happy than I have ever been before."

He came across the seat to me, his mouth seeking out my lips, his right arm going around my shoulder.

I like to think that it was because of the drinks but it may have been something far deeper than that, a sudden urge to prove that I was a woman. There was only one way, I reasoned, in which I could overcome my fear of the male—belong to the male, to a decent man, and find out for myself if love were as good as the girls had said it was in school. They had said that it took you out of this world, into a world filled with wonder and satisfaction, that it created in you a new sense of life.

"George," I said and went to him. This time my mouth was partly open and waiting for him. "George, darling."

He tried to be gentle with me but he was too anxious.

"I never have," I cried.

"I know you haven't. Don't fight me," he whispered.

Another sensation flooded through me. I wanted to be a woman, all woman, but I had doubts; and if this were the only way I could end them, it had to be. Still uncertain, I helped him as much as I could, fighting down the disgust and the revolt that threatened to ruin this moment for us. I clung to him, whimpering, saying that I loved him, loved him, trying to convince myself that this was as it should be, that there was nothing beyond this that a normal girl could desire.

More than anything, I prayed that I was in truth a woman, a real woman.

"I won't hurt you," he said. "I won't hurt you any more than I can help."

But he did hurt me. The pain slammed through my whole body and I think I may have screamed. I begged him to stop, not to go on, but it was too late. All I could do was sob, wishing that I hadn't had so much to drink, and pray he would quickly dispel his desires, for his caresses aroused only my disgust.

It must have been a long time later that he moved away from me. My legs were numb. I felt hollow inside, so hollow that I could have cried. Where was all the beauty? Where were all of the wonderful sensations? I didn't know. I had given myself for the first time and I had found nothing. Nothing. At last I had belonged to a man and it was nothing like the girls had said it would be. My body had been sullied and used and I was no longer a virgin. I had reached out for sex and had found an emptiness even worse than the pain had been.

"You don't have to worry," he said, lighting a cigarette. "I didn't take any chances with you."

I was grateful for that and asked for a cigarette.

"It will be better the next time, Doris."

"Yes."

"Once you get used to me and I get used to you it will be better and better. And there'll be other nights," he said as he started the car.

"Yes."

There would never be this kind of a night again, not for me. I would find something else to do with my time.

We didn't talk much on the way back to Benton.

Somehow, there didn't seem to be very much for us to say.

3

I packed the car early the next morning and was about to leave when I was interrupted.

"I heard you get up," Laura said as she came down to the living room. "I just wanted to tell you that you deserve a lot of credit. Most girls would hang around—girls whose parents had money—and not do anything."

"Thanks."

She was wearing a blue negligee that didn't hide much of her body.

"There's something else I wanted to tell you, Doris. Your father and I are getting married. We decided on it last night."

I was still wearing George's ring but I kept it out of sight.

"Luck," I said. "I hope you're very happy together."

"I hope you mean that."

"I mean it."

"I'm still going to keep my dress shop. I worked too hard

for it to let it go. And at this time of the year, with school just getting under way, we won't be able to take any honeymoon. We'll have to let that go until sometime during the winter."

"All right," I said.

Laura followed me to the door.

"You think I'm a tramp, don't you, Doris?"

"I didn't say that."

"No, but I can tell. Well, I can't blame you for that. But I will try to be a good wife to him and you can count on that."

"I'm sure you will."

"Watch the boys," Laura said as I opened the door.

She waved to me from one of the windows as I was getting into the car and I waved back, not because I wanted to but because it seemed only fair. In a short time she would be my stepmother and there wasn't anything I could do about it.

Traffic was light and I had no trouble of getting through the town and reaching the highway. I guess I thought of Laura during the whole drive. She had been wrong when she had said I thought she was a tramp. I didn't think any such thing. And I thought she had the most lovely figure I had ever seen.

It was hot driving and I pulled the skirt of my dress up over my knees. It had been higher the night before, and George had known me as no other man had ever known me, or ever would again. As I drove along I glanced at his ring on my left hand. If I accepted marriage I could expect the same thing every night. There would be dinner, television, perhaps a few drinks and then sex. I reached over with my right hand and removed the ring. I couldn't face it. When I wore the ring I was living a lie. But I assured myself that my lack of response to George hadn't been my fault. He had been too abrupt with me, too anxious to satisfy his own demands. I was just a young girl who didn't know what it was all about.

I passed through a small town and stopped for a red light. I had nothing to worry about. I was going away to school and I had money to spend. I could think about George again when I was more rational and calm. I didn't have to rush into marriage with him. There was time for that in the future and by then I might find myself, know in my own heart what I wanted to do and what I expected out of life.

The light changed and I resumed driving. I had made up my mind to one thing, however. I wouldn't go home for weekends.

I would stay at the school and if George sought to visit me I would find an excuse to put him off. He would be after the same thing again and I wasn't ready for that just yet. In some way I had to seek the truth about myself and learn what I was.

Eighty miles isn't much in a new car and the road was fairly good. Only in one other place did I have to slow down and this was a spot where they were putting in a new bridge. It had rained the night before and the detour was thick with mud but the Ford rode easily through it. Another driver, I noticed, hadn't been so fortunate. The car, not a late model, was down over the bank with the front of it sticking into the water.

A couple of miles further on and not far from Cedarcliff I came on a young man trying to hitch a ride. My father had told me many times never to pick up strangers but, as I slowed, I saw that the young man had a pleasant face and I couldn't see any harm in picking him up.

I brought the car to a stop by the side of the road, watched him approach in the rear-view mirror, and pulled the hem of the dress down over my knees.

"Thanks," he said as he opened the door and got in. "Thanks a lot."

He had sandy hair and a ready smile. His teeth were white and I judged his eyes a pale blue. He was wearing a T-shirt and slacks, both brown, and a pair of tennis shoes.

"You're welcome," I said and pulled the car out onto the highway.

We rode a short distance in silence.

"You see my car back there?" he asked.

"I saw a car that was over the bank."

"That was mine. I skidded down there about four this morning and I've been waiting ever since for a wrecker. I couldn't wait any longer. I'm late enough for work as it is." He laughed. "I'm so late I don't know whether or not I still have a job."

He seemed decent enough and I was glad to have his company.

"You work in Cedarcliff?" I asked.

"Out at the school."

"That's where I'm going."

"Are you?"

"Yes. It's my first year."

He asked me my name and I told him. His name was Hank Herbert, he was twenty and he lived in the village with an aunt.

"She'll raise hell about the car," he said.

"Why?"

"Because it partly belonged to her."

He settled back, lighting a cigarette, and I knew that he was watching me. For some reason I didn't seem to mind. My dress was slightly tight but it was high in front and there wasn't anything that he could see.

"You're lucky you didn't get hurt," I said, breaking the silence.

"I suppose so. But I wasn't going fast and the car just slid down the bank. I got my feet a little wet when I climbed out but they're dry now."

I couldn't think of anything else to say.

"You were out here during the summer?" Hank inquired shortly.

"Yes."

"Did they tell you who you're rooming with?"

"Nina Wilbur. She's in her third year."

He threw his cigarette outside and lit another.

"I know her," Hank said.

"She seemed like a nice girl."

He hesitated.

"You'll find out soon enough," he told me finally. "Some of the girls like her and some of them don't." He hesitated again. "There's always a reason for that sort of thing."

Hank went on to tell me about his job at the school. He took care of the grounds when such work was necessary and during the winter he had a room in the cellar of one of the buildings where he painted screens and things like that. He was saving his money for college and he hoped to go away in a year or so. I got the impression, although it wasn't from anything that he said, that he dated some of the girls at the school and that this is where much of his money went. I decided, listening to him, that he would probably never go to college. Even if he did, twenty-one or twenty-two would be pretty old to start. I felt slightly ashamed that I had so much and he had so little. It didn't seem quite fair.

We drove through Cedarcliff and there wasn't much to the town. Somebody had told me during my visit that it had a population of eighteen hundred and there couldn't have been many more citizens than that. There were a bank, a hotel, a few stores, a couple of bars and that was about it.

The school was about a mile outside the village and the grounds and buildings were well kept. There was a huge parking lot, partly filled with cars, and I pulled the Ford in there. Most of the cars were new and fairly expensive. You had to have money to go to Cedarcliff School and you had to have it on the line. Only the rich could afford it.

"I want to thank you again," Hank said as he got out. "If it hadn't been for you I might still be walking along the road."

"You're welcome, I'm sure."

He started away from the car and then came back, leaning on the door.

"Perhaps I could see you some night," he suggested.

"I was told the girls weren't allowed out."

"On weekends they are." Hank poked his head inside the car. "And you can manage on other nights if you know how to do it."

"I'll think about it." I didn't think I was interested in him but there was no point in injuring his feelings. "And I'll let you know."

"You do that."

I watched him as he walked away from the car. There didn't appear to be anything wrong with him and it might be fun to go out once in a while. The weekends would belong to me and, except for the Saturday night dances, there wouldn't be anything else to do.

He disappeared from sight around one of the buildings and I think a little sigh escaped me.

He wasn't bad.

He wasn't bad at all....

The rest of the day was taken up with class assignments and I was glad when I was finally excused to go to my room in Massey Hall. A porter helped me with my bags. He was an elderly man and complained of the heat and all the work that he had to do.

"Been runnin' all day," he added. "Upstairs and down. That Miss Lily don't understand that a man's legs can wear out. All she knows is that you're supposed to be on the jump from eight until five.”

Massey Hall was a three story brick building, long and wide, and it housed all the girls attending the school. Miss Lily, her eyes hidden by dark glasses, had said it was the policy to put a new girl in with an older girl, thereby making it easier for the new girl to acquaint herself with the grounds and buildings. She called it a form of progressive education. I hadn’t known what she had meant by that, not exactly, but it hadn’t been important. During the forty-five minutes she had addressed us she had said a lot of things that I hadn’t understood.

“She talks in circles,” one girl had complained. “You’d think we were a bunch of babies.”

My room was on the second floor, at the rear of the building, and I was surprised to find Nina Wilbur already there when I arrived. I hadn’t seen her in the main building or at the meeting.

“Greetings,” she said, standing near the window. She was wearing a robe, belted tightly around the middle. “Greetings from another world.”

“Hi.”

She waved me to the bed to the left of the door and I put my things on that. The porter stacked what he was carrying at the foot of the bed and I thanked him. He lied, said it had been a pleasure, then went out and closed the door behind him.

“I should have had my robe off,” Nina laughed. “Old Bill likes to walk in on the girls when they’re half naked. Don’t ask me why. They say he has a wife in town and he can’t even take care of her.”

Nina was a tall girl, brunette and willowy, and her legs beneath the line of the robe were straight and well-formed. As she came away from the window the robe parted and I could see her golden thighs, as lovely and smooth as the calves below.

“You weren’t at the pep talk,” I said.

She made a face as she sat down on the edge of her bed.

“I heard it twice before and I didn’t want to hear it again. She goes through the same routine every year. Study hard and get high marks. Forget about boys. Isn’t that what she said?”

“Something of the sort. I have an appointment with her for seven tonight. What’s that for?”

“Another pep talk, only she’ll get more personal when she has you alone. She’ll want the history of your family starting with the Revolution and she'll bear down on the rules of the school. But don't worry about it. All you do is answer the questions you feel like answering and let the rest go."

It took me a long time to unpack and put my things away and Nina helped me. Nina had untied the belt around her middle and more than once I got a glimpse of her body. She was tanned from the sun, tanned all over, and when one of her breasts came into view I sucked in my breath. She didn't bother to cover herself up and before we finished she had removed the robe.

"Might as well be comfortable," she explained.

I tried not to look at her body but I couldn't help myself. I had the same sensation as when I had looked at Laura Stevens, only Nina didn't have the full blown beauty that Laura had. But in spite of this, her body had rich lines and I drank it all in. I lit a cigarette, afraid that she was aware of my interest, and walked to the window.

"I picked up a boy on the way in," I said. "Hank Herbert. Do you know him?"

"Hank Herbert? Oh, sure, everybody knows Hank. At one time or another he's made time with lots of girls at the school."

"Really?"

"He's one of those fellows who can't get enough of a good thing. Any girl who goes out with him is a nut."

"I see."

"Or lets him into her room. Miss Lily has given him the run of the place and he's taken advantage of it. Not only in a girl's room but in his own place. You have anything to do with him, honey, and you're asking for it."

It was hard for me to believe. He had impressed me as being regular but Nina should know what she was talking about. I had to take her word for it.

I resolved that I would stay away from Hank Herbert. I had had one experience with a man and that had been sufficient.

"You might relax and get out of your clothes," Nina said. "It's an hour before dinner."

"I don't think I'll eat."

"Neither do I. This is the first day and I know just what it will be like. Cold cuts and salad. It takes the cooks a few days to warm up and then the meals aren't so bad."

There was a package of cigarettes on the dresser and she

walked over to pick it up. My stare followed her movements, the full roll of her hips, and then lifted to her reflection in the mirror. She was lovely, very lovely, and she was all girl. She had sounded so sure about Hank Herbert, and I wondered if she had ever had anything to do with him. I also recalled that he had been rather vague in discussing her. It was possible that they had at one time been lovers and then had drifted apart.

"You needn't be bashful," she told me. "I don't bite."

I got out of my dress and placed it over the foot of the bed, thought about the half slip and then pushed it down over my hips. All that remained was the bra and my panties, garter belt and shoes. I kicked off my shoes and unhooked my stockings, rolling them down my legs. She watched what I was doing and I saw her smile.

"You've got a nice shape," she said.

"Thanks. You aren't so bad yourself."

Nina opened a drawer of the dresser.

"Care for a drink?"

"No, thanks."

She opened the bottle and poured some liquor into a glass.

"We aren't supposed to have it in our rooms," she explained. "But most of us do. You get done with an assignment from Paul Blanding and you need a shot of something or other."

"Who is Paul Blanding?"

"He teaches history. You must have seen him. Tall and dark and with a slight limp."

"Yes, I guess I did."

"He loads it on and the only way you can pass if you don't do your work is to see him on a weekend. If you know what I mean."

"I think I do."

"He lives in town and he's married but that doesn't stop him. More than one girl got through his course by climbing into the back seat of his car."

I removed my bra and struggled out of the panties. I had dressed hurriedly that morning and I had put on a pair too tight.

"I thought this was a nice school," I said.

"It is."

"And yet things such as you mentioned go on?"

Nina poured a second drink.

"What do you expect? You take three hundred girls shut up alone and something has to happen." She laughed. "And a lot of things do. Take my word for it. A lot."

She kept talking about the school and I listened to her but most of my attention was directed at her body. Her beauty was striking and I tightened up inside just thinking about her.

"You aren't paying any attention to me," she said.

I felt my face grow hot.

"I'm sorry."

"I was talking about Paul Blanding. With your build he's sure to make a pass at you. It's up to you whether you fall for it or not."

"I won't."

"Don't be too sure. He's rather charming and the marks he gives out are important. I'm not in his class any longer but when I was he practically offered me the sky if I would go to bed with him. I told him to go to hell and I worked my skull thin getting passing grades. Another girl I knew took care of his needs and she wound up with the highest mark in the class."

"She was lucky she didn't get something else."

"True. But the next year she didn't come back. I heard she married some guy in the army and went to Germany with him. For all I know she may have had a kid before her nine months were up."

We talked some more and at a quarter of seven I dressed for my appointment with Miss Lily. I was nervous, though there was no reason why I should have been. Nina assured me that the interview wouldn't amount to much and that it shouldn't last more than fifteen minutes.

"She looked you up before you got here or you wouldn't be here," Nina said. "You can be sure of that."

Nina was still naked and I felt wave upon wave of excitement rush through me. For the next few months I would be sharing the same room and I could glory in the observation of her body, dream that I was embracing her and holding her tight, my fingers running over her wonderfully tanned skin. I knew that it was crazy, that it was the wrong feeling for me to have, but it was there and I couldn't control it.

"Luck," she said as I left.

"Thanks. I'll probably need it."

It wasn't a long walk to the main building so I didn't hurry. There was something wrong with me, something terribly wrong and twisted, and even though I searched for the reason I didn't know what it was. Now that I thought of it, it had been with me for a long, long time, starting with those nights when I had heard my mother cry out as my father had claimed her. I had come to think of the male as a beast and my one attempt to prove that the male wasn't had ended in dismal failure.

Miss Lily was waiting for me in her office and without her dark glasses on she didn't appear to be so old. I guessed her to be in her early forties, rather attractive in a dark sort of way, and her figure amply filled out her white blouse and gray skirt.

"You're late," she said.

"Sorry."

"Being sorry isn't any excuse, Miss Foster. When you're told to be a certain place at a certain time you're supposed to be there."

"Yes, Miss Lily."

She sat down behind a large desk and waved me into a chair alongside. I sat down.

"How do you like your room?"

"Fine."

"And Miss Wilbur?"

"She's very nice."

Miss Lily nodded.

"You should get along well with her, I think. She's a better than average student and she can show you much about Cedarcliff School. She has been helpful to other girls in the past."

"I'm sure she'll be a good roommate."

My session with Miss Lily was very short. She asked me questions about my family but I got the impression, as she followed a form on her desk, that she knew almost as much about my father as I did. Finally she said she welcomed me to the school and that she wished me all good luck.

"I'll do my best," I promised.

"I'm sure you will." Miss Lily pushed the form aside. "You may go now."

I left the main office but I didn't return to Massey Hall right away. I walked about the grounds, not caring where I went, and tried to think.

Nina, I thought.

God.

Laura, I thought.

Oh, God.

I found a bench, sat down, trembling all over, and began to cry.

Anything, I thought, was better than this.

Anything.

4

I enjoyed my first two weeks at school. The food was generally good and the classes were interesting, although I found there was a great deal of work to do in the evening. Paul Blanding was the toughest of the lot and there wasn't a night that went by that I didn't have to write page after page of information relating to the birth of our country and its growth. Much of this, however, I had had in high school and therefore it wasn't too difficult.

"I'm going to get a typewriter," I said to Nina one night. "A typewriter would be easier and faster."

Nina seldom wore any clothes in the room and she was sitting exactly that way on the bed. This was perhaps one of the reasons that it took so long for me to do my work. I would write a little and then I would look at her and when I looked at her nothing I was doing seemed very important. Not until she lay down, covering herself with a sheet, was I able to study the way I should.

"I wish I could type," she said, yawning, putting her hands behind her head and thrusting her breasts straight out. "But I don't know the first thing about it. If you get a machine perhaps you could show me."

"I'll try."

But after the lights were out, were the worst times. I would think of her in her bed, and I would have the awful, terrible urge to go to her—or to have her come to me. In moments such as this my head would ache and I would think that I would never be able to sleep again. Often we would talk in the darkness, frequently about the school and sometimes about boys, but my listening and replies were purely mechanical. My eyes would be closed, seeing in my mind how she walked around the room, and more than once I thought of Laura standing without a stitch in the hall at home. I tried to compare the two but that was impossible. They were different, both beautiful, and whether I liked it or not I was drawn to them. Then I would think there was something dangerous in the way I was reacting and I would try to think of George. But thinking of George didn't help. I could feel his hands upon me again, and I knew that wasn't love. It was nothing but animal lust.

"You have a boy friend?" Nina asked me during one of our talks.

"Well, there was a boy I went with back home but you couldn't say he was a boy friend. He works for my father and we only went out on a few dates." I didn't know why I felt it necessary to lie. "Movies and like that. The usual things."

She laughed. "The usual?"

"You know what I mean."

I met other girls at the school who wanted to be friendly but I didn't have the time for them. All I wanted to do was get back to that room with Nina. Her classes ended before mine did and she was always stripped when I joined her.

George wrote to me every day and I answered a couple of his letters. He was doing fine in his job of running the lumber yard and my father and Laura were being married in two weeks. Was I coming home for the event? I wrote that I couldn't, that I had too much to do at the school, and I wrote both to Laura and my father and wished them luck. There was no reply from Laura but my father dropped me a card, saying that if I needed any more money to let him know and he would send it. I guess he thought money was all a daughter wanted from a father.

On Monday my last class was with Paul Blanding and he asked me to remain after the others left. All the other girls got their Thursday papers back but mine wasn't returned.

"You're a hard worker, Doris," Blanding said.

"Thank you."

He had my paper with him and he glanced at it a moment. Then he turned his head and smiled at me.

"You can have a hundred on this or you can have seventy-five," he said. "Which do you want?"

He had me confused.

"A hundred would be better," I replied finally.

"So it would be."

"But I don't see how you can give me a hundred if I don't deserve it."

"I didn't say you didn't deserve it. I said you could have one or the other. Being deserving has nothing to do with it."

I was still confused.

"I'm not sure I understand," I said.

He pushed the paper aside and reached for a cigarette.

"You're by far the most beautiful girl in the class," Blanding told me. "Did you know that?"

"I hadn't even thought about it."

"Maybe you haven't but I have. When I'm talking about the discovery of America I'm wondering what it would be like to discover you." He inhaled deeply. "You know that Saturday you won't have anything to do. Miss Lily will put on a dance but you don't have to stick around for that. You could meet me in town and we could have dinner together."

So there it was. Of all the girls in the class, he was after me. And I knew it wouldn't stop with dinner. There would be drinks and a hotel room. He was, to be sure, rather handsome but no man appealed to me that way.

"You're married," I said. "Or I heard that you were."

"Yes, I'm married. But what has that got to do with it? My wife knows of these things but she doesn't mind. She has a nice apartment and she has her own friends—some of them male. I don't tell her how to live her life and she doesn't tell me how to live mine."

"The modern arrangement?"

"You could call it that." He leaned toward me. "I can help you, Doris. I can help you a lot. Or I can hurt you. Whatever I do is up to you."

I didn't have to consider the situation. I knew what I was going to do and what I had to do.

"I'd rather take a zero," I said, getting up. "I don't know what kind of a girl you think I am but you're all wrong. If I have to make my passing marks outside of class I'll just fail."

Blanding didn't argue with me about it. He merely took his pen from his pocket and gave me a seventy-five.

I took the paper and walked from the room. Tears burned my eyes.

I thought of going to Miss Lily but rejected the idea. Others had probably gone to her before and it was doubtful if it had done them any good.

Outside, I threw the paper into a trash can. Hank Herbert was very busy pruning one of the bushes but he called out to me.

"Hello, Hank," I said.

He was stripped to the waist—it had been a hot day—and his huge chest was covered with sweat.

"How's school?" he wanted to know.

"All right. Fine," I added. "Just fine."

"Still rooming with Nina Wilbur?"

"Still."

He had a pair of pruning shears in one hand and he dropped these on the grass.

"I only work half a day tomorrow," he said. "Could I interest you in a ride in the afternoon? We've got the car back on the road again and it seems to run okay. We could drive around and I could show you some of the country."

"Thanks, but I'm busy," I said.

He lost some of his grin.

"Perhaps the next time?"

"Perhaps."

I walked on and I could hear the chop of the shears as he resumed cutting away at the bush. The tears, I knew, were still in my eyes. Paul Blanding had been very unfair. I wondered, vaguely, how I would make out in his class after this. Some of the girls, I felt sure, would have welcomed his attention.

Nina was in the room. She was her usual undressed self and standing at the dresser pouring herself a drink.

"Have one?"

"I guess I could use it," I admitted.

She arched her brows.

"Troubles?"

"Yes."

"From home?"

"No, not that."

I got out of my dress and slip and while I was doing this I told her about Paul Blanding.

"The bastard," she said when I had finished. "But it was to be expected. You can't look the way you do and not invite attention."

I accepted the drink from her and it burned as it went down my throat. I coughed and gasped for breath.

"Not used to it, huh?"

"Not very."

"Try another. The second one is better."

"I—hope—so."

It was and we had several drinks. The dinner hour came and went and we talked about Paul Blanding. Nina agreed with me that there was no use going to Miss Lily. Miss Lily would only say that I had invited his offer and she would tell me that I had to leave the male teachers alone.

We emptied the bottle and Nina got a fresh one from the dresser drawer. I was sitting on my bed, my glance fastened upon her. She was all curves and lines, the sweeping, glorious lines that made her a woman.

"You look hot," she said, bringing the drink over to me.

"I am, a little."

She put her glass on the night stand, bent over me and unhooked my bra.

"This will help," she said softly.

Nina took the bra from me. Her hands had only touched my skin for a second but it had been enough to send a thrill through me.

"Thanks," I murmured.

She picked up her drink.

"What about the rest?" she inquired. "We've got nothing to hide from each other, have we?"

"I guess not."

I stood up and pushed the panties down over my legs. Once I was out of them I placed them at the foot of the bed.

"Any man would want you," she said, sitting down on her own bed.

"Would he?"

"Yes. Any man. All a man has to do is look at you and he's certain to get the urge."

"What about yourself? You look like man-bait to me!"

Nina laughed and tasted her drink.

"I've had my moments. Men are always making passes at me. The first time was when I was sixteen—to tell you the truth, I haven't been able to stand a man since. We had a cottage upstate at the time and my father had invited this couple for the weekend. They didn't know the way but I did and my father told me to ride with them. At the last moment the wife couldn't go—she got sick or something and I made the trip alone with the husband. We hadn't gone fifty miles when he pulled off into a side road and raped me."

I didn't know who this man was, had never seen him, but I hated him for what he had done to her. How could any sane man violate a young girl?

"Why didn't you tell your parents?"

"I did tell my mother but she didn't believe me. She said that he wouldn't do such a thing, that I was just making it up. Three months later she found out that I hadn't been lying. I was pregnant. But I lost the baby that same month and nothing ever came of it. Later the couple moved away and we never heard of them again."

"You poor kid!"

She walked to the dresser and poured another drink.

"It taught me one thing," Nina said. "It taught me to hate men and all the ugly things they want from a girl." She returned to the bed and sat down again. "They go out with you for one purpose and one purpose only. They talk about love but they don't mean love. They mean sex. Nobody can tell me otherwise."

We had a lot to drink but it wasn't just the drinks that did it. She came to me and sat beside me on the bed, her thigh against mine, our need the common need of two girls alone.

"You know what I want to do," she said, her voice low and throaty. "You know, don't you?"

"I'm not sure."

"Don't tell me that. You know and I know that you know. You wouldn't be here like this if you didn't." She spoke hurriedly and with passion. "The moment I saw you I knew that it had to be you. It couldn't be anybody else. It had to be you or no one at all."

Her hands sought my body and she pushed me back on the bed. I felt my foot hit the glass on the floor and upset it.

"Please, Nina."

But I didn't fight her. I couldn't fight her. I wanted her as badly as she wanted me.

"Say it again," she commanded, her mouth close to mine.

"Please!"

Her mouth came down over my lips, lips that were waiting for her. I opened my mouth, inviting her. She began to moan, crying out that she loved me.

We kissed for a long time and then she told me to be patient, that she would make me live as I had never lived before. I was twisting on the bed now, all restraint gone, wanting her to please me, begging her to hurry.

Nina pleased me.

She turned my body into a savage thing of desire that knew complete satisfaction as she brought love to me again and again.

Afterward, she slept beside me but I could not go to sleep.

I had ventured into the world of the unknown.

I had become, to put it bluntly, a lesbian.

5

It was late when we awoke the next morning, much too late for breakfast. Nina was still in the bed with me, up close, the heat of her body making it seem hot in the room. I was on the inside against the wall, and she stirred as I crawled over her.

"You're lovely," Nina said sleepily, a smile on her lips.

I walked to the dresser and searched for a cigarette. I had had a most miserable night after our affair, lying awake and knowing that she was beside me, afraid to accept the truth but at the same time afraid to accept anything else. I had achieved satisfaction with her and I knew that this had been wrong.

Nina sat up, stretching, and I could see the reflection of her smile in the mirror. I could also see the wonders of her shape but when I thought about what we had done it make me a little sick. She had pleased me where George had failed. It didn't seem right.

"It mustn't happen again," I said, trying to sound firm.

"But it will," she assured me.

"It would be better if I got another room," I said.

She got up from the bed and crossed the room.

"That's up to you, Doris."

I turned and faced her.

"I don't mean anything bad by it," I explained. "We had a little too much to drink and we went too far. It could have happened to anybody."

Her lips twisted.

"You enjoyed it," she said. "You were out of your head."

"But it isn't human," I protested.

"It is human. It's the most human thing in the world. Girls have been loving girls for years and years. What's so terrible about it? You have your fun and there's no danger of some man making you pregnant."

I didn't answer her but got clean underthings from the dresser and put them on. She was experienced and I wasn't but that didn't mean that I had to listen to her. I had to fight this battle myself, to conquer the unnatural desires which had claimed me, and I could only do it if I were left alone.

"We're going to be late for class," Nina said, obviously convinced that I wasn't going to pursue the conversation further. "Both of us will get hell."

"I'm going to see Miss Lily about another room."

"Suit yourself."

"But I won't tell her what went on between us."

"You had better not." Nina's tone became hard. "You were asking for it, honey, and I only pleased you. Besides, your word wouldn't be any better than mine."

"I know."

I left the room before Nina did, carrying my books and hurrying as fast as I could.

Hank Herbert was working in front of the building and he already had his shirt off. He was doing something with the plants, putting leaves around them, and the sweat glistened on his broad shoulders.

"Run like hell," he said to me.

"What?"

He grinned and leaned on the handle of the rake.

"Your first class English?" he asked.

"Yes."

"You might as well not go at all as be late. They count it against you."

"Do they?"

"Sure. You could talk to me a few minutes and you won't be in any more trouble."

I paused, breathing deeply of the clear air.

"I want to see Miss Lily," I said.

"She'll only raise a fuss with you."

"That I can't help."

His shoulders lifted and fell and he poked at the leaves with the rake.

"You think any more about going out with me?"

"Not much," I admitted.

"All you have to do is follow the path across the campus and over the brook. That brings you out to the main road and I could wait for you in my car. You can come back the same way and nobody would know the difference."

I shifted my books from one arm to the other and bit my lower lip. It would be one way of getting away from Nina and the school for a few hours and I felt compelled to do both. What harm could come to me? He wouldn't try anything the first night out, I felt sure. And if he did all I had to do was make him stop. No man, I reasoned, would force a girl beyond her wishes.

"I'll see," I said, turning away.

"Well, I'll take a chance on that. I'll be there at eight and I'll wait for you."

I went on toward the main building. I had a long wait before I could see Miss Lily and when I finally entered her office I saw she had my schedule on the desk.

"You missed English," she said as I sat down.

"I know."

Miss Lily was wearing her dark glasses again and I couldn't follow the movements of her eyes.

"We don't miss classes at Cedarcliff," she said. "We make all of them."

Now that I was in her office I felt rather silly and I wasn't sure about what I wanted to say or how I wanted to say it.

"I'm sorry," I murmured.

She toyed with her glasses and tossed the schedule aside.

"Well, we'll overlook it this time." She removed her glasses and she was rather attractive when she wasn't wearing them. "Something of importance must have brought you here."

"I want to change my room," I said.

"Oh?" She raised her eyebrows.

"I thought you could help me."

"Is there a reason?"

"I don't know," I said. "If I were in with somebody who was taking the same subjects I was taking—the same interests—

it might work out better."

"You have any trouble with Miss Wilbur?"

"No," I lied. "None at all."

She leaned back in her chair.

"Miss Wilbur is a very nice girl, Miss Foster."

"Oh, I'm sure of that."

"She may not be the best student in the school but she has a great deal of common sense and she can answer many of the questions which are bound to arise for a new girl. That is the reason I assign the rooms the way I do—a new girl in with a girl who has had some experience on the campus."

"I'd be willing to pay extra to move into another room," I said. "Money isn't any object."

Miss Lily smiled.

"Do you think you are the only girl with means at the school?"

"No, of course not."

She arose from her desk and walked to a distant wall. There was a chart on the wall and she studied this in silence for a few moments.

"There aren't any other rooms," she said finally, turning away from the chart and facing me. Her dark dress was severe, making an attempt to hide her natural curves, but she had a rather interesting body. "Everything is taken. I'm afraid you'll have to stay where you are at least for the time being. Once in a while we have a girl drop out, though not often, and if this should happen I'll keep you in mind."

I was disappointed. I knew what it would be like to go on living with Nina and I wished to free myself from the trap into which I had walked, a trap which, I now realized, had been waiting for me a long, long time.

"Thank you." I said, getting up from my chair.

The lines around her mouth became hard.

"If you wish to see me again don't miss a class to do it. I'm here when classes are over with for the day and that is time enough for you discuss anything which you may have on your mind. I hope that is clear to you, Miss Foster."

"It's clear."

"Parents send their girls here because we offer a fine educational system but we can't accomplish our purpose if a student begins to skip classes."

"Yes, Miss Lily," I agreed meekly.

I excused myself before she could make another speech and left the main building. I checked my watch and found I was just in time for my next class. However, I did not hurry. I was thinking of many things. If I could not get a room away from Nina it might be better if I gave up college. But if I did that, what did I have to return home to? Laura and my father making love? Once they were married it would be worse than ever. To George, to the man whose ring I carried in my pocket-book? I didn't know. Something had happened to me the night before, something very terrible and also very beautiful, and it had left me in a state bordering on panic. I knew if I continued to live with Nina that the same thing would quite possibly happen again. There would be drinks and our bodies and I would be tempted to forget myself, to tread even further into the world of the unknown.

It was a long day and while our teachers were very good I got hardly anything out of their lectures. My mind was in a state of turmoil and more than once I felt that I must flee my present life. I had three thousand dollars, a new car and I would be able to get a job. I was a rapid typist and I knew something of the new method of taking dictation. If I went to New York I could lose myself in its millions and at the same time find myself and learn what I really was.

"Miss Foster?"

"Yes, Mr. Blanding?"

"You weren't listening."

"I'm sorry."

"Do you know the assignment for tomorrow?"

"I'm afraid I didn't hear it."

"You may stay after class and I'll give it to you then."

"Yes, sir."

Mr. Blanding's was the last class of the day and after the others had left he came down to my desk. He was smiling.

"There wasn't any assignment," he said, sitting down opposite me.

"Then why was I kept?"

"Because I wanted to talk to you." He crossed his legs. "I would still like to see you some evening or weekend."

I placed my books in a pile.

"No, thank you," I said.

He grinned at me and he was rather attractive when he grinned. I wondered, vaguely, how he had developed his limp.

"Am I so repulsive?" he demanded.

"It isn't that. You're married and I don't go out with married men. I never have and I think it's too late to start now."

"If I should give you below passing marks you would be restricted to the campus each weekend until the marks were improved."

"I know that."

"And it doesn't matter?"

"Not in the least." I considered what I had said and made an effort to soften the impact of it. "Well, it does matter. Of course it does. I may want to go home or get away for a day or so."

"That's to be expected."

"But I don't see why you pick on me. There are other girls in the class who would be flattered by your interest."

"And you're not?"

"Oh, I won't go so far as to say that. A girl wants to be attractive to men."

"You certainly are. We've had a lot of beautiful girls pass through here but I would say that you are the best."

I arose from my desk and he did the same.

"Thank you," I said.

I felt a little desperate. "I don't see why you can't grade my papers the way they should be graded and let it go at that. Nothing you can say or do can force me to do something I'm not willing to do. And I'm not willing to date a married man. It seems to me that if you are married you should stick to it."

He walked with me to the door.

"That isn't always possible," he said. "You see somebody who is very beautiful and you want to know them better. Being married doesn't have much to do with it My wife has her moments and I have mine."

I felt that he was lying to me, that his wife was ignorant of his playing around on the outside, but I said nothing. Eventually, I decided, he would become discouraged and he would seek out somebody else.

Blanding suggested I think over what he had said to me, and the door closed behind me.

I dreaded going to Massey Hall but I didn't have anywhere

else to go. I walked toward the building, hoping to see Hank Herbert, but he was nowhere in sight.

Nina was in the room when I arrived. She lay upon her bed, her glorious body revealed.

"You're late," she said.

"I had to stay after class."

"Paul Blanding again?"

I put my books on the dresser.

"Yes."

"He'll get next to you yet."

"No, he won't."

I wanted to get out my clothes and relax but I was afraid to undress in front of her. As she remained silent my glance drifted toward her bed. Her eyes were closed and she was smiling faintly. A strange tide rose within me as I watched her breasts lift and fall.

"I got two more bottles today," Nina said.

I sat down on my bed.

"Two bottles? How did you do that? None of us can go off the grounds, not during the week."

Her eyes opened and her smile became wide and wise.

"Hank Herbert," she said. "He brings the stuff out in his car for a price—two dollars a bottle extra."

She rolled over, sat up for a second and then got to her feet.

"Let's break one open," she said, going to the dresser. "Let's drink to what happened to us last night."

"I don't want anything."

"Are you sure?" She got out a bottle from the bottom drawer of the dresser. "A belt in the belly will do you good."

I shook my head as Nina looked at me. I didn't want anything to drink. I knew what would happen if I did.

"You're blaming yourself," Nina said, opening the bottle and pouring a drink. "And hating yourself. You shouldn't do that. There's no reason for blame or hate. What we did was as natural as the sun coming up."

"No, it wasn't."

She swallowed the drink and coughed a couple of times.

"Sex is natural," she said, pouring another drink. "Any form. The only difference is that it's cleaner between two girls than it is between a man and a girl. A man violates you and makes you dirty."

I lay down, stretching out, feeling the softness of the bed beneath me.

I knew she was drinking heavily and I didn't like that. What if she wanted to make love to me again? Would I be able to resist her?

"I had a letter from home today," Nina said.

I yawned. The lack of sleep the night before was telling on me.

"Did you?"

"Yes. The old man is in the hospital with a gut-ache."

"Too bad."

"Well, it's his own fault. He has an ulcer and he knows he shouldn't drink but he puts it away by the gallon. He dates some of the young girls in his office and he doesn't know where to stop—with sex or anything else."

"Your mother must like that."

"Like it? What the hell does she care? If he gets his lumps on the outside he doesn't bother her at home. Sometimes I think she's glad he has a wandering eye. He comes home stinko and he just flops into bed."

"I wouldn't like a marriage like that."

"I wouldn't like any kind of a marriage. All you do is sit at home and wait for the master of the house to come in from work and take you to bed."

I lay on the bed and Nina raved on and on. She hated men and there was no doubt about that. I tried to imagine how I would feel in the same position and I couldn't. I had willingly accepted George's advances. I had not been forced. Perhaps he had been too anxious and that may have been why I hadn't felt any real sensation from our contact. I had heard that it could be that way with a girl, that some girls were colder than others. I remembered the night before with Nina and I wished that George had brought me the same delight, thrilling me until I wanted to scream because of the beauty of it. But, I reasoned, perhaps I wasn't cold. Another man might awaken the sleeping emotions within me, drive me into a frenzy that would far surpass anything I had ever known. It would be a desperate attempt, a long shot, but it would be better than living in a world of fear and doubt—fear that I was a girl-lover, and doubt that I was not all woman. If only George were near I might go into his arms again. But he was not near—he was eighty miles away—and I had to do the best that I could on my own.

"Time to eat," Nina said.

"You go ahead. I'm not hungry."

"Worried?"

"A little."

"Stop worrying. You make me nervous."

I made every effort not to watch her dress but I failed. My head began to pound.

"I don't want to eat but I may have that drink," I said.

She waved toward the bottle on the dresser.

"Help yourself." She smiled. "Anything I have belongs to you. Anything."

"The same goes for me."

She came over to me, bent down and kissed me on the mouth.

"Anything?" she wanted to know huskily.

I moved my lips away from her mouth.

"You know what I mean," I said, my head aching harder than ever. "Clothes and things like that."

"Oh."

"But not—"

"The other?"

I wanted to. God, I wanted to so badly I hurt all over. "No," I replied, hardly able to speak.

Nina left me lying on the bed.

"You'll change," she said. "You see if you don't."

I was almost asleep when she left the room but after she was gone I got up, quickly changed my clothes and prepared to go out.

Something, I knew, was going to happen that night.

Perhaps something I had not bargained for.

6

I knew, even without thinking about it, that spending an evening with Hank Herbert was a foolish thing to do but I had to get away from that room and Nina. I couldn't live with myself if the same thing happened between us again. I would lose all my self-respect, and after that is gone a person doesn't have much left.

"A walk might do you good," Nina said when I told her I

was going out. "You can think better when you walk and after you've thought over what we can mean to each other you'll know how right I am."

She had returned from eating a few minutes before.

"I like to walk," I said. "I may be gone quite a while."

"Take your time. I'll be here when you get back. I'll be here—waiting for you. If I should be asleep all you have to do is come to bed with me."

"I'm in a hurry," I murmured, walking to the door.

I had to get out of there. Why hadn't Miss Lily been able to find another room for me? With another girl I could talk about our homes and our studies and there would be nothing like this. If the girl didn't have any shape and she wasn't attractive it would be so much the better. I resolved I would see Miss Lily again about a different room. If I bothered her enough she would have to do something. At the moment I would have paid a thousand dollars to have been able to part from Nina.

"I'll be thinking of you," Nina said as I closed the door.

I had little difficulty finding the path which led across the campus and into a clump of woods. The path narrowed and it was darker under the trees. I could hear the sound of water running and soon I was on a little bridge, the water hurrying beneath me. I stopped and stared down at the water. There is something peaceful about running water, something that eases the cares which may be troubling you.

I'm not a lesbian, I told myself. I can't be a lesbian. One tiny mark doesn't make a black streak. One breath doesn't assure life. One mistake isn't the end of the world. It takes many marks, many breaths, many mistakes to change a person from what he is meant to be. But—I couldn't help wondering what Nina was doing at that very moment. Was she drinking? She shouldn't drink so much. As time went on she would drink more and more and it was bound to have some effect on her studies. You couldn't learn with a drunken mind. All you could do was love.

I looked down at myself and I was sorry I had worn the sweater. The sweater made my breasts seem bigger, more prominent. Without thinking I put up my hands and touched them. They felt swollen, as though filled with some crying need. Some day, after I married, they would become even larger. They would fill with the milk of life and after I gave birth I would be able to nurse the child. There would be none of that drying-up process for me. I would give my baby all I could give.

Feeling weak, I leaned against the railing. Who was I kidding? I knew the answer to that one. I was kidding myself. I didn't want a baby. I never wanted to have a baby. I didn't want to die the way my mother had died.

"Kiss me," she had said when she had left for the hospital.

I had kissed my mother.

"I won't see you again."

And she hadn't. She had died and the baby had died and now my father was going to marry a girl young enough to be his own daughter. No, that wasn't for me. A man used a girl for one purpose and the girl paid for it with her life.

I lit a cigarette and dropped the match into the water, watching it until it rushed out of sight. The thoughts I had been thinking were crazy thoughts without foundation. Very few girls died in childbirth and it was possible to have a physical relationship with a man over a long period of time without getting pregnant. Why hadn't my father been careful with my mother? There was certainly no logical explanation for this. Perhaps he had tried to be and something had gone wrong. He had never offered an explanation and I had never asked him for one.

I glanced at my watch. It was ten minutes of eight. Now that I was near the highway—I could hear the cars going by— I was undecided about the wisdom of what I was doing. The little I knew about Hank Herbert hardly complimented him. But I was sure I would be safer with Hank than I would be in my room. Nina was a temptation I wasn't certain I could resist. If we shared our love together again it would simply make it harder for me to stop. Because—well, I *had* enjoyed the thrills she had brought to me. During those moments with her I had lived in the brightness of romance, a romance which had left a deep impression in me. I had heard of girls who loved other girls and I had found such relationships both amusing and fantastic. Now I found them neither. I knew what society said of them. Society tabooed them. And if that taboo were the only reason for me to want to avoid such relationships, then that was reason enough. I didn't want to put myself into the position of having another incident with Nina. What if we were discovered? We would have been kicked out of school as morally unacceptable, and that stain would sully the rest of my life.

I dropped my cigarette into the water and it followed the course of the match, lingering for a second in a little whirlpool and then sweeping from sight. It was like my affair with Nina. It was there one second and gone the next.

I left the bridge and went on toward the highway. As I emerged from the woods I paused at the side of the double ribbon of concrete. Would he stand me up? It didn't seem quite possible. He had appeared to be anxious for the date and if he didn't meet me this time he might know he wouldn't have a second chance.

I was surprised when Hank approached from my right, not from the direction of town. He had been out to a farm, he explained, to pick up some eggs for his aunt and he had to deliver these to her home.

"She's baking a couple of cakes," he said. "She makes a lot of cakes for money. Why she does it, I don't know. She's got enough to live on."

"Maybe she just wants something to do."

"That must be it."

He was wearing blue slacks and a blue sport shirt open at the throat and I could smell the odor of his shaving lotion. It wasn't expensive, not the kind my father used, but it had a clean smell to it. When he wasn't in working clothes he was rather handsome.

It took us only a couple of minutes to get to Cedarcliff. Even at this early hour of the evening the town appeared to be dead. We passed the theater and I noticed the film there had played in Benton several weeks before. I had gone to the movie with George and while the movie had had good reviews I hadn't cared for it. The actress who had carried the lead had been a sex-pot and I guess she had made the movie a success. The newspaper in Benton had classed the movie as immoral and this may have been the reason why so many people had gone to it.

Hank's aunt lived on a quiet side street in a rather old house in fairly good shape. The house was painted white and it had green shutters.

"Coming in?" he asked me as he stopped the car.

"Do you think I should?"

The two cartons of eggs were on the seat between us and he

picked them up.

"Well, I'd like you meet my aunt."

We found Hank's aunt in the kitchen, sitting at the table and looking through a magazine.

"Hello," she said when she saw me.

She had a pleasant face and gray hair and she was inclined to be short and stout. Her face wasn't pretty, though it may have been at one time, and she had a genuine smile.

"You're a very pretty girl," she said as Hank left the kitchen.

I felt at ease with her motherliness which seemed very close.

"Oh, come now," I laughed.

"No, I mean it. You're the prettiest girl he's ever brought here."

We didn't stay at the house very long and when we pulled away from the curb he asked me where I wanted to go.

"I don't know of any place to go," I said. "This is all new to me."

"The movie is out."

"Yes, the movie is out. I had a hard enough time watching it once without going through it twice."

Somebody was burning leaves and I almost choked on the smoke as we passed the blazing pile.

"The burning of leaves is quite a project around here," Hank said. "Nobody seems to know what else to do."

"Well, it is a small place."

We reached the main street and he turned right. The engine had a skip to it and he had to change gears.

"We can always stop at a bar for a drink," he suggested. "We can have a couple and we can talk and I can get to know you better."

"It's up to you."

I thought he would stop at one of the bars in town but he continued to drive out into the country.

"How are you making out with Nina?" he asked me.

"All right."

"She's no bargain. They shouldn't have put you in with her. They shouldn't put anybody in with her," he added, slowing the car as bright neon lights appeared ahead of us. "But maybe she isn't any worse than some of the others in the school. She isn't the only one."

"Only what?"

"Lesbian," he replied. "You'd be surprised at how many there are out at Cedarcliff. But it may not be the fault of the girls. They're thrown together day in and day out and something out of the ordinary is bound to happen. Most of them hate themselves for what they do."

I was glad it was dark and he couldn't see my face. I knew that my cheeks were flaming.

"Let's talk about something else," I said.

"Sure. Anything. Anything as long as it concerns you."

"Why me?"

"Because I only know your name and nothing else."

"There isn't much to know."

"There's always a lot to know."

"I could say the same about you."

"Not as long as you're rooming with Nina. Nina must have told you plenty of things about me, most of them bad."

"Well—"

"I'm even surprised that you met me. I told myself you were just trying to be nice and you didn't want to come right out and say no. I'm glad I was fooled."

He parked the car in front of the bar and grill and we went inside. There were only a couple of people in there and they sat at one of the tables. We took stools at the bar and while the bartender was fixing our drinks—rye and soda—I examined the display of guns hanging on the back bar. I didn't know anything about guns but some of them appeared to be very old, possibly weapons used during frontier days.

We had a lot to drink and we talked a good deal about the school.

"But there's nothing much doing out here during the week," Hank was saying. "Saturday night they have a band and you can dance your fool head off. Some of the girls from the college come here and the local boys know it. They have more fun than they would at the dance at the school and they can rush the bar for all it's worth."

At ten I said I thought I had better go but when he ordered another round of drinks I didn't protest. It hadn't been much of an evening, nothing exciting, but, it was better than being in that room with Nina. Here I was safe and in the room I wasn't.

"You're very quiet," Hank said.

"Sorry."

"Did you tell Nina you were seeing me?"

"No."

"Well, I wouldn't. She can get mad at you over nothing and carry stories to Miss Lily." He lit a cigarette. "Now that we're out here and you're with me I'm wondering if I did right by asking you."

"I'm glad you did."

"Are you?" His eyes searched my face.

"Yes. Very."

I don't know just when it was Hank kissed me. The couple at the table had long since left and the bartender was in back, possibly in the kitchen. Hank simply brought his mouth over to my lips and pushed down hard and sure.

"Don't," I said, twisting away from him.

"Why not?"

"Because we don't know each other very well and I don't kiss every boy I meet. I—I believe a kiss should be something important."

"It was important to me."

The bartender returned and we resumed our drinking. I can't say I was getting helpless but I did feel the drinks. His kiss hadn't been bad, not bad at all. His mouth had been soft and warm and just wet enough to send a tingling sensation up and down my spine. George hadn't ever kissed me that way. George had just bored in, his passion exploding, his hands reaching out to touch me.

"You fill out that sweater," Hank said.

"Do I?"

He grinned and pushed his empty glass across the bar.

"The way it should be filled out," he replied.

At a few minutes past eleven we left the bar and Hank held my arm. I was acutely conscious of his presence, of the pressure of his fingers. I told myself it was the rye but I knew it was more than that. I was trying to find in myself something that admired the male, that would make me think as other girls thought about the male. I knew that a boy and a girl were meant to be together, not two girls. Why hadn't they taught us more about it in high school? They had talked about everything from the founding of our country to figuring the height of a standing tree but there had been nothing about sex.

"Nice night," Hank said as he backed the car out onto the highway.

"Not bad."

There was something wrong with the low gear in the car and it ground terribly but after he finally shifted into high the thing didn't make much noise. My window was down and I could feel the cool air whipping around my face and messing up my hair. I didn't care.

"How do you make out with Paul Blanding?" he inquired.

"Half and half."

"Half good and half bad?"

"You could call it that."

"He try to date you?"

"The first day."

"That follows. He dates all of the pretty girls. And he gets them to give him what he wants." Hank paused. "One guess as to what that is."

"I don't need one guess."

"But maybe you can't blame him too much. The hours when he's at school his wife is handing it out right and left. If a salesman goes to his house and doesn't make more than a sale he's out of his mind."

"Someday they'll both be sorry."

"Maybe. Maybe not. She gets hers and he gets his—but not from each other."

I leaned back and closed my eyes.

"Do we have to discuss sex?"

"It's an interesting topic."

"But not for two people who hardly know each other."

He reached down with his right hand and touched my left thigh, his fingers probing the softness.

"We could know each other better."

I took his hand away.

"Don't do that," I said.

"Why not?"

"You know why not."

"You've got a nice leg. In fact, you're nice all over. Of the three hundred girls at the school you're the best."

Even before the car slowed and we pulled off the road I knew he was going to park with me. However, I said nothing. What was the harm? Nina would still be awake and I wanted her to be asleep when I returned to the room.

"Nobody can see us here," he said as he shut off the lights and engine. "There's a big hill of clay between us and the main road."

I smiled into the darkness.

"No doubt you've been here before."

He wasn't offended.

"I don't deny it. I've been here lots of times."

"With lots of different girls?"

"A few."

"From the school?"

"Some of them. Some from town, but I like the girls from the college best. They know why a fellow parks."

I got a cigarette from my pocketbook and he held a light for me.

"And why does a fellow park?" I asked.

"Because he likes a girl."

"You can like a girl without parking."

"But not with the same results."

"Must there always be results?"

"What's the point of it if there aren't?"

I thought of having been with George and the old fear returned to me. I had been silly to accept Hank's invitation. He was out for all he could get and nothing short of the limit would satisfy him. That didn't mean I disliked him. I didn't. A boy sets a goal for himself and he's entitled to try for it. A girl takes her chances when she's parked in the country in the darkness. But that doesn't mean that she has to surrender herself as a tramp might do.

"You've got the wrong girl," I told him.

"I don't think so. You're not as innocent as you were the day you were born."

George, I thought; George, you didn't please me. Why was that? Did I expect too much or did you give too little? Then I thought of Nina. Admit it or not, my relationship with Nina had been a touch of heaven. She had brought life to my hungry body, a form of life frowned on by all the best people. Perhaps I could find the same thing with Hank. Perhaps he could turn me into a raging inferno of desire. Perhaps...

"Don't, Hank," I said thickly.

He had one hand on my knee.

"Your skin is smooth. Smooth. It's like a piece of silk," he said.

"Don't please!"

"I'm pretty nuts about you," Hank said.

I tried to free his hand but he held firm.

"We shouldn't be doing this," I said, throwing the cigarette out of the car. "This is for a girl who wants this sort of thing and I don't."

"Don't tell me you never have."

"I'm not saying that, but I hardly know you and you don't know me much better. We had a few drinks and a nice evening and we should let it go at that."

"I know something that would make it better." His face was very close to mine. "I know something that would make it a hell of a lot better."

His mouth found my lips, a mouth wide open and filled with passion, a passion which, although I fought against it, forced my lips apart. A good portion of my life passed before me in that second. Who was I? What was I? Should I belong to a girl or to a man? I thought of what Nina had done for me and I began to tremble, my arms moved up to encircle his neck. I would never be a girl's girl. I would find the path that a girl was meant to follow and some day I would be a respectable wife. But I would not find it in a parked car and with a boy I hardly knew. There had to be something decent in my life, something worthwhile.

"No," I protested, pulling my mouth from him. "No more, Hank."

"I get what I go after," he muttered.

"Not tonight."

"Tonight is no exception."

"You're drunk, Hank. It's the liquor. Let me go and in the morning you'll feel different."

"Yeah. I'll feel as though I missed something."

"There are other girls who wouldn't mind."

"True. But I happen to want you."

While we had been talking he had been working on my sweater with his free hand. I let out a little sob as he touched me.

"They're lovely," he said.

"Don't," I whispered. I was crying by this time. "Don't do

anything we'll both be sorry for."

He bent and kissed them, lingeringly.

"You won't be sorry," he said his voice muffled. "And I know I won't be. I've wanted you from the second you picked me up on the highway."

"Hank—"

"It's better than Nina. Anything is better than Nina. And don't tell me she hasn't at least tried. I've worked at the school long enough to know better. She gives you a few drinks and then she takes over. That kind of stuff isn't for you. With your body you're meant for only one thing."

I began to fight him, clawing and biting and scratching, but he didn't seem to mind it at all. Then his body struck in all its fury, his mouth crushing my lips.

"Live," he told me. "Live, baby! Live!"

But I didn't live. I almost died. I almost died because of what he was doing to me and because I knew he wasn't being careful.

I sobbed when, much later, he drove me toward the college and the path which led through the dark woods.

I had proved nothing to myself.

Nothing at all.

7

Nina was still sleeping when I left the room the next morning. I was early for class but I had been unable to sleep and I thought a walk might do me good. I only glanced at her before closing the door. She had a gentle smile on her lips. She had been that way when I had come in the night before and I had not disturbed her.

I left the building and the glare of the sun nearly blinded me.

"Good morning," Hank said.

He had been waiting for me at the front door. I tried to brush past him. He caught my arm.

"I don't want to talk to you," I snapped. "We don't have anything to say to each other."

"Even after last night?"

"Even after last night."

His grip relaxed.

"You were as much to blame as I was."

The way he said it made me angry.

"I didn't park the car," I reminded him. "I didn't buy the drinks. And I asked you to quit. What more could I do?"

He let me go but I continued to stand there. It was pointless to run away from him. All he could do in the daylight was talk and talk couldn't hurt me.

"You could have given me a baby," I said. "You know that, don't you?"

"Are you worried about that?" He was faintly amused.

"Who wouldn't be worried?"

Hank looked out across the campus. No one was there, just the grass wet from the night's dew and the mist rising from it.

"I lost my head," he said after a while.

"Thanks. That helps me a lot."

"It's one chance in a million that anything happened."

"What if it did?" I insisted.

"I'd stick by you."

"Am I supposed to believe that?"

"Why wouldn't I?" he retorted. "You're a beautiful girl and I think a lot of you."

"How many other girls have heard the same thing?"

"Well—"

"You don't have to excuse yourself, Hank. I was a fool to go with you in the first place and now I've paid the price. You got what you wanted. If I live to be a hundred it won't happen again."

I walked away from him, letting him stand there. In a way I was glad to know I could depend upon him if I turned out to be pregnant but the thought of being married to him was rather bleak. I didn't know the amout of money Hank made at the school but I was fairly sure it wasn't much. And I would die, simply die, if I had to live the rest of my life in a town like Cedarcliff. I was used to the better things in life, all the things with which he would never be able to provide me.

I found a bench and sat down. It was useless to cry but I did. I cried because I didn't know what I was and nothing I did ever seemed to turn out. I had given myself to Nina and I had permitted Hank to know the favors of my body. Right now, this very minute, I could be pregnant and this made me cry all the harder. My mother had died in childbirth and I felt the same thing might happen to me. I didn't want to die. I wanted to find myself and be decent and grow old with the passing of the years. Even if I had to grow old alone, with no love to please me.

I had breakfast in the dining hall but I didn't eat very much. I had a bad headache and the noise of the girls chattering all around me didn't help it very much. One of them had sneaked out the night before and met a boy from town, a boy she had met during her visit to the school during the previous summer. He had been a dream, a perfect dream.

"God," she said, "he was all man."

"If Miss Lily finds out he'll turn out to be a nightmare."

"How's Miss Lily going to find out? The old goat locks herself in her room and hits the bottle."

"Honest?"

"So help me. How else does she stand it out here? She isn't an old woman and my guess is that she knows what a man was made for the same as any girl."

Sex, sex, sex. Sex was everywhere, all around me. Why was it so important? There were other things to do. But the girls would rather talk about home and boy friends and, sooner or later, sex. I doubted if there were a girl in the school who hadn't gone to bed with a boy, and now that the opportunity was denied them they missed it. My further guess was that if they were all given the opportunity to throw their restrictions here aside they would take it—instantly.

The day was much the same as any other day, except that we were given a load of English work to do, and at noon I received my mail. I had three letters, one from my father, one from Laura and one from George. They all said about the same thing. My father and Laura were being married on Saturday and they hoped I would come to the wedding. Only George's letter went into greater detail. He missed me, missed me terribly, and he asked me why I didn't give up college and marry him right away. He was doing fine in his new job, better than he had expected, and he could get a loan on a beautiful house just outside of Benton. After the conclusion of his letter there was a note in which he said he had wanted to drive out and see me that weekend but he felt he should stay in town and attend the wedding. He hoped I would be there so we could spend some time together.

I didn't quite know what to do about it and I spent most of

the afternoon thinking things over. The marriage would soon be a fact and I had to accept it. I hoped, for my father's sake, Laura would make him a good wife. The thought of having a stepmother only a few years my senior rather amused and annoyed me. I prayed silently they wouldn't have a baby. I didn't know how I would take that. But I concluded my father wouldn't want a child at his age, and Laura wasn't marrying him so she could become a mother. My father wanted his sex and Laura wanted his money. It was, to my way of thinking, as simple as that.

Paul Blanding kept me after class, and as he came limping down the aisle I let out a sigh.

I watched him as he lit a cigarette and sat down on top of the desk opposite me. He swung his bad leg back and forth and for the first time I noticed the knee was stiff.

"Why can't we be friends?" he asked.

"I thought we were."

He filled his lungs with smoke and blew a cloud of it toward the ceiling.

"I saw you last night," he said.

"Did you?"

"You used the path across the campus and then you went through the woods."

"I didn't see you."

"That's possibly due to the fact I was in the woods, off the path."

I didn't know what to say.

"Still have a mind of your own?" Paul Blanding inquired.

"Very much so."

"But not so much that you didn't sneak off with Hank Herbert?"

Again I didn't know what to say. If he told Miss Lily what I had done she would believe him and I would be in real trouble.

"You're very foolish to run around with Hank," he said. "He's got other girls in the school into trouble and you could be next." He leaned forward. "Would you like to be carrying Hank's baby around inside of you?"

I felt compelled to defend Hank, not because he had treated me as he should have but because I didn't want Paul Blanding to guess what had gone on between us.

"There was nothing wrong in it," I said.

"But you know the rules of the school?"

"Yes."

"On weekends your time is pretty much your own but during the week you live by the code as set down by Miss Lily. And if you escaped from what Hank wanted to do to you last night you were lucky. You won't be so lucky the next time, of that I assure you. He has a way of forcing a girl to his will."

"What about you?" I flung at him. "Isn't force the basis of your methods?"

He shook his head.

"There's a difference. Hank can only do one thing for you and I can help you in your school work. If you are nice to me I will be nice to you." The ashes from his cigarette fell on his pants leg.

I gathered my books in my arms and stood up.

"I'd rather take my chances," I said. "I'd rather work until four in the morning than get my marks the way you want me to get them."

His face showed no expression at all.

"Suit yourself."

I turned my head as I left him.

"I certainly will. And please don't keep me after class again. I don't want the girls talking. I'm not that kind of a girl and I don't intend to become that kind of a girl. As long as I do my work I don't know what else you want from me."

He followed me toward the door.

"You know what I want," he said.

The color rose to my face, burning. But I determined the next time a man knew me physically would be when I wanted the man.

Once outside I walked slowly toward Massey Hall and reread the letters from home. By Saturday night Laura would be my stepmother and everything would change. I didn't know exactly how it would change but I felt it would. She would bleed my father dry and in the end she would cast him aside. It would cost him a lot for the divorce and there was a good chance she would get alimony. It had happened to other men before and there was no reason to believe that my father would be an exception. A young girl, I was sure, didn't marry a man in his forties for love. She married for security and what she could get out of him.

I spent most of my time on George's letter, trying to imagine myself being married to him and rearing his children. It was impossible to imagine, or even to consider. I had never been in love with a man and I didn't know what love was but I was sure I wasn't in love with George. I mentally berated myself for having accepted his ring. A ring was only a piece of metal that had to stand for something or otherwise it was useless. You bought a ring in a store but you couldn't buy love there. Love had to come from inside you, had to have a meaning, had to represent the ultimate in life. True, I respected George, but my emotions for him didn't go beyond this point. He could have been earning a thousand dollars a week and it wouldn't have changed me. Money, no matter how much there was of it, couldn't bring love.

Hank was working in front of Massey Hall, trimming the shrubs into neat cones, and he stopped me as I started past him.

"You still mad at me?" he asked.

"No, I'm not mad." What good was it for me to be mad? I had accepted his invitation and he had collected his reward. "No, I'm not mad at all."

"What about tonight?"

"No." I was firm.

"The same thing wouldn't happen. I promise you."

"No."

He clipped a couple of stray branches.

"Isn't there anything I can say to change your mind?"

"Not a thing."

I left him there by the bush.

Nina was in the room when I entered. She was seated on her bed and working on a project.

"You made a night of it last night," she said.

I placed my books on a chair.

"Well, I walked and walked and time just slipped by me."

She fluffed out her hair and smiled.

"Or Paul Blanding slipped you one?"

"No, not that."

"I'd like to keep score for him. He must have more girls in the course of a year than you can shake a stick at." Nina got to her feet and unsnapped her bra. "Jesus, it's hot in here."

"You should have opened the window."

"Well, I forgot."

She wasn't using the desk and she invited me to help myself. I sat down almost immediately. I had a great deal to do and when she spoke of going to eat I told her I wasn't hungry.

"Neither am I," she said, opening a dresser drawer. "Let's have a drink and to hell with the damned school."

I had thought the window being open would help cool the room but it didn't. My hand, gripping the pen, was sticky and I was hot all over. It had been one of those September days that creeps up on you, getting warmer and warmer, and then smashes into you head-on.

"We should have a fan," I said.

"You strip down and it isn't so bad. If there's any air at all you get it."

Nina had fixed me a drink and she placed it on the desk but I didn't touch it right away. I had missed several things in my classes, thinking about home, and I had to do some reading to catch up. I was intensely aware of Nina's undraped form in the room and I could smell her perfume. Finally I reached for the drink and tasted it. It wasn't bad. The drink was gone before I realized it and Nina poured me another one.

My English was a snap and it didn't take me long to finish it. By this time the second drink had gone the way of the first.

"I had a phone call from the city this afternoon," Nina said.

"Did you?"

"About my father. They're operating on him and they're going to take out a piece of his gut. My folks thought I ought to be there but what can I do for him? I'll run down this weekend. He'll feel better then and he'll be able to talk."

I thought of spending the weekend without her and it was an absolute void. I'd be alone in the room and there would be only the Saturday night dance to amuse me. I saw then I was closer to her than I had suspected. Even though I knew it was wrong I looked forward to being with her, of having her near. Yes, I could've gone home to see my father married. But the house would be filled with drunks and George might expect the same thing from me I had given him before. It was a weekend that I didn't want to spend at home.

"I hope your father gets along all right," I said.

"Well, he's got a good doctor. He wouldn't have anybody

but the best. But he'll probably have to give up his drinking, like it or not. I knew a fellow once who had the same kind of an operation and he had to stick to milk."

I put my books away, far from being satisfied with my efforts, and pulled the sweater over my head. What was I fighting? What was I running from? One girl got her pleasure with a boy and another girl got her pleasure with another girl. Was it so terribly wrong? It wasn't something that had to last, that had to become an internal part of my life. We shared a few short hours and the secret was ours. No one need know.

I got out of my skirt and put in on a hanger. Then I removed the rest of my things and threw them in my laundry bag. I turned and faced Nina who was watching me closely. Our bodies were alive and glowing.

"You could make a fortune in a night club," she said.

"How?"

"By stripping."

"I'd never do that."

"Why not?"

"And show myself to men? Besides, I don't have to."

"You said something about being a teacher."

"That's right."

"Teachers don't make much money. A good stripper does. A good stripper can name her own ticket."

This time I poured my own drink and I didn't use any ginger ale. The liquor burned my throat as I swallowed it and it made me cough.

"You really bounce," she said after I had stopped coughing. She laughed. "If half the girls had half of what you've got the world would be a better place."

"There's one girl in my history class who isn't far behind me."

Nina nodded.

"She's the one who put out for Paul Blanding last night."

"How do you know?"

"Oh, word gets around. She lives with an old roommate of mine and she came in at midnight crying. She figures she might have got herself knocked up. The roomy told her to stop worrying, that Blanding never takes a chance. But she wasn't convinced and she won't be until her month is up."

I wished I was as sure and I treated myself to another drink.

Becoming pregnant was all that had to happen to me. Suddenly, in a state of near-frenzy, I felt the need of talking to someone, anyone.

"I went out with Hank Herbert last night," I said.

Nina didn't seem surprised.

"I thought as much. He wouldn't let a pretty girl like you slip through his fingers."

My eyes were clouded with tears.

"And he went the distance."

"That follows, too."

"We had a few drinks and he parked and he wouldn't let me go. I tried to fight him but he's awfully strong and he—well, just took me."

"You aren't the first one. And you won't be the last."

"But—"

"The thing to do is not worry about it. What's done is done."

"But—but he wasn't careful."

Her face clouded.

"The bastard!"

"Supposing I had a baby?" I wailed, reaching for the bottle. "Do you know what that would mean?"

Nina brushed the suggestion aside.

"You can get rid of a kid," she said. "Other girls have and you could do the same. The thing to do is not let it go too long after you know. The longer you wait the more dangerous it is."

"Oh, my God!"

She came over and put her arm around my bare shoulders.

"Don't get so upset," she advised. "Probably nothing happened. When you're sure it didn't you'll be angry at yourself for being so scared."

"I hope so." I was in tears. "Oh, I hope so!"

She kissed me on the cheek.

"But that doesn't excuse a man for being careless with a girl."

She led me to my bed and we sat down upon it. I was crying my fool heart out, ashamed of myself and ashamed I had told her. Such a thing was very personal with me and I wasn't like the other girls who seemed to glory in talking about their sex lives. It was something to conceal, not something to make conversation about. But I had been lonely and miserable and confused. I hadn't been boasting about my association with Hank Herbert. I had been confessing.

"You poor damn kid," Nina said as her mouth sought mine. "You poor kid."

It was the best kiss I had ever had, the very best, and I think I cried out as she forced my lips apart and her tongue became a spear of blazing fire. I fell back on the bed, pulling her down with me, our bodies meeting in solid contact.

"I love you," she said. "I'll love you until the end of time."

I knew what she was going to do and I wanted her to do it.

"I love you, too," I moaned.

She was good to me after that—oh, how good she was to me!—and I cared nothing about anything else. I was a captive of the flesh, a willing captive, and my body rose, trembling, to the magic of her love.

We had just parted—she was sitting upon the edge of the bed and I lay upon it—when the door opened and Miss Lily came in. It was still light in the room and I remember reaching for the sheet with which to cover my nakedness.

"Miss Wilbur?" she asked.

"Yes," Nina said. "Is something wrong, Miss Lily?"

Miss Lily had on her dark glasses and it was impossible to see her eyes. I didn't know whether she was looking at us or at the empty bottle.

"You'll have to leave right away," Miss Lily said, her voice calm. "They called from New York. Your father died on the operating table."

"Died?" Nina echoed.

Miss Lily nodded. "Just a few minutes ago."

Nina got up and moved stiffly across the room. In that moment she looked very tired and very old for her age.

"Thanks," she said.

After Miss Lily had gone I helped Nina pack. We kissed once, holding each other as though we were the only two people in the world.

"I'll be back," she said. "Wait for me."

I told her that I would.

I knew, kissing those lovely lips, that I would wait for her forever and ever.

Rightly or wrongly, Nina was in my blood.

8

Nina was gone for ten days and I was so terribly lonely and miserable I didn't think I could endure the separation. I tried to lose myself in my work, doing more than I had to do, and several times I had Hank bring me in a bottle from town.

"I won't charge you the extra two dollars," he said. "Let's say I was paid in advance."

Two days after Nina's departure I learned I wasn't pregnant and I cried with joy. That night I drank almost a whole bottle of rye by myself and collapsed in a drunken stupor on the bed. When I awoke the next morning it was so late I had already missed two classes and when I reported to the third class I was told Miss Lily wanted to see me.

"Sit down," she said after I entered her office.

I sat down and wished that she wasn't wearing her dark glasses. I wanted to see her eyes.

"You aren't doing very well," she told me. "You're getting off to a bad start."

"My clock didn't go off."

She smiled.

"Or the liquor was too much for you?" she inquired.

I pretended to be hurt.

"I don't know what you're talking about," I said.

She waved my protest aside.

"It doesn't matter," she said. "We have regular classes and you are supposed to attend them. What is the point of coming to an expensive school if you aren't going to make the most of it? There are thousands of girls who would give ten years of their lives just to be a part of Cedarcliff. The only reason you are here is because your father was able to afford it."

I fingered the books in my lap and stared down at the floor. She was quite right. I had been somewhat foolish and I would have to be careful not to be so again.

"There's another thing I wanted to see you about," Miss Lily went on. "We have two girls who are leaving—one by choice and one because she is hopelessly inadequate for us— and that will mean an empty room. You mentioned before you wanted to move but at the time I couldn't do anything about it. Now, if you wish, you may have a room by yourself."

The news came so suddenly I didn't know what I wanted to

do. Right or wrong, whether or not I liked it, I was tied closely to Nina. The thought of being away from her left me cold all over. Yet—and this was the important part—I had to do something. Our relationship couldn't go on and on without leaving me covered with scars, scars which no one would be able to see but which would be there just the same.

"Thank you," I said. "I'll take the room."

"There will be an extra charge, Miss Wilbur."

"That's all right. As soon as I get a bill I'll give you a check."

I moved my things that night and sat in a large chair, drinking. Where was Nina now? Did she miss me as much as I missed her? I had another drink and shook my head. I had to get over this lesbian problem. I had to bury it.

I drank quite a lot that night but I didn't get drunk— something prevented me. And long after I went to bed, turning out the light and lying nude in the darkness, I wished Nina was there with me. I could talk to Nina and she would understand. She would help me. Or would it be help? No, it wouldn't be. It would be love, the glorious love of two bodies seeking and finding each other, bringing a beauty to the world that the world—my world—had never known before.

The next morning I met Hank on my way to breakfast and I told him to bring me in a couple of bottles from town.

"You must be throwing a ball," he said.

"There isn't anything else to do," I explained lamely.

"Not since your roomy went home?"

"I now have a room by myself."

"How convenient."

"I'm afraid I don't understand you."

"You will in time."

Paul Blanding didn't bother me the rest of the week and he gave me a ninety on a paper I had thought terrible. But I was sure he hadn't forgotten about me. He was only waiting for the proper time to approach me again. While he was doing this he was amusing himself with another girl in the class. She didn't seem to be overly bright and I felt sorry for her.

I thought of going home for the weekend—I had had another letter from George—but I rejected the whole idea. I didn't want to see my father married and I wasn't interested in seeing George. I would have had to put on the ring, and to have worn it would have been to live a lie. If I could get up the courage I would return it to him and he could look for another girl who would appreciate it more than I did.

Saturday I played two games of tennis and lost both. I have never been a very good tennis player and the girl on the other side of the net was terribly fast. Later I found out she had won several trophies and then I didn't feel so badly about losing.

I spent the afternoon working on my assignments, especially my history, and while I was doing this I had a few drinks. I didn't bother eating that night and about seven-thirty I got ready for the dance. I had never been to one of Miss Lily's dances, of course, but I didn't feel as if I wanted to go into town and wander about alone.

But the dance didn't amount to much. There were about fifty girls there and only half as many boys. Music was provided by a record player which refused to change records as it should have and Miss Lily spent most of her time trying to keep it running.

Sunday was a dull day and so was the following week. My schedule followed the same pattern every day—drink into work. Some girls tried to become friendly, dropping into my room, but I didn't encourage them. All during my waking hours I was thinking of Nina, what she was doing, and how soon she would be back. On Thursday I had a letter from her and she said she would return early on Monday morning. She said the funeral had been sad and that she missed me. I thought of writing to her, to tell her I had missed her, too, but she had neglected to include her return address and I didn't know where to write.

By Friday I couldn't endure it any longer and I decided on going home for the weekend. Anything was better than the emptiness of my room and the bottles of liquor I had been drinking. A change, I further decided, might do me good.

I got away from the school at four and it seemed wonderful to be driving the Ford again.

There was a lot of weekend traffic but the road was good, except for the place where they were building the bridge, and I made good time.

Shortly before six-thirty I arrived home, left my car parked in front of the garage and walked into the house through the back way. I hadn't considered the reception I would get but now as I stepped into the house I did. Would I be welcome? Or wouldn't I?

My questions were soon answered.

"Well, darling," Laura greeted me, "what a wonderful surprise."

"Hi."

She was in the kitchen and I could see she was in the process of making herself a drink. She wore a pale blue robe, though she hadn't bothered to belt it around the middle, and I could see through the opening she had nothing on underneath. I tried to glance away from her and couldn't. It was like throwing a match in an empty gasoline drum.

"Have one?" she asked.

"What is it?"

"Gin and orange juice. It isn't bad."

"Well—"

"One won't hurt you. You probably need it after that ride."

"I am a little dry."

She reached up high in a cabinet for another glass and her figure was perfectly outlined by the robe. I had to admit to myself that her body was lush and ripe and in that instant I couldn't blame my father for having wanted her. Any man would have. Or any woman.

"I'm glad you came," she said. "Your father and George will be away overnight—they have a chance to buy some standing lumber upstate—and I was at a loss to know what to do with myself."

I watched her while she mixed the drinks.

"I thought your store stayed open Friday night," I said.

"Well, I found out being married and running a store doesn't fit. I hired a woman who seems to know her business and she's taking care of it for me."

"That makes sense."

"It was partly your father's idea. He doesn't want to have me working and he even insists I sell the store. I may at that. If I can only make a deal, possibly with the woman I now have, we can take that honeymoon that we weren't able to take. He's anxious to get away for a little while and I honestly don't blame him. George can take care of things here and he can relax."

She handed me the drink and I tasted it It was pretty good and I told her so.

"I like it," she said. "You can drink them and not get plastered. But, then, I've always been a gin drinker. I used to swipe my father's bottle at home to see what it was like."

We carried the drinks into the living room and I walked behind her. Her hips had a sassy, heady motion and I hated to think of my father taking all this beauty and spoiling it. Some night, no matter how careful they were—if they *were* careful— he would make her pregnant and much of her shape would be gone. I don't know why the thought disturbed me so much but it did. They were both old enough to know what they wanted from their marriage and it was none of my business whether they had one or a half-dozen kids.

"We missed you at the wedding," Laura said after we were seated on the davenport.

"Well, you know how the first week of school is. You don't know whether you're going or coming. And," I added, "I didn't think I'd be missed at all. When two people are getting married they only have eyes for each other."

She smiled and leaned back. I could see the curve of one breast. I had been told many times I was built in that department but she had much more up there than I did.

"George was unhappy about you not coming," Laura said. "All he did was drink and moon around. We had quite a few people to the reception and one girl made a play for him but he wouldn't have anything to do with her. He claims he's going to marry you."

"He gave me a ring."

She examined my left hand. "You're not wearing it."

"No."

"Any good reason?"

It was strange I should feel close to her. I don't mean as a daughter would feel about a mother or a stepmother—but as a friend. And the fact that she was so lovely may have had something to do with it.

"I'm not sure that I'm going to marry him," I said.

"Does he know that?"

"I haven't had a chance to tell him."

"You could have written."

"I thought of that but it didn't seem to be the thing to do. That's the easy way out. I think it's only honest I tell him face to face. I'm sure he would do the same thing with me."

"No doubt. He seems straight."

I toyed with my drink.

"It isn't that," I said. "I'll be in college four years and that's a long time. People change in four years. Everybody does. It isn't fair to tie him down that long and it isn't fair to me."

Laura left for the kitchen to get a couple more drinks and I closed my eyes. I tried to grasp the picture of Nina and I couldn't. All I could see was Laura, Laura yielding, granting me my every wish. My face turned hot, then cold, then hot again. I thought I must be going mad. Better that I had stayed at Cedarcliff with my bottle and my loneliness.

She returned from the kitchen and as she bent over to hand me my glass she fell all open in front. Nina had fine breasts but nothing like these. These were the very fruit of life, their centers as dark as the lipstick on her lips.

"I was afraid you might hate me," she said, sitting down. "I thought that was why you didn't come to the wedding."

"No, I don't hate you. Why should I? You're my father's choice for a mate and if he's satisfied I should be too."

"Some of the neighbors don't like me."

"That's to be expected."

"They think I married him for his money but it wasn't just that. If it had been money I wanted I could have had that without marriage. I can show you dozens of checks he gave me I never cashed. What I gave him wasn't for sale. What I've tried to give him is the love he needed so desperately."

"I think I understand," I said.

"Every man wants love. We all want love. We can be rich or poor but it is really love and health that count."

She lit a cigarette and went on.

"There's one thing you don't have to worry about," she said. "There won't be any babies. I don't want any and it's too late in life for him to start raising another family now. If we had one he would be sixty-three before it got out of high school."

I don't know how it eventually happened. I can't tell you how it happened. We had had only one drink but she sat down quite close to me, our thighs nearly touching. I had a terrible struggle with myself, trying not to put my free arm around her, but I couldn't resist. And she responded the way I hoped she would, her lips parted, almost smiling, waiting for my kiss.

"I won't stop you," she said softly.

We both spilled our drinks, dropping our glasses to the floor as we embraced. A wave of panic and fear surged through me, making me cold all over.

"You're going to hate me," I whispered.

Laura's eyes took on a new shine.

"Hate you? Why should I? It won't be the first time that it's happened to me and I hope that it won't be the last."

My left hand found the front of her and she was all I had expected she would be. I became frantic with desire.

"When was the first time?" I demanded, breathing heavily.

"In school. I was a senior and the other girl was older. The next time was when I was selling dresses from house to house. I had to fit this girl for a dress but it went beyond that. I thought I would die when she moved away."

"Yet you've been—that way—with my father."

"To escape. You try to run from yourself but it's impossible to run. You only fool yourself. There's nothing quite like this. Nothing. This is the beginning and the end of love."

"The beginning and the end of everything."

I was wild that night but not as wild as Laura. She undressed me there in the living room, kissing me as she did so, her lips burning with passion and need.

"I'm glad he went away," she cried. "I'm glad they both went away."

It was an exhausting night. First in the living room and then upstairs in the big bedroom. Minutes that stretched into hours, love as I had never known it before—even with Nina. It was a love that carried me up into the clouds, tearing away all my past life and giving me something new, something more real than anything I had ever experienced.

"It has to be this way every weekend," Laura said as we lay side by side.

"How can it be? My father will be home."

"After he has gone to sleep I can come to you."

"What if he should catch us?"

"He won't catch us. We'll be smart. He's a sound sleeper but if that doesn't work out we can always take a ride into the country."

I sighed and closed my eyes.

This was my father's wife.

And my lover....

I couldn't look my father in the face when he returned home later the next afternoon. Laura and I had spent the entire morning in bed, making love and promises. During moments when we lay panting upon the bed I tried to compare her with Nina but I couldn't. Both her flesh and love were far superior, beyond anything I had ever dreamed of knowing.

"Love me," she had encouraged me once.

And I had, hardly able to breathe, my every action clumsy and showing my inexperience. However, she had been patient with me and she had told me it would be better the next time. She had been sweet about that. I knew I hadn't pleased her, not the way she had pleased me, and she had seemed contented enough to return to the role of being my lover.

We were in the kitchen when my father came into the house.

"Well, hello there," he said, smiling. "The two of you look fine."

I glanced at him, then away, but not before I saw Laura kiss him warmly on the mouth. I didn't blame her. She was living a dual role and she had to be the affectionate wife. We hadn't talked about it much the night before but I was sure now she had married him for his money. She had confided to me she hated the sex act with the male, probably more so than I did, but she accepted it as a price she had to pay for marriage. She had also confessed she had had several female lovers but that some of them had got scared and others had moved away.

"You appear well," my father said to me.

"Yes, I'm fine."

"How is school?"

"Oh, it's all right."

He raised his eyebrows.

"Just all right?"

I felt nervous being so near him. I had received the love of his wife and I was afraid I might show it.

"Oh, I didn't mean it the way it sounded," I assured him. "It's a fine school but it takes a while to get used to it."

"How is your money holding out?"

"Very well."

"Just say the word if you need more."

"Thank you, I will."

He had his arm around Laura's waist—she was wearing the robe again—and he was digging his fingers into her stomach. I hated my father for that. He hadn't been in the house five minutes and he was after her, unable to wait for the darkness of the night. I thought of him going to the same bed with her, of what he would do to her, and I resented him all the more. Laura was mine. If only we had discovered each other before the marriage she could have refused my father. But now she couldn't. She was his wife and since he was her husband he had certain physical rights to her.

"George will be glad you're here," my father said, his fingers in the softness of Laura's flesh. "He hasn't said much but I know that he's missed you. And he thought you should have written more often."

"I was rather busy."

"That's what I told him. I said you had to get settled and all that stuff. He said he understood."

I wasn't wearing George's ring and I wondered if my father noticed it. No doubt I would see George that night and I would return it to him. I couldn't go on being a love-cheat. I knew, without any question at all, what I was and what I would always be. I was a lesbian, perhaps even more so than Laura or Nina, and there was no place in my life for a man.

"Let's go upstairs," my father said to Laura. "We can talk while I change."

"Well—"

"And you ought to put on something yourself. George is going to stop out later this afternoon and that robe doesn't cover you very much."

I watched them go and I blinked back the tears. I knew what would happen when they reached the bedroom.

They were upstairs a long time and when they finally came down Laura was wearing shorts and a halter and her face was flushed.

"I'm going down to the office for a short while," my father said. "George is going to meet me there and we're going to outline the details of the lumber purchase." He paused at the door. "We got a good buy upstate but I'm going to have to go up there from time to time to set up the mill. I can't expect George to do everything and he's busy enough here."

As soon as my father left Laura fixed us drinks and we sat

at the table drinking. The woman who did the cleaning was in another part of the house and was hard of hearing. We could talk in privacy.

"He's a bull," Laura said.

"I know," I said, remembering the nights I had heard them in the room across the hall.

"I told him I didn't feel like it but he wouldn't listen. He had to hit the sheets before he would do anything else." She sighed. "Sometimes I don't figure men. They attach so much importance to money and sex you'd think they were the only two things in the world."

"Well, money and sex are important for marriage."

"True enough," Laura admitted.

"Without either one you're lost. But—"

"But?"

"Well, you have to be really sure of both."

Laura smiled at my remark.

"The money's easy to identify," I said.

"But is the sex?" she pointed out.

"Well, some aren't sure of the sex they really want."

"A lot of them aren't. The divorce courts are filled with people who won't admit what they are. Some of them, afraid of being alone, stick to marriage to the bitter end, bringing up kids who are as confused as they are. The others, the smart ones, find an outlet such as we have found."

Laura fixed another drink and calmly surveyed me.

"I never thought it of you," she said.

"Thought what of me?"

"What you are."

"Well—"

"But I wanted you to be that way. I prayed for it. You have a right in the house and it isn't dangerous. For me to find somebody on the outside might mean the end of my marriage. There are girls who will blackmail you if you have money."

We emptied the gin bottle and started on a fresh one. I knew my father wouldn't say anything. He liked to drink himself and he didn't object to anybody else seeking the same enjoyment.

"I don't know why we sit down here," I said, recalling the wonders of the night and wanting them again.

"Because of that old bitch upstairs. She may not be able to hear very well but she's got the eyes of a hawk. And she hates me. She's been with him so long she looks down on me because I've brought a little pleasure into his life."

"I don't know how you stand it," I said. "The sex part."

"Why do you think he married me?"

"I guess he must have loved you."

"No, it wasn't that. Any girl who would have been willing to share his bed could have had him. He has to prove to himself time and time again he's a man and it takes a girl to help him do that." She lit another cigarette. "I'm being honest with you, Doris. He bought me just as he would buy a new car and I have to give him his mileage. I moan at the right times and once in a while he gets beyond the barrier I've set up for myself. There are times with him I do get a certain lift. But when it's over with I feel angry and dirty. It isn't the kind of love we shared and it never will be. The only thing is he never complains. I may have a strange streak of blood in me but your father and I can go on and be happy. The only thing is I have to get my kicks on the outside."

I tried to feel sorry for my father but the feeling just wouldn't develop. He was getting what he was paying for and nothing else. There was a good chance that he would eventually stray from the marriage-bed and find somebody else. He was old enough to know better and young enough to have the urge. I said nothing to Laura about my thoughts and I saw no reason I should. I might be wrong. For her sake, I hoped I was.

Our conversation was interrupted by the arrival of my father and George. George greeted me warmly, kissing me lightly on the cheek, and he insisted we have dinner at Moon Lake Inn.

"Steak," he added. "To celebrate."

I hesitated but my father encouraged me and, I suppose because she thought she should, so did Laura.

"Take the Caddy," my father said. "Laura and I are going to spend a quiet evening at home. I'm tired of driving."

On the way out to the lake, George and I talked about many things, mostly his progress in the business and my work at school.

"I wrote you about the house," he said. "It's a very nice house. I wish you would look at it with me."

"We'll see."

"We could get the keys tomorrow."

"Not tomorrow. I'm leaving early for the school." I tried to soften the refusal. "Perhaps next weekend."

He seemed disappointed.

"It won't stay on the market long," George said. He drove a short distance in silence. "I put five hundred dollars down on it," he told me. "But that's only a ten-day option. If we don't take it somebody else is bound to snap it up."

"And you lose your five hundred dollars?"

"Well, that part isn't so bad. It didn't come out of my savings. Your father gave me a thousand dollar bonus for digging up that lumber deal."

"I'm in college," I reminded him. "Four years is a long time."

He slowed the car for a truck in front of us.

"I don't know why you insist on college," he said. "I may have said it before and I may not have said it but I think it's foolish for you to go on with it. College is for a girl who is going to go into a profession and that isn't true in your case. It isn't that your father can't afford it. He can. But there's more to it than that. It's four years out of your life and four years before we could start raising a family."

"Family?"

"That's what marriage is for, isn't it?"

"With most people."

"And the younger you start having children the better it is. I've done some reading about it. A girl's best years are between eighteen and thirty and it's best to space children about two years apart."

I wasn't even wearing his ring—he hadn't noticed that—and he had me pregnant already. Well, I had news for him. He wasn't going to make me pregnant. No man was. With the attitude I had I'd be an unfit mother from the very start.

The inn was deserted this time of the year and we sat at a table that overlooked the lake.

We had a cocktail while waiting for our steaks and it was then George saw that I wasn't wearing his ring.

"Where is the ring?" he asked.

"In my pocketbook."

"But—why?" His face had a worried look to it. "Why, Doris?"

I gave it to him straight.

"Because I don't believe in wearing something that isn't real to me."

He waved for another drink and I reached into my pocketbook for the ring.

"I don't follow you," he said.

I placed the ring on the table near him.

"I don't know how to say this," I began. "I honestly don't. You've been sweet to me and you're an awfully good man but I don't feel about you as I should feel. I—I can't explain it. You're ready to settle down and I'm not. That may be because you're four years older than I am. I don't know. All I know is I couldn't marry you."

He picked up the ring and put it down again.

"You met somebody at school," he said.

"How could I? It's a girl's school. It—it's nothing personal. Believe me. It's just that marriage means so much to you and I can't see it."

The waiter brought our second drink.

"I'll let the house go," he said. "I can wait, if that's what you want. Probably my trouble is I've tried to make you do things my way. I forgot you have a mind of your own. If you want a degree the thing for you to do is to get it. I'll still be there waiting when they hand you your diploma."

I shook my head.

"It won't work," I said. "My feeling for you goes just so far but not far enough."

"I work hard."

"I know you do."

"I'd provide you with a good home and I'd never be dishonest with you."

"Yes, I'm sure of that."

"Maybe my talking about a family has scared you off but it's better to discuss this before marriage than afterward. We have a man who works in the yard who is nuts over kids. His wife isn't. It's a marriage that doesn't belong and if they had looked at all sides of it at the start they probably would have found mates more suitable for each other."

The steaks arrived, beautiful steaks that could be cut with a fork, but I didn't eat much and George didn't either. We had several more drinks and he smoked incessantly. I felt as if I were the meanest person in the world, but what I had done had been the right thing. There were other girls who would give anything for a chance with George, girls with whom he could find the love he could never find with me.

"I'm not taking this as final," he said at last.

I pushed my plate aside. It was a shame to waste such a wonderful steak but when you aren't hungry you can't eat.

"But it is final, George. It has to be. I've been over it again and again and I always come up with the same answer. You wouldn't want me to marry you if I didn't love you, would you?"

"You may not recognize love." He was stubborn.

"That's possible. I don't deny it. A year from now I may wish I didn't make the decision I just made."

But, in my own heart, I was positive I would not alter the decision. A new sort of life had opened up for me and it was the one I wanted. To be honest, I wanted to continue with it more than anything else in the world. I may have been a little mad on the subject but at least I was being honest with George.

"I'm going to keep the ring," he said, placing it in his pocket. "And I'm going to keep on asking you to marry me every time I see you."

"Please don't. The past is gone and we should both forget it."

"There are things you can't forget."

"You can forget anything if you try." I knew this was a lie. Some things lingered, things that should and things that shouldn't. "You'll find somebody else," I said gently. "You have all the qualities of being a good husband—you're handsome, you earn good money—more than one girl would be more than glad to share your life with you."

"But I'm in love with you," he protested. "I've been in love with you for a long, long time and you don't just kick real love out the window. If it were just marriage I wanted I could have had that long ago."

We sat at the table, drinking and smoking, and he pleaded with me. Wouldn't I reconsider? Wouldn't I wear his ring and try to decide that there was something for us? He was firm but I was just as firm. And the drinks, in view of the fact we hadn't eaten much, didn't help matters any. One moment he was practically crawling at my feet and the next moment he was nearly shouting. I had never seen him this way before and I didn't know how to handle him. He blamed the school for what had happened and he insisted I had met somebody else. I attempted to assure him that none of this was true but the more he drank the more bitter he became.

"I think we should go," I said.

"I guess you're getting tired of my company."

"It isn't that. Why should we sit here and fight? There isn't any sense to it. Your mind goes one way and mine goes another. I can't help it. What if I were in love with you and you weren't in love with me? It would be the same thing in reverse."

"No, it wouldn't. Any man would be in love with you, Doris. All a man has to do is look at you and he's in love."

"In love with the idea of love? Is that what you mean?"

He ordered another drink.

"You're trying to confuse the issue," he said. "You might as well come right out and tell me I'm not in love with you."

"I didn't say that. You must be or you wouldn't say so." I leaned my elbows on the table. "I don't know why things have to end this way. We can be friends, can't we? It isn't the end of the world, either yours or mine. In a month or so you'll forget all about me and you'll meet another girl, a girl who can be as sincere with you as I want to be. In a few months you'll look back upon this as just another incident that shouldn't have happened."

He resumed his pleading, promising me anything if I would only marry him. I was only half-listening. I was thinking of Laura and my father back there in the house and the thought made me almost ill. She would have to do anything he wanted her to do, do it time and time again, and my eyes filled with tears of pity for her. George thought I was crying for him and he told me not to cry.

"I don't intend to be brutal," he said. "I only know what I want and I'm doing everything I can in an effort to get it. From the day I met you I thought of you as being my wife. I can't get over it."

"Please." All this was going too far and it was getting us nowhere. "Can't we talk of something else?"

"I guess I'm boring you."

I wanted to go but he kept up his drinking, sometimes talking to me and sometimes, I thought, talking to himself. I had never seen him drink this much before and although I could have had drink for drink I refused many of them. I wanted to be sober when Laura came to me after my father had gone to sleep, her body soft and tender, her lips hot and wild. I thought of where she had bitten me and I hoped she would bite me again.

We left the inn as they were getting ready to close. George staggered as we walked to the car and I asked him if he wanted me to drive.

"Nonsense," he muttered thickly. "I drove the thing out here and I'll drive it home." He stumbled and almost fell. "Won't be anybody able to say George Richards got so far down the ladder he couldn't drive a car."

Frankly, I was alarmed but I didn't argue with him. There was hardly any traffic on the road and if he drove slowly there wouldn't be too much danger. I lit a cigarette and waited while he fumbled around for the key.

Once on the road he drove carefully enough, saying nothing until we reached the cut-off known as Pantie Lane.

"Gonna park," he said, slowing the car.

"No, George."

He laughed at me.

"Why the hell not?"

"You know why not. You're drunk and you don't know what you're doing. I do. And I don't want to park. I want to go home."

I begged him to go on, to forget whatever it was he had in his mind, but he pulled the car in under some trees and stopped it.

"You were here with me once before," he said, shutting off the engine and the lights.

"That was before. This is now. There's a difference."

"Like salt water and fresh water?"

"That's a good description."

"It was the first time for you."

"I lost my head."

He came toward me across the seat.

"Lose it again," he encouraged. "Even if we aren't engaged there isn't any harm in it."

"There is to me."

"Why? Did I scare you the first time?"

"It isn't that."

He tried to kiss me and I jerked my head aside. All around us was the darkness of the night. I could feel the heat of his breath on my neck, the search of his hands as he reached for me.

"You wanted me before, Doris."

"I said I lost my head, didn't I?"

"But once more—hell, it doesn't amount to anything. And I'll be just as careful of you as I was before. Honest. I won't take any chances with you."

"No, George." I pushed his hand away from my bosom. "No."

"You didn't have enough to drink. That's your trouble. You could have run up your batteries until they were overcharged."

This time his hand was more successful and he hurt me. I pressed against the door, getting as far away from him as I could. His hand fell to my thigh.

"Be a good boy," I said.

I heard him sneer.

"Why be good? What did it get me? A ring tossed back in my face? Nuts to it. If I can't have the real thing I'll take second best."

He was determined and I knew he could force me.

A man after sex is a man out of his mind. I reached down and touched his hand.

"If you go any further," I said, "it'll be rape. And you won't get away with it, George. I'll go to my father. Think of that, will you? You have a good job, a fine salary. You wouldn't want to lose all that, would you?"

"You'd go that far?" He was astonished.

"I most certainly would. I went out to dinner with you and I gave you your ring back. It ends there, not here on the front seat of a car. I don't want a cheap affair, George. All I want is for you to let me alone and find somebody else."

He withdrew his hand.

"Sorry," he said stiffly. "I'll drive you home."

"No, I'll drive you."

"Have it your way."

We didn't speak on the way back to town and when I stopped in front of his house I had to prod him awake.

"Forgive me," he said as he got out.

"You're forgiven."

But he wasn't forgiven. He claimed he loved me and all he wanted from me was what all men wanted from a girl. A girl, I thought, was good for only one thing—to throw all shame aside and to please a man physically.

The house was dark when I arrived home and I immediately went upstairs. The door across the hall was closed and I wondered if she were as anxious for us to be together as I was.

I undressed in the darkness and lay on my bed, waiting for her. It seemed as though I waited a long, long time before my door opened and closed again.

"Doris?"

"Yes."

"Thank God!"

Laura lay down beside me and when I kissed her I tasted the salt of her tears.

"You're crying," I said.

"You would be, too."

"Why?"

"I missed you until I could hardly bear it any longer."

"You don't have to miss me now," I whispered. "I'm yours."

And I was.

For the rest of the night.

9

I returned to the school early Sunday afternoon. I couldn't stay in the same house with Laura and my father, knowing what my father wanted to do to her and knowing what she had to do for him.

"Next weekend," Laura said, following me out to the car. My father had remained in the house. "We'll find time for each other."

"Or you might come to Cedarcliff," I suggested.

"Yes, I might do that."

"There's a hotel in town and we could be alone."

"I'll have to write to you about it, Doris. I'll have to ask him and see what he says."

There were a lot of things I thought about during the ensuing drive. How, I asked myself, would I react to Nina? I didn't know. She was lovely and wonderful but she wasn't anything like Laura. There wasn't anybody like Laura. But as I drove along, approaching the school, I knew I was sorry for myself, sorry that I was different from most girls. I was caught in a web of shame and love, a web that drew tighter around me with every passing second. I tried to think of some of the things I had read about lesbianism but what little I remembered made very little sense. I knew it was a disease, a disease which had its roots deep within me, but I knew of no way of curing myself. And I wasn't at all sure I wanted to be cured. I had enjoyed the love act with Laura and, to be perfectly honest about it, I had enjoyed the same thing with Nina. But, I thought, I couldn't love two girls at once. Or could I? Of this I wasn't certain, and I felt lost and alone. I had read a girl could love two men at the same time, the love for each based on different reasons. But here there was only one reason—the crying need for the satisfaction of a forbidden desire.

And yet—and yet—I felt no dislike toward George. He had been drinking too much the night before and the blind desire for sex had taken over his mind. I had been his before and he had had every reason to think I might belong to him again. You couldn't hold it against a man for trying and a man couldn't hold it against a girl if he failed to achieve his goal.

There were but a few cars in the parking lot when I reached the school. Most of those who had cars either went home for the weekend or into town or got away for the day. Nina's car wasn't there either.

I had left my room unlocked and I knew as soon as I got inside that it had been a mistake. My clothes were all over, scattered from one end to the other. The dresser drawers were open and my underthings were in a pile at the foot of my bed. Putting down the suitcase, I began to examine the amount of damage. I soon discovered the extent. Everything was ruined. Everything. Whoever had been guilty of such an act had used a very sharp instrument, perhaps a razor, and had cut most of the things into shreds.

Weakly, I sat down on the edge of the bed. I wasn't worried about the loss—I had plenty of money with which to buy new clothes—but I couldn't understand why anybody would want to do such a thing. To my knowledge I hadn't made any enemies at the school and there was no good reason why anybody should destroy my personal property.

I left everything where it was, just as I had found it, and went to seek out Miss Lily. Of course, her office was closed on Sunday but I knew she had a room at the rear of the building and it didn't take me long to locate it. I knocked and waited for several moments before she opened the door. I was rather shocked at her appearance. She wore black panties and black bra and nothing else.

"I'm sorry to bother you," I said, "but somebody has been in my room."

"You were away for the weekend?"

"Yes, I went home."

"Did you lock your door?"

"No, I didn't."

She rubbed her eyes as though she had been sleeping.

"Then it's your fault and I doubt if there's very much I can do about it. Locks are put on doors and they are meant to be used."

"But all my clothes have been ruined."

"All?"

"They're in shreds. The only things I have that are any good are the things I had with me."

"It may teach you better next time."

"But—"

"You must have made somebody angry with you. It's happened to others before—I never found out who was responsible—and it will probably happen again."

Miss Lily had a very young-looking body for her age and her breasts appeared to be firm and round. My glance drifted down to her legs. They were perfect and if I had been judging her age on the basis of her legs I would have said she was not much past twenty.

"Will you come in?" she asked me.

"No, thank you. I only wanted to tell you what had happened."

She hitched at one of her bra straps.

"I'll do what I can," she promised. "If I should find out anything I'll let you know. And if we catch whoever it was they'll have to pay for the damages."

"Thank you."

I left her, highly unconvinced anything would ever come of it. From now on I would lock my door whenever I was out of the room. But the more I thought of it the less sense it made. Why would anybody do such a thing? I could understand it if the clothes had been stolen but to simply destroy them was beyond me.

It took me an hour to clean up the room, putting the things in a pile for old Bill or somebody else to take away. I had just finished when the door opened and Nina came in.

"My God," she exclaimed, "what happened?"

"Somebody did a job on my clothes. They cut them all up."

She frowned.

"But why?"

"You tell me."

She was wearing a bright red skirt and a bright red sweater. She looked very pretty. She had one side of her brunette hair pushed back over one ear and the other side fell forward, partly framing her face.

"I came back yesterday," Nina said. "I thought you would be free and we could have a little fun. But you had gone home."

"Yes."

"And you moved out on me. I was surprised about that and I haven't been able to understand it. I thought we were getting along very well."

"I wanted to be by myself," I said. "I wanted to think things out. Haven't you ever wanted to do that?"

"Lots of times. I've been thinking things out ever since the funeral."

"I'm sorry about your father. It isn't pleasant to lose somebody close to you."

She walked to the dresser and took one of my cigarettes.

"He bought his own ticket," she said. "He knew what his drinking would bring but he wouldn't quit. He was told a hundred times it would only lead him to his casket and a hole in the ground."

"That should be a lesson to you, about drinking so much."

"Well, I'm young and he wasn't. When you're young there are lots of things you can do you can't do after you get old."

I didn't know how I would feel if my father died. Certainly his death would make Laura free and we would be able to live together. But you don't wish death on your own flesh and blood and I didn't wish it on my father. I just hoped Laura and I would be able to continue with our love. Perhaps she could get a divorce and she would still be free.

"The bars are open in town," Nina said. "They open up at one o'clock."

"So?"

"I thought you might like a drink. I killed the last of what I had and the liquor stores aren't open on Sunday. You have to go to a bar if you want a drink and we'll be shut up here at the school for the rest of the week."

I considered her suggestion and saw no reason why I shouldn't accept. I had intended to bring a bottle from home but had forgotten to.

"All right," I said.

We took my car and Nina wanted to go to the bar where I had gone with Hank Herbert. It didn't matter to me. We would have a few and return to the school. It didn't have to go beyond that. She had her room and I had mine and I was so positive I was in love with Laura I couldn't think of anybody else. Yet, in spite of this, there was something fascinating about Nina. She was a girl and so was I. How did I know that Laura didn't have another lover? To be sure, I didn't know. All I knew was we had spent some wonderful moments together.

The bar was crowded and Hank was sitting next to a girl with flaming red hair. The girl was wearing shorts and halter and she had a nicely formed body. She had one hand on Hank's knee and I made up my mind she would get what she was looking for before the day was over.

"Local talent," Nina said as we sat down at a table.

"Who?"

"The girl with Hank. She used to clean at the school and she puts out right and left. When he can't find anybody else he picks on her. She's already got one kid with no father—no known father, that is—and if she doesn't watch out she'll be getting another one."

"I feel sorry for her."

"Why should you? Some girls like to get pregnant. It makes them feel superior or something. I've got a friend back home and the more kids she has the better she likes it. There's only ten months difference in the ages of her last two so you can see she doesn't waste much time. All she has to do is look at a pair of her husband's pants and she gets sick in the morning. It must be a hell of a life. She just gets part of her shape back and she starts getting big all over again."

It was stuffy in the bar, the smoke hanging against the ceiling, and it took us a while to get waited on. Nina ordered a vodka and orange and I had an orange and gin.

We were on our third drink, the juke box making a terrible racket, when Hank came over and asked me to dance.

"What happened to the redhead?" I wanted to know.

"She had another date." He smiled. "One with money attached."

I don't know why I danced with him but I did. Somebody turned the juke down and we were able to talk.

"Let's cut out of here," he said.

"I'm with Nina."

"To hell with Nina. She's nobody for you."

"And I suppose you are?"

"Well, I'm not the world's best but I'm better than she is."

I was glad when the dance was over with and I was back at the table. Hank had returned to the bar and now he was talking to another girl.

"He's on the make for you," Nina said.

"A lot of good it will do him," I retorted, draining my glass. "We're as far apart as the moon and the sun and we're going to stay that way."

"There're a few things we ought to talk about," Nina said. "Things that are important."

"I don't know what they could be."

She leaned forward.

"You've changed, Doris. Do you know that?"

"In what way?"

"Moving out on me was one of them. It wasn't a nice thing to do and it made me quite angry. But that's over with and I won't go into how I felt. The main thing is what we're going to do from this point on."

I knew what I was going to do. I was going to study like mad, keep up my marks, and go home to Laura every chance I got. It burned me that we were kept on the campus during the week. The round trip to Benton was only a hundred and sixty miles and I could do it easily in the middle of the week. Laura could always find an excuse to get away from my father and we could meet in secret, if only for an hour or so. I knew in that second I would miss her, miss her terribly. Nina couldn't take her place. Nobody could.

"I want out of the school," Nina said when I made no response. "If it hadn't been for my father insisting I would never have gone to any school."

"What about your education?"

She made a face and the twist of her lips didn't add to her beauty.

"Who needs an education? What do most of the girls do after they get out of here? They meet some jerk and they marry. It's a waste of time and money."

"Not to me it isn't. I intend to teach."

"For peanuts?"

"No, not for peanuts. Some of the jobs are pretty good. It used to be you worked for practically nothing and boarded yourself but it isn't that way any more. A teacher, if she gets in the right school, has real security."

"Don't tell me you have to do that."

"It isn't what I have to do. It's what I want to do. When I was in high school I saw what a good teacher could do and, to me, it's something worthwhile."

"I suppose you would like to live with another teacher?"

"I don't know. I might. It's too early for me to think about that now. I have four years to go and then I have to get a job after I get out of here. I haven't made any plans. When the time comes I'll do what I have to do."

Hank started to leave the bar with a girl, not the redhead, and they kissed near the door. Everybody was a little drunk and nobody cared what he did.

"Another slut from town," Nina said, following my glance.

"He gets around, doesn't he?"

"In a way a man wants to get around. He's had enough girls to start a harem." She laughed. "For all I know he's got one— a harem and a dozen kids he wouldn't recognize if he stumbled over them on the street."

Hank and the girl went outside and they paused in front of the door to kiss again. He was a man all right and there was no doubt about that. He was a man and before the girl got back to town he would prove it to her. I pitied the girl who would eventually marry him.

"You interested in him?" Nina asked me.

"Not at all."

"Yet you seem to be interested in what he's doing."

"I'm just curious. I wonder what makes him tick."

"Never mind that," Nina said, opening a fresh package of cigarettes. "I've got big news." She lit one and blew the smoke out of one corner of her mouth. "My old man left me a neat bundle of cash."

"That's nice." I didn't know what else to say.

"A hundred thousand. I'll have it in thirty days."

"Say, that is a lot of money."

She leaned forward intently.

"That's why I wanted to talk to you. We could have a ball on a hundred thousand and Miss Lily can put her school where a lot of people put things. We could budget ourselves and live on ten thousand a year. That way the money would last ten years."

I knew then what she was after. Nina had plans to quit the school and wanted me to go away with her. A few days before I might have been tempted—what future was there in becoming a teacher, anyway?—but now—now I could think only of Laura.

"I couldn't," I said.

"Give me one reason why not."

"Well, for one thing, my father would object and, for another thing, I'm not sure."

"The last is why you changed rooms?"

I had had just enough to drink to be honest.

"Yes."

"You can't escape it," Nina said. "You know that, don't you? Once you have experienced the greatest love of all no other love can please you. I know. I've tried. I stayed away longer than I had to in an attempt to forget you but I couldn't. Even when I was standing at my father's grave I wanted to be with you. And that night, instead of crying, I longed for you. Then I came back to find you had left me. I thought I would nearly go out of my mind."

"Please," I said. "This isn't the place to talk about it."

"Then we should go."

"I'm ready if you are."

We paid our check, splitting it down the middle, and walked outside. The parking lot was filled when we returned to the school and I parked the car on the grass under some trees.

Nina was feeling the vodka and she wanted to make love in the car. I refused, saying I was tired and wanted to get to bed.

"The car is no place," she said on second thought. "Let's go to my room."

"No."

"Or your room."

"No."

Nina finally realized it was no use and we parted in the hall but not before she had extracted a promise from me that I would see her the following night.

I knew, however, I wouldn't.

I never would, never again.

I was in love with Laura.

I managed to avoid seeing Nina on Monday night, pleading a headache and a great deal of work to be done. I lied about the headache but not about the work. My history took me over two hours and my English was almost as bad. It was nearly twelve by the time I finished and I simply fell into bed, dead tired.

On Tuesday I had a letter from Laura. She started out by saying how wonderful the weekend had been and how much she missed me. She was alone at the time of writing and she was drinking to kill the loneliness she felt. Then she came to the point in which I was interested. She had mentioned coming to Cedarcliff to my father and he had told her he wished she would wait until another time. On Friday he was leaving with George for upstate, to complete the purchase of the lumber, and an accountant would be at the office to go over the books. He wouldn't leave the office keys with anybody except her and, for this reason, she had to remain in Benton. But, she pointed out, we would be able to be together and, she added, she couldn't wait until Friday night when I would reach home.

I read the letter several times, the ache in me getting bigger for her every moment. I was disappointed she couldn't come to Cedarcliff but as long as my father was going to be out of the house we would be able to share our love.

I went through the afternoon in sort of a trance. How could I wait until Friday? Only part of my mind was on my class work. I wanted to sit down and write to Laura, to assure her of my love, to promise her the coming weekend would even be better than the last.

"You aren't paying attention, Miss Foster," Paul Blanding said during my last class.

"I'm—sorry."

"Are you ill?"

"No, I'm not ill."

"Then stop dreaming, will you? It's very important you absorb as much of what I'm talking about as you can."

"Yes, sir."

He didn't keep me after class and for that I was grateful. He had given me an eighty-five on one of my papers and I was grateful for that, too. I didn't want anything to happen to prevent me from going home on Friday. If for any reason at all I was restricted to the campus I was sure I would die a hundred deaths.

Hank Herbert was in front of the building when I emerged and he called me over to him. I hadn't seen him since Sunday at the bar and grill but I had thought about the girl who had been with him several times.

"Busy?" he inquired.

"Frightfully." I had more work to do that night than I had ever had before. "They load it on," I added, smiling. "You give them a foot and they take a mile."

He nodded.

"That's Miss Lily for you. She claims a girl's mind should be active for five days out of the week."

"Well, she's the boss."

He kicked a stone out of the way and shoved his hands deep into the pockets of his pants.

"They haven't moved the path," he said.

"I don't follow you."

"The path across the campus. It's still there. I could meet you on the road later tonight and we could have a few drinks."

"Thanks, no."

"My aunt thought you were a very lovely girl. She keeps asking me why I don't bring you back to the house again."

I shifted the books in my arms.

"I'm really too busy," I said. "And the fact I was rather foolish once doesn't mean that I intend to be foolish again. You know plenty of girls if you want a date. What about the one you took out of the bar?"

"Oh, her."

"You don't sound very respectful."

"Why should I be? She's just a chippie and everybody knows it. If a guy buys her a couple of drinks he can go the distance."

"And you think the same thing of me?"

"No, I don't. Not at all." He kicked another stone. "I might have started out thinking about you in that way but I've changed my mind. I think you're a pretty decent girl and I would treat you as one. No parking. No necking. Just a little talk. What harm is there in that?"

I started walking away from him.

"I've got too much to do," I said. "Far too much to do. I have no time for anything but work."

My clothes were still in a pile in my room, back of the door, and this annoyed me. We certainly paid enough at Cedarcliff to get service and instead of service we got nothing. I got out of my clothes, put on my robe and plunged into my school work. I finished my English theme and gave myself a seventy-five or an eighty on it, and tore into my history. Most of the questions were easy and I remembered the answers from high school. If my first year history weren't any more difficult than this I would be able to breeze through it. Anybody who flunked it deserved to be thrown out of the school.

I don't know what time Nina entered the room but it was just after I had completed my work. She wore a red robe and as soon as she had closed the door she reached under the robe and produced a bottle. The bottle was full and the seal hadn't yet been broken.

"Relax," she laughed. "You'll kill yourself with all the effort you're putting into your studies. Relax and live a little."

Nina opened the bottle. Then she looked for glasses on top of the dresser but there weren't any.

"Don't you have glasses?"

"No."

"You must drink straight from the bottle."

"I haven't had a bottle."

"Hell of a thing. You need a bottle in this stinking hole in order to stand it."

"I haven't found it to be so." That, to be honest about it, was a lie. I was all right while I was busy doing something but after I got into bed and started thinking about Laura I could have used a stiff jolt. "It only gets me confused when I'm working on a paper," I continued. "A good mark requires a clear head."

Nina walked over to me and held out the bottle. She had unbelted her robe, although I hadn't seen her do it, and it hung open down the middle.

"You first," she said.

"I don't want any."

A tiny smile played at the corners of her mouth.

"Say, what the hell is the matter with you, Doris?" she demanded.

"Nothing's the matter. I just don't feel like it, that's all. I get started and I don't know when to stop so the best thing is not to get started."

Nina tipped the bottle to her mouth and took a long drink. All her interesting features were fully exposed and I made every effort not to look. All I had to do was think of Laura and I didn't want to look. All I had to do was think of my father's wife and my whole stomach churned, creating a delightful pain that spread all through me.

"You don't want me," Nina said, carrying the bottle to the bed. She sat down on the edge of it. "I can tell when I'm not wanted."

I didn't have the courage to hurt her. I prayed she would leave me alone. Then I thought of the nights that had been glorious for us and I wasn't sure what my wishes were. I had heard a lesbian seldom knew her own mind and I was inclined to agree. Laura was eighty miles away—what was she doing this very second?—and I had a girl in my room who wanted to love me. Nina had pleased me before and I knew it was her desire to please me again. I thought of the other girls in the school and I wondered if there were many like me. I hoped there weren't. I lived in the shadow of beauty and on the edge of hell, a hell that swept up toward me to claim the good days of my life.

"Christ, it's hot in here," Nina said, putting the bottle on the floor and pulling the robe down from her shoulders, revealing both tilted breasts. "Miss Lily should furnish us with fans, that's what she should do."

"I agree."

She picked up the bottle and took another drink. She was seated upon the robe but she had flung it away from her legs. She was lush, though not as ripe and full as Laura, and she made no effort to hide any of her charms.

"Have you thought about going away with me?" she inquired.

"No. I told you what I want to do. That part hasn't changed."

"I'll have a hundred thousand dollars," she reminded me.

"I know that. You told me before."

She yawned and stretched and I knew that she was showing herself off for my benefit.

"I've read a few things about Mexico, Doris. You can live there for almost nothing and have so many servants you can't count them. You could hand your old man some bull about studying down there and he wouldn't be the wiser. Why should we rot away in this dump?"

I won't say I didn't think about what she said. I did. The situation at home had a hair-trigger attached to a loaded barrel and despite my love for Laura I was smart enough to realize it. We might not be caught this year or next but some day we would be. What would happen then? I dreaded to think about it. Benton was just small enough so that everybody knew what everybody else was doing. If a girl were a prostitute, and there were some, everybody in the community knew about it. Being classed as a lesbian would be even worse. So few people understood the motives which guided a lesbian. I was one and I didn't. I only knew I felt sick when I thought of a man in the sexual sense. The pleas of my mother came back to me and I saw her lying dead and still in a casket, the result of trying to have a baby that should never have been planted within her. I think the fear generated by this was what bothered me most, that and the fear I might, if I did become pregnant, die the way she had died.

"I should have stayed in my room and talked to the four walls," Nina said. "At least I'd have gotten an echo."

"Sorry. I was just thinking about what you said."

"Ever been to Mexico?"

"No."

"They say it's nice. And there's a lake outside of Mexico City—I can't think of the name of it—where a lot of people like us live. The boys team up with boys and the girls team up with girls. But we wouldn't have to go there. You can get a house for under twenty a month, furnished, and the help you hire work for almost nothing. All you have to do is love and raise hell."

We talked for a long time and she continued to drink. I was evasive in all my replies and this seemed to disturb her. Once she came over to me and she tried to kiss me but I told her I wasn't in the mood. That bothered her even more.

"She must've made you," Nina said, slurring her words. "She must've made you like she's made most of the others."

"Who?"

"Miss Lily."

"You're out of your mind," I retorted. "Whatever gave you that idea? You're out of your mind," I said again. "Completely."

She took a long, long drink from the bottle.

"Have it your way," she said. "You fool, you don't know what it's all about. You don't know and you won't listen. To hell with you. You'll wake up soon enough and then you'll be glad to come running back to me."

She left about twelve and I was glad to have her go. She was drunk on desire and booze and I was very tired.

Laura, I thought as I lay down on my bed. Laura, honey. Laura, honey, if you were only here, if you could only be with me.

I went to sleep with a pillow clutched tightly in my arms.

The next day, Wednesday, was uneventful. I attended my classes and tried to get as much out of them as I could. But Thursday was different. On Thursday I had another letter from Laura. She loved me. She loved me in a way that far surpassed any feeling she had ever felt. When Laura was with my father, giving herself to him, she thought of me. It was the only way in which she could tolerate him. There wasn't a night he left her alone. The night before she had written the letter she had got awfully drunk, thinking of me, wanting me, and she didn't know how far he had gone with her. She was worried about it, frantic. However, as for the other things at home, everything was going all right. The woman who had taken over the management of her store knew her business and sales were good. The fact that Laura had been able to make such an arrangement had caused my father to start talking about taking an extended trip. He had been to Europe at one time, taking a small part in a movie, and he wanted to go back. He thought it would be a wonderful honeymoon for them, and if they went they would be gone several months. He had already talked to a travel agency about his plans and as soon as he had turned all the affairs of the lumber yard over to George, Laura felt sure he would go ahead and buy the tickets. This last bit of news left me stunned and I knew I had to see her as soon as I could. I had to be with her every second of every day possible. And when she was gone, I knew, I would miss her, miss her terribly. I was glad I was in school. It would be something for me to do. I would lose myself in my work, possibly take an extra course, and somehow, somehow, I would manage to wait for her return.

Once I had accepted the contents of her letter as something which couldn't be avoided, I was able to pay attention in my classes. Tomorrow night, I told myself, I would see her. Tomorrow night we would belong to each other. And if my father and George stayed overnight Saturday in that town upstate, or wherever it was they were going, Laura and I would live with all the fury and the passion of the flesh.

God, it was something to look forward to, something that would be greater than anything either one of us had ever experienced.

I was surprised when Paul Blanding kept me after his class. He had been keeping other girls, a different girl each day, and I had heard he was making time with them. I had felt sorry for the girls but I had been grateful he had left me alone.

"I have some bad news for you," Blanding said after the last girl had gone out and the door had closed behind her. "I've been going over your papers and I must say they could stand a great deal of improvement."

I was even more surprised this time. I had been very careful with his assignments, checking everything from beginning to end, and while I hadn't seen my marks I had thought they must be pretty good.

"I don't understand," I said. "I've really put a lot of effort into your course."

He came down the aisle and his limp seemed to be more pronounced than ever.

"Effort isn't always enough," he said, standing over me. "A man who works hard at building a barn doesn't create a thing of beauty."

I didn't know what he was driving at and I regretted having worn a dress with such a low neckline.

"You'll have to stay on the campus this weekend," he went on. "I'll give you some extra work and perhaps you can get your marks in line."

He might as well have struck me with a stone. I had so many plans with Laura for the weekend—and now this.

"I can't," I whispered. "I simply can't!"

"Can't what?" He was smiling. "What can't you do?"

"I have to go home," I said, close to tears. "If it were any weekend but this it wouldn't be so bad, but—well, I can't. I have to go home. There's something I have to—do." I was pleading with him now. "Don't make me stay. Please don't! I'll work harder than ever if you'll only be reasonable about this."

It became quiet in the classroom and I fought back my tears. Of course, I could always quit the school, I could always walk out, but if Laura went to Europe with my father I had to have something to occupy my mind.

"There's a way around it," Paul Blanding said. "I think you know what it is."

I knew. All I had to do was give myself to him and I would have a passing grade.

"I—couldn't!" I gasped. "I just couldn't."

He shrugged and reached for a cigarette.

"It's up to you. You know the path across the campus and I park my car off the road, about a hundred feet to the right of the path. No one can see my car from the highway and no one has to know you ever met me."

"Please. I—"

"I'll be there about eight, possibly a few minutes before. You think it over and make up your mind about coming to me." He paused. "You know what I want in return for a passing mark. The decision is yours."

He turned away from me and I got up from my desk. My legs were weak and heavy and I felt as though my heart were doing double duty. If I were going to see Laura this weekend— how could I go on living if I didn't see her?—I would have to permit him to take advantage of me, would have to give him the most treasured possession a girl could give any man.

All I wanted to do now was reach my room and shut myself away from the world, a world filled with madness and sex and all the things a girl could easily hate.

But I found out that once I was in the room I couldn't run away from what faced me. If I didn't do as Blanding asked I wouldn't see Laura. And if I quit the college he might give me such a bad mark it could make it difficult for me to get into another school. Paul Blanding had me right where he wanted me and there wasn't a thing I could do about it.

I cried a long time, lying there on the bed, but the tears didn't change anything. I thought of the hours I had put in on my history and I hated every minute of them. Then I thought of what it would be like to be with Blanding and this made me feel ill.

I skipped supper—how could I eat?—and left the building about seven-thirty, following the path across the campus and toward the woods. How, I asked myself, could I hold up my head after this? But my course was clear and there was no avoiding it. I would do anything to be with Laura again. Anything.

I entered the woods, crossed the bridge over the stream and turned to the right. There was no turning back now. I had arrived at my decision and I had to go through with what, I was sure, would be some of the worst moments of my life.

Paul Blanding had backed the car down the narrow, weed-filled road, probably so that it would be easier for him to drive to the highway after darkness set in, and I noticed his smile as I came up to him.

"I knew you would come," he said, getting out of the car. He was carrying a blanket. "I knew you were just as ready for this as I am."

"You're wrong in that."

"Wrong or right you're here, aren't you?"

"Unfortunately, yes."

He led me to a small clearing a short distance from the car. The grass in the clearing was deep and thick and he spread the blanket on the grass. I stood there, watching him as he limped around straightening out the blanket, and I didn't believe it was I who was really here. It was somebody else and I was only dreaming this was happening to me. In a few seconds, I told myself, I would wake up and he would be gone.

"What are you waiting for?" Blanding asked.

I came back to the present. I wasn't dreaming. In the fading light of day I was in the woods with this man who was more animal than human.

"Nothing," I replied. "Nothing at all."

"Then take off your clothes."

"Take off my clothes?" I repeated.

He grinned.

"The other girls do. I like it better that way. And, frankly, I want to see you. I want to see you before—"

I don't know how I did it but I did. With trembling hands I stripped myself, showing him all my beauty. All the time I was doing it I was crying. I couldn't help crying. I felt more ashamed than I had ever felt.

"You're better than the others," he said.

The shame of what I was doing went deeper and deeper.

He came to me, taking me in his arms, kissing me, first on the mouth.

"You're made," he exclaimed thickly. "Oh, how you're made!"

Soon I was on the blanket. The sight of him revolted me. I glanced away. I didn't have to wait long. He was after me before I realized it, his body claiming me with a wild fury that drove the breath from my lungs. My lips parted and I cried out with the pain but he soon sealed my lips with the violence of his mouth, telling me as he did so I was the most beautiful girl he had ever known.

He begged me to relax, but my body was as a thing of wood. All I knew was an awful thing was happening to me, that I should never have gone this far, and several times I tried to get away from him. But that was impossible. During the minutes that followed I was a slave to his demands, but a slave who gave her flesh, not her heart.

"You weren't worth it," he said much later. "You weren't worth it at all."

I sobbed as I found my clothes band began to dress. No man had ever reached me and no man ever would. I belonged to my own kind.

I was in a world apart.

10

I couldn't wait to get away from the school on Friday and I couldn't look at Paul Blanding as I left his class.

There was the usual Friday traffic but I pushed the Ford all the way to Benton, stopping only once for gas and another time for a soft drink. I had missed lunch and I was hungry but I had to get to her.

I thought of the night before and after careful consideration I decided it had been worth submitting to Paul Blanding, thereby assuring myself of a weekend I would never forget. I couldn't have stayed at Cedarcliff, knowing Laura was only eighty miles distant. I would have left the school rather than suffer such a penalty, but I also knew I needed the school and had to cling to it.

"I won't bother you again," Paul Blanding had told me the night before. "You can be sure of that."

"Thanks."

"Most of the girls enjoy it but you don't. There's something wrong with you, Doris. There's something a great deal wrong with you."

"And I suppose you're normal?"

"I don't say that, but when it comes to sex I know what I was built for. You don't. You're living in a shell. My guess is Nina brought you into her club and you can't escape from it."

As I approached Benton I knew this was so. Nina, although I no longer cared for her, had brought me a new kind of love, a love that had the full bloom of a flower in early spring.

I arrived in Benton shortly after six and drove straight to the house.

Laura came out on the back porch and waved to me as I parked the car in the driveway. She was wearing red shorts and a red halter and her legs were nice and straight. My heart pounded, pumping my blood faster and faster, as I got out of the car and walked toward her.

"He's not here?" I asked.

She shook her head.

"No. They left this morning, right after they got the accountant started on the books. I just got here by taxi after locking up, and I have to open up for him again in the morning."

I mounted the steps. I had the insane urge to kiss her but I knew I couldn't do it out in the open.

"I didn't think accountants worked on Saturday," I said.

"They don't usually, I guess, but your father is anxious to get started on that trip he's been talking about. He's paying extra for a fast job."

We entered the kitchen and I saw the bottle sitting on the table. I didn't blame her for drinking. I had only been with men twice in my life and I could imagine what it was like to have to put up with one every night. The picture sent terror through my heart.

"They won't be back until Sunday," Laura said, getting a glass for me from one of the cabinets.

"Oh, good."

"One of the men who owns the land lives in New York and he couldn't make it until then. And the other man was going away for the weekend so they had to leave today. It worked out fine."

"I should say so."

She poured two stiff drinks.

"It's been a long week," she said. "A hell of a week. I just had to write you."

"I'm glad you did and I'm sorry I didn't take the time to answer."

I took the glass from her.

"It's just as well," she said. "I leave things lying all over and your father might have found anything you might have written. That wouldn't have been good." She lifted her glass. "To us, baby. To hell with men."

We drank and she asked me about school. I didn't tell her about Paul Blanding but I did tell her about my clothes being destroyed.

"Who would want to do that?" she inquired.

"I don't know."

"Have you made any bad friends?"

"Not that I know of. In fact, I've hardly made any friends at all. The classes aren't too tough but I'm kept busy at night. There just hasn't been the time to meet anybody and become very friendly."

Our glasses were empty and she poured two more drinks.

"It's nothing to worry about," Laura said. "We can run

down to the store and you can pick out anything you want."

I knew she had at one time kept the store open on Friday night but that the practice hadn't paid and she had given it up.

"It's closed now," I said.

She swallowed her drink quickly.

"Well, what of that? I have a key and I own it. I can do as I please. And I'd like to help you select your things. I want you to look out of this world."

We had one more drink and then I drove her downtown in the Ford. She said my father had a car ordered for her, an Olds convertible, but it hadn't yet arrived.

"It's a waste of money if we're going to Europe," she said. "You can't very well take a car with you."

"Some people do."

"Yes, but it's cheaper to rent one over there. He says he's going to rent a hotel room, lock the door and spend most of our time in bed. I doubt if he intends to do much driving."

"I hate to think of you going," I said.

"Don't think I don't, too. There'll be just sex and more sex and I'm wondering if I'll be able to stand it." She laughed a little and lit a cigarette. "For a man his age he's got a lot of ambition in one direction. All he has to do is look at me and he gets the yen."

"He isn't alone," I confided.

"But it's different with you. You're a girl and so am I. He's a man and there isn't a night that goes by he doesn't try to convince me. Now he's got me worried sick. I don't know what we did that one night and neither does he."

"What if he gave you a baby?"

Laura threw the cigarette outside as I made a right turn to the main street.

"Don't talk like that. Who wants a baby? Jesus, can you imagine me with a baby? I'd jump off the roof or something before I had one."

Laura's store was in a good location. The farmers and rural people came into Benton Friday night to do their shopping but the type of merchandise Laura sold didn't appeal to the more ordinary people. The ones with low incomes shopped in the chain stores, trying to pick up bargains and getting cheated for their pains. None of Laura's dresses sold for less than sixteen or eighteen dollars and even her bras and underthings were expensive. She had told me once she was interested only in the better customer and this was the type that came to her.

The window lights of Laura's store were on and the gowns displayed were truly beautiful. Apparently the woman running the store knew her business.

Laura unlocked the door and we went inside. The lock snapped as the door closed behind us.

"We can go into the back room and I can bring the things to you in there," she said. "If I turn on the lights in here I'll have some farmer woman knocking on the door for a two dollar dress."

The building was long and narrow and she led me toward the rear, past racks and racks of dresses which left little room. It seemed to me she ought to have a bigger place but I didn't say anything to her about it. I figured she knew what she was doing. She'd started with nothing and she was a success.

The back room was separated from the front by a heavy curtain and after she turned on the light I saw a cot against one wall.

"I used to sleep here," she said, following my glance. "When I first opened up I worked alone and I worked day and night. Things weren't very pleasant for me at home and staying here was cheaper than a hotel room. Lots of nights I was still knocking myself out at two and three in the morning."

She had good judgment as to the kind of clothes I should wear and it wasn't long before I had been fitted out with a dozen dresses, as many skirts and sweaters to match and a few half-slips.

"They should do you for a while," she said.

"They're fine."

She was close to me and she leaned forward and kissed me on the mouth, not a kiss of fire but just a kiss that told me I was needed. I sighed and returned her kiss. Then, when she touched me, I could hardly control myself.

Laura laughed and strained toward me. My hands were overflowing with her loveliness and I cried out, "I don't care if tomorrow ever comes. Tonight is ours, all ours."

We stumbled to the cot and fell upon it, our mouths fastened together in a moment of fierce desire, a desire that became more intense with each passing second.

"I love you, Doris," Laura murmured.

"And I love you."

"With all your heart?"

"With all my heart."

It was a frantic night there in the back of the store and we didn't leave until long after one o'clock. As soon as we returned to the house it started all over again, a frenzy which knew no bounds, nothing but the hopeless, terrible craving of flesh that must be satisfied.

At nine the next morning we went down to the lumber yard to let the accountant into the office. He was a small man who wore glasses and had little to say except that he would be finished by noon, that he could snap the lock on the door himself, and that he would call my father at the place he was staying upstate.

We spent the morning in the house, both of us stripped, and by noon we were drinking heavily, sitting in the living room and paying no attention to the television. Laura had given the cleaning woman the day off and there was nobody to bother us. Once somebody rang the front door chimes, possibly the paper boy, but we didn't bother to answer. We were too happy the way we were, drinking and kissing and touching each other. We talked about a great many things but mostly about how we could continue our relationship. She thought I ought to quit school and go along with them on their European trip. However, I wasn't sure about that. I wanted to go, yes, and school wasn't that important to me, but I thought my father would be with her most of the time and we both would be running a risk. She was his wife and she belonged to him and we both had to accept that. We finally decided we would have to suffer our separation silently.

"We'll find an excuse to get away together when I get back," Laura said. "You can pretend you're ill, in need of a rest, and we'll take a cottage some place. We'll make up to each other for all we'll have missed."

"Again and again," I agreed.

The afternoon wore on and we continued with our drinking, sitting on the davenport, our bodies close, the desire, satisfied the night before, building up again inside of us. Presently we were drinking less and our kisses became longer. I knew we would find love there in the living room.

"I want you," she said finally.

"And I want you to want me."

It had been good in the back of Laura's store but not as good as it was this time. The liquor had killed any restraint Laura might have had and all my emotions were keyed to the breaking-point, emotions which knew only one outlet for the torrent of expectation which filled me.

"Now," I told her as she kissed me. "Oh, now!"

I don't know how long it went on. I didn't think. I didn't care. I alternately rose to the heights of untold happiness and then fell into the depths of despair, telling her it wasn't right, we shouldn't do what we were doing, then wanting her worse than ever.

I wasn't aware of my father or of George being in the room—much of the time my eyes had been closed—until I looked up and saw them standing there. My father's face was livid and George's face was white.

I screamed, throwing myself away from Laura, and tears swept into my eyes. Laura saw them then, too. But she didn't scream. She merely sat up, her nakedness there for them to see.

"Lesbians," my father said, his voice harsh. "A couple of lesbians. My wife and my daughter."

"Dad—" I began tearfully.

"Shut up!" He reached down and slapped me across the face but I was so nervous and frightened I didn't feel the blow. He slapped me again and the effect was the same. "Maybe it was a good thing the accountant came up with a shortage and I had to come home. This could have gone on for years and I'd never have known."

I saw the pain in George's eyes and I looked away from him. Laura now was crying softly, bent over, her face hidden by her arms.

"Shortage?" I wanted to know.

"The shortage George created," my father said. "Ten thousand bucks down the drain."

"I was going to put it back," George said. "I told you how it was at home, the folks determined to live it up. I was only trying to help them—not myself. I wouldn't have taken a dime for myself. I—"

"Oh, can it," my father said. "There's something else here that has to be settled first. Laura?"

She wouldn't look at him.

"Laura!"

She still wouldn't look at him and he leaned down and gripped her by the shoulders.

"You're getting out of here," he said. "Today. Now. Get your clothes and take off. I'll make the arrangements for a divorce. That ought to satisfy you. Then you can have all the girls you want."

I thought she would fight back, argue with him, but she didn't. She just got up from the davenport and left the room. She didn't look back and I didn't watch her as she left. I continued to sit there, numb and sick, trying to find words to express myself. But the words wouldn't come. Nothing would come except the tears.

"I'm going," George said.

"So long," my father told him.

"And I'll pay you back."

"I expect you will."

The door closed.

"You go, too," my father said, walking over and turning off the television. "I'll leave a check for you on the way out and you can pick it up on your way to the car. It'll be enough for you to finish your education, and what you do with your spare time is no concern of mine." There was a ragged edge to his voice. "Your mother would die if she knew what I had brought up. I mean, she would die a second time."

"You killed her," I accused.

"I killed her? How?"

"By making her pregnant."

"No, I didn't kill her. That's part of life, part of marriage. It's a chance you take and sometimes the chance isn't a very good one. Don't think I haven't missed her. I have. Nobody could ever take her place."

Slowly, I got up from the davenport and made my way to the stairs. He was putting me out of his life and there was an emptiness I couldn't explain even to myself.

It took me quite a while to pack my things. The prices were still on the dresses and I decided I would total up the amount due and send Laura a check from the school. I knew the amount would be high, possibly more than I could afford, but I had accepted them from her and I couldn't take them back now.

No one was downstairs as I carried my luggage out to the

car. All my good luggage was at the school and I was using battered suitcases I had once taken to summer camp.

There was a check on the kitchen table made out to me in the amount of five thousand dollars. There was no note, nothing. I picked up the check and dropped it in my purse, deciding it had been an expensive day for my father. He had lost a wife—or he was throwing her aside—and George was short in his accounts. I wondered, vaguely, if my father would ever go on his European trip. It didn't seem as though he would.

I didn't drive far that night. I was still feeling the liquor and I didn't feel safe on the highway. I put up at a motel about twenty miles out of Benton, shutting myself up in my room and having a good cry.

I had to learn, for once and for all, just what I was.

It was the most important thing in my life.

Was I a lesbian?

Or wasn't I?

11

It was about the middle of Sunday afternoon when I drove my car into the parking lot at Cedarcliff. I knew old Bill was off on Sunday so I began to unload the luggage myself. I had to make three trips but soon I had everything up in my room and I started putting the clothes away, first writing down on a piece of paper the amount due on each item. I wrote out a check to Laura, not sure whether I should use the name of Stevens or Foster—I eventually decided on Foster since she was still married to my father—put the check in an envelope, sealed it, addressed it and added a stamp. Then, with nothing else to do, I sat down on the bed.

The night before at the motel had been a miserable one. A couple had been fighting in the room next to me and their voices and curses had come through the paper-thin walls. This, on top of what had already happened to me at home, had made me frantic. I had twisted on the bed, crying and hating myself, and even after the couple had stopped their fighting I had been in no way relieved. I had asked myself dozens of times what I was and I hadn't come up with the answer.

Now, back at my room at Cedarcliff, I knew only that a normal girl didn't go to another girl for love and I had done just that. Laura and I had drunk a great deal of liquor and we had made love and we had been caught. My father believed I was a lesbian and I was sure George shared the same belief. What else, I asked now, was there for them to believe? I had been there with Laura, hadn't I? I had been letting her make love to me and I had done nothing to stop it.

I arose from the bed and walked to the window. I had made a mistake, a horrible mistake, and it would stay with me the rest of my life. No matter where I went it would follow me. There would always be the memory of the look on my father's face, of George standing there looking down at Laura and me. I felt, in spite of what I had heard, that all wounds did not heal. And if the wound did heal there was always the scar to remind you of what you had done.

There were a few girls out on the grass and they seemed to be laughing and joking. Why couldn't I be like them? Why was I different? Why had I plunged headlong into a mess from which I would never be free?

Two girls walked toward the entrance of Massey Hall, their arms around each other, their bodies pressed together. My sympathy went out to them. They were possibly on the verge of doing something they should never do.

I left the window and got a package of cigarettes from my handbag. My hands were shaking as I lit a cigarette and the more I tried to stop them the more they shook. I had hurt my father—both Laura and I had hurt him—and he hadn't deserved that. He had been generous with us and we had returned his generosity by being unfaithful. Once again I sat on the bed and tried to think of things as my father would think of them. He had lost a daughter and a wife, and George had betrayed him. All he had left was that beautiful home and his business. Would they be enough? Would they ever come close to filling the void I knew must now exist in his life? I doubted it. Money made things possible, many of the good things in life, but money by itself had little meaning. As I thought of this I looked again at the check he had left me on the kitchen table. Even after paying Laura I had a considerable amount of money in the bank, and when I added this five thousand to it I would be far from poor. If I managed properly, I could go through four years of college and into the teaching profession. As I realized this, tears filled my eyes. Even in his moment of anger my father had lived up to his paternal responsibilities. How many other fathers, I asked myself, would have done the same? Most of them would have thrown me out without a dime.

I lay down on the bed and cried until there just weren't any more tears. It was hot in the room and I eventually sat up. I had to get hold of myself. I had to go on and build a new life, a life in which I could at least take some pride, a life which would bring me the better things which went with wise and moderate living.

Was I a lesbian?

Was I?

I honestly didn't know and when it came to questions of sex I was frightfully confused. Somewhere along the way I had got on the wrong track. But I did have sufficient funds to seek out a good doctor and find out what was wrong with me. I didn't believe my problem was too different from that of many girls who had come to fear the male and his reproductive powers. The death of my mother during childbirth had created a block somewhere in my mind and it had caused me to regard my father in an abnormal light. Perhaps much of the fault had been mine but until the feeling I had about my father was gone I didn't stand a chance of becoming normal.

I was on my fourth cigarette when the door opened and Nina came in.

"I saw your car," she said. "What brought you back so early?"

I folded the check and returned it to my pocketbook.

"There was nothing to do," I lied. "And since there wasn't anything to do I decided I might as well do it here. I can always study and try to get ahead of the teachers."

She came over and sat down beside me.

"The hell with that," she said. "Let's take a run out to that bar and have a few drinks. You're supposed to relax over the weekend and forget about school."

But I didn't want a drink. No matter how much I drank it wouldn't solve anything. I had been drinking the day before and I had made the biggest error of my life. I didn't intend ever to make such an error again.

"You go ahead," I said. "I don't care for it at the bar. There's too much smoke and too much noise. I'd rather stay here with my books."

"You won't get out again until next weekend."

"I know that."

Nina smiled. "Unless you sneak out," she said.

I arose and carried my pocketbook over to the dresser.

"I don't intend sneaking out," I said. "I'm here to learn as much as I can and that's what I'm going to do."

"The model student?" she inquired.

"You needn't get nasty about it. This may be a lark for you but it isn't for me."

"Don't tell me you intend staying on?"

"Indeed I do."

"Have you thought any about going away with me?"

There was no doubt I had thought about it. I had thought about it the night before. It was an easy way to escape but I knew it would only be running away from reality. And I had to face reality. I had to face it now or never.

"No," I lied. "No, I didn't think about it."

"We could have a wonderful life together."

I was smoking too much but I lit another cigarette. My hands were no longer shaking.

"You had better get somebody else," I said. "A lot of girls would jump at the chance. I'm just not one of them."

Nina got to her feet and I could see her eyes were bitter.

"I made you happy before," she pointed out.

She had made me happy but she lived in a world apart and I no longer wanted to belong to it. It was a world of disgrace and terror, a world filled with the forces of love on which most people frowned.

"You go ahead," I said again. "Enjoy yourself. I'll spend the rest of the day working on my history and English and several other things I know will be coming up. I'll get the jump on the teachers."

The anger was all over her face, her eyes blazing.

"I could claw you blind," Nina said between clenched teeth. "The time you moved out on me I knew you had been playing me for a sucker. Why do you think I ripped up all your clothes? Because you had it coming to you, that's why. What do you think I am, anyway? Somebody who brings you love you can just kick out of your life? Well, don't kid yourself. I don't give up that easily. What's good one day is good the next." She forced a laugh. "Sometimes it's even better."

"Please. I don't want to talk about it." My voice rose and I was more determined. "You should realize I'm not that kind."

"The hell you aren't. You're that kind—all the way through."

We argued for a while and Nina begged me to go with her. I refused. Once she came close and tried to kiss me but I slapped her face and she called me a vile name. I was glad when she was gone, and in a way I wasn't glad. She had brought me love, the forbidden fruits of the flesh. In the blindness of her love she had destroyed my clothes. I tried, without much success, to understand.

I went to work on my English but my mind wasn't on it. In disgust I threw the book aside.

Although I had opened the window the heat in the room was intense. Thinking I would be left alone, I got out of my dress. I felt a touch of pride I hadn't gone with Nina. I was one step on the long road back. But, I felt, there would be many steps and I would have to take them one at a time.

I was deep in my history when I heard the door open and close behind me. I pushed the book away and turned to see who it was. It was Miss Lily.

"You seem to be busy," she observed, smiling.

"A little."

Miss Lily moved slowly toward me across the room and it was easy to tell she had nothing on beneath the dress.

"I saw Nina drive out alone," she said.

"Yes."

"I thought you might be going with her."

"I didn't want to."

"Nina is a very pretty girl," she went on.

I said nothing. I didn't know what she was driving at. I knew, of course, she had come to my room for something but what it was I couldn't guess.

"How do you like the school?" she asked.

"It's all right."

"Anything wrong?"

"No, nothing is wrong."

"What about your teachers?"

"They seem to be competent."

"And Paul Blanding?"

I wondered if she guessed or if she knew about him. But, I

assured myself, there was no way she could know.

"Mr. Blanding is included," I said.

There was a chair close to my desk and she sat down on that. She crossed one leg over the other and the skirt of her dress rode above her knee. She didn't bother to fix it.

"He has an eye for pretty girls, Miss Foster."

"Does he?"

"And so does Nina." Her tone was soft and she smiled again.

"Isn't that rather—unusual?"

Miss Lily hesitated a moment and reached for one of my cigarettes.

"Not so much," she replied. "This is a school for girls and we don't always live up to conventions."

"I see."

She watched me through the smoke.

"You're a very beautiful girl."

"Thank you."

"Perhaps the most beautiful in the school. You have a lovely shape and the face to go with it."

I suddenly regretted having removed my dress. She was staring at me, not just at my face but my entire body. A cold chill ran up and down my spine, a chill that ended in a sudden flash of fire. I toyed with a cigarette, but my mouth and throat were so dry I couldn't bear the thought of inhaling.

"I'm busy," I said.

"There is no need to be busy at Cedarcliff. It is a very easy school if you are willing to cooperate." She leaned toward me and the top of her dress flared. "You aren't a child, Miss Foster. You are a girl who has a mind of her own and who knows what she wants."

"Well, I hope so."

"As I recall, you said you wanted to be a teacher."

"That's right."

She nodded.

"It is a good field of work," she said. She leaned closer to me. "If you do as I suggest—and I think you will—I could possibly find a place for you here upon your graduation. We pay well, more than most larger schools, and we have an excellent pension-plan. It means real security to those selected."

"I appreciate your confidence in me," I murmured.

She leaned back in the chair and, thank goodness, removed the view of her breasts.

"It isn't confidence. It's sense. You do as I say and you'll have nothing to worry about."

"I'll do what I can."

She regarded me thoughtfully.

"Can I be practical with you, Miss Foster?"

"I don't know why not."

The cigarette was almost burning her fingers but she still clung to it.

"I said before you're beautiful and I meant it. You have the kind of beauty a woman can respect and enjoy. Do I make myself clear?"

"Not very."

She leaned forward again but only to crush the cigarette in the ash tray. I glanced out the window.

"We could be very happy together," she said. "You could be nice to me and I could be nice to you. You wouldn't have to work as hard as the other girls and I would see that your marks were high. You might take on some additional subjects and you could graduate in three years instead of four. Then I would equip you with a teaching position and we would still be together."

It was then I knew what she meant. She was one of them, too. Miss Lily was the same as Nina, except she was in control of the school and if a girl didn't bend to her will the girl would fail. Miss Lily hadn't threatened me with that but I was sure it was true. No wonder she didn't care what Paul Blanding did. What she did was just as bad.

"Where are you going?" she asked as I pushed my chair away from the desk.

"I'm going to pack and I'm going to get out of here. Right away."

"You won't get in another school at this time of the year."

"I don't care if I don't."

We had an awful scene after that. I got out my best luggage and she followed me around as I threw things first into one and then into the other. Miss Lily begged and pleaded with me. She would do anything for me, anything at all. She would pay me eight thousand a year in the teaching job she would provide, and if she could manage it she would pay me more.

"Just stay with me!" she cried. "Just stay with me!"

I was so numbed and shocked by her offer I nearly left the room in bra and panties. I had to open one of the suitcases to get out a dress and I pulled it down over my head, hardly able to wait to be free of her. She seized the opportunity to disrobe herself.

"Look at me," she commanded. "I'm not bad for being over forty. And you wouldn't have to love me. I'd love you. I'd love you until you went out of your mind with the wonders of it."

I put everything I had in the hall and made the first trip down to the car, throwing the bags in back and not caring how they landed. She might still have been in the room when I dashed upstairs to obtain the rest of the stuff but I didn't look inside to find out. I had seen all of her I wanted to see and I never wanted to see her again.

I can't fully explain why I drove toward home but I did. I guess I wanted to see my father again, to confess all my sins to him and hope he would somehow be able to understand. But the closer I drew to Benton the more doubtful I became, and I know I slowed the car so much I impeded the Sunday traffic. More than once I angered drivers and they blew their horns at me. In practically a stupor I pulled over to the shoulder of the road and let them go by. I rested awhile and then drove on.

In one respect I was grateful to Miss Lily. She had made me see how ugly my life had become, and from this realization came my urge to do something about it, something clean, right, and lasting. By the time I reached Benton I knew what I had to do, what I should have done at the start.

I didn't go home but took a room in a decent hotel. I tipped the man a dollar for bringing up my luggage and as soon as I was alone I put in a call to George.

Yes, he was home. Yes, he would come to see me—if I still wanted him to come after what he had done.

"I'll wait for you in the bar," I said before I hung up. "And don't be too long."

He wasn't long. I was on my second drink when George arrived and he didn't have much to say until he had tasted his rye and ginger ale. We were alone at the bar, the bartender at the other end reading a paper.

"Your father came out to see me this morning," he said. "He's a very right sort of a guy. He said he thought he could understand I had helped my folks with the money I took from time to time, and he said I deserved another chance."

"That's wonderful!" I was pleased for him.

"I'll still be the manager but twenty-five percent of my pay will go to the company until the full amount is paid. I think it's a real break. He could have sent me to jail." George seemed to consider this. "Hell, he could have ruined me. But it isn't in his heart to hurt anybody."

"I think he hates me," I said.

"I don't know. I honestly don't know, Doris."

The drink tasted like water in my mouth and I didn't really want it. I pushed the glass aside.

"And what about you, George?" I asked. "What about you?"

He appeared uncomfortable.

"Well—"

"You were there. You saw us. You saw what we were doing. It must have affected you in some way."

He nodded.

"It did. It made me a little sick."

"And what did you think?"

"I didn't think. I tried not to think. I knew Laura wasn't any good but I didn't think she would go that far. I didn't say anything to you but when your father had decided to marry her he asked me what I thought. I told him but he paid no attention to me. He said she had had some bad luck during her life and she needed some good. I didn't argue with him."

"Now I suppose he'll divorce her."

"Of course he will. He was very firm about that when I talked with him this morning. He was a beaten man, Doris. Everything he had believed in had gone up in smoke. I don't think he blamed you as much as he blamed her. He said she was older and wiser and you were probably just a victim of circumstances."

I picked up a cigarette and again my hands shook. I could pretend my father's deduction had been right but I was beyond pretending.

"She wasn't the only one," I said, fighting to keep my voice from breaking.

It isn't easy to confess. It never is. But I did. I told him everything, about Hank Herbert and Paul Blanding and Nina and, finally, Miss Lily. I didn't drink while I was doing it. I had found an inner courage and my courage didn't need a stimulant.

"I just packed up and drove away," I concluded. "I couldn't stand it any longer. I had to face things—and myself."

George waited until the bartender had brought him another drink before he spoke.

"You've got a lot of guts," he said. "Nine out of ten girls would never admit what you have."

"It's the truth."

"Only in one respect."

"How is that?"

"Because the girl all those things happened to wasn't the real you. The real you is the person sitting beside me, a girl who can speak of herself in such a way that what she says is more than enough payment for her mistakes."

My eyes clouded over.

"Do you mean that, George?"

"I mean it very much."

I finished my drink and had another one. I wasn't drinking to hide anything. I was drinking because I felt good and because I felt honest with myself. I saw what had happened to me as something that could have happened to any girl who has the slightest doubt in her mind about love. Love comes to you from many directions and it's up to you to recognize it. Love has certain obligations and responsibilities and unless you can accept these you cannot accept love. Love, to a girl, isn't the endless search of another girl's lips. Love, to a girl, belongs to a man and to a man alone. Love is the pressure of a man's arms around you; love is his strength and yours; love is the knowledge that your man and you are meant to be together and to create and bring life into the world. Without this real kind of love there would be no homes, no marriages, and nothing enduring.

When we left the bar George didn't ask me if he could come up to my room. He just took my arm and steered me into the elevator and I knew this was what I wanted, wanted even more than the next breath which meant my life.

It was a wonderful night, a glorious night, a night which knew no bounds. He was gentle, never forcing me, and each time was better than the one before.

"I want your baby," I gasped. "I want your baby terribly."

He kissed me hard on the mouth.

"Are you sure?"

"If you're going to marry me, yes."

"Well, I'm going to marry you."

It was daylight before we got to sleep.

Not that we had any inclination to rest, but the human body can stand just so much of desire and pleasure.

We had had our share of both ...

More than a year has gone by, now, and the doctor tells me I will be going to the hospital any day. George wants a boy and I want a girl but I guess it doesn't really matter as long as the baby is healthy.

I don't think any longer of dying in childbirth. I am happy with George's baby—our baby—growing inside me, and the doctor says I have nothing to worry about. He is the best doctor in Benton and I have decided he ought to know.

We live in a lovely neighborhood. It isn't the finest in town but George and I are satisfied. My father refused to take back the money he had given me, and our furniture is paid for. George is doing an outstanding job at the company and he is slowly paying back the debt he owes. My father comes to the house frequently for dinner and he insists on writing off the loss but we insist, even more strongly, that the debt should be met. He is divorced from Laura and she is still running the store. I never see her but she has a young girl working for her and I've heard they are very much in love. They may be, but sooner or later they will realize their tragedy.

You may have read that Cedarcliff School has been closed down. There was some trouble between Nina and Miss Lily, and Miss Lily was stabbed. When the police investigated they uncovered the whole rotten mess, including Paul Blanding and how he had treated some of the girls. The paper stated Miss Lily would recover from her wounds, and a couple of days after that I read one of the girls had charged Hank Herbert with rape. I still have the clippings around the house but I never read them.

"Get rid of them," George tells me. "What good are they to you?"

I think he's right and I think I'll find them and go out and

burn them as soon as I'm finished writing this.
I am not living in the past.
Today holds too much for both of us.
And tomorrow promises to be even better.

The End

THE
STRANGEST
SIN

Sharon Doyle felt dirty when she woke up in Jimmy Slade's bed, but that wasn't unusual. She always felt dirty after a night of passion in Jimmy's cheap room on West Avenue and sleepily she wondered why she continued to see him. He didn't work; he was a liar; and—let's face it, she told herself—their relationship didn't make much sense. She had such a lovely apartment on Park Place and, until now at least, her bar on Bently Street had given her a nice profit every week. Of course, there were rumors that the shoe factory was moving upstate and that would hurt her business a lot. More than half her steady customers worked in the factory and most of them made good money.

She yawned, glancing at the alarm clock. It was a little after seven and she opened her bar at eight. She did that every day, except Sundays when the time was one; and Tuesdays, Lucy's day off, she worked a double shift, sticking it out until closing time, three in the morning.

With casual interest she glanced around the room, seeing the faded paper on the walls and the junky old furniture that kept falling apart. The rent was five dollars a week and most of the time she had to give Jimmy the five so he could pay the woman. In fact, this past year she'd given Jimmy a lot of money—he was constantly broke—and though he promised to pay her back, he never did. Twice she had broken with him, and twice she had come back. She smiled; there was no use wondering why she did it. She had returned to his bed because he was just about all the man a girl could possibly want. Still, she knew that it wasn't right. She had to admit to herself that the whole thing was only cheap sex, nothing more, and love ought to mean something far beyond that. Besides, there was always the chance of getting in the family way and having Jimmy run out on her. Like that fellow had run out on Lucy last spring. Lucy had lost the baby, and since that time she had entertained dozens of men in her upstairs room over the bar. Sharon didn't know if Lucy charged for her favors, but she guessed it was none of her business if the girl did.

She yawned again, listening to Jimmy breathing heavily beside her. Often she had thought he had heart trouble because of the way he breathed, but at twenty-six, four years her senior, he seemed to be healthy enough. Probably he had some kind of obstruction in his nose that caused it.

She stretched, then got up from the bed and began hunting for her things. She had been stoned the night before and Jimmy had undressed her. She'd drawn a blank and didn't remember much of what had happened after that. No doubt he had made love to her and then cursed her for being drunk and unsatisfactory.

There was a cracked mirror over the old dresser but she didn't look at herself in it. She knew what she was like without looking. She was forty-two inches at the bust, her breasts tilted and firm, and down below that she was only twenty-four. At the hips she flared out to thirty-eight and her thighs and legs were perfect—better than most of the ads she saw in magazines. As for her face, men said it was beautiful; her lips were full and red, and she hoped that they weren't kidding her. And her blonde hair helped; it cascaded below her shoulders in long, natural waves. When she was working she wore a band to keep it out of the way.

She dressed slowly, her mind on Jimmy, and then she had trouble with the bra. Lucy, although she was not quite as big, never wore a bra, and the men liked that. Lucy was a nut on blouses, and wore the transparent kind that let almost everything show through. As for Sharon, she was content to dress decently and let the men use their imagination. The only time she wasn't decent was when she was with Jimmy. On Saturday night she dated Carl Evans—he had an apartment across the hall from hers and he sold hardware supplies across the state—but he never asked anything from her. She supposed that was partly why she went out with him, that and the fact that he was rather handsome in a blond, clean-cut way. When she dated him, she could dance and drink and then come out of the night feeling clean, untouched by the proddings of conscience.

"You sure tied one on last night," Jimmy grunted from the bed.

"I was worrying about business. You've heard the talk about the shoe factory moving away?"

She pulled the dress down over her head and checked the seams of her stockings. For once they were straight.

"I told you before that you should have sold out. You had

something to show, a business making a profit, but now if the shoe factory moves, what have you got? A bar with no customers, no business. You couldn't give it away."

"Then I'll get a job and let it die. Take it from me it's no picnic behind that bar. And, speaking of getting a job, when are you going to hunt for one?"

"I've been talking to Bert Robinson. Or were you too drunk to hear me say that last night?"

"He's a crook, Jimmy. You know he controls the rackets in Sanderstown."

"So what? It's a living, isn't it?"

"A living for a while, and jail after that. He may have money but he can't buy everything. Take that house he had uptown. The police raided that, didn't they?"

"Sure but the joint's back in operation again, and with the same girls. It cost Robinson some dough, but he made it back in a hurry. The whole deal was just for show and nothing else."

She turned now and looked at him. He was a big man, well over six feet, and he lay stretched out on the bed in his shorts. He always wore shorts, even when he made love.

"I won't be seeing you tonight," she said.

"Why not?"

"Because what we have isn't any good and it never was. You won't work, and you cost me money. After the money there's only one thing that you want and you make it seem cheap. It's ugly. I hate the way you make me feel."

"I suppose it's better with that hardware salesman."

"He's a gentleman, Jimmy."

"And I'm not?"

"You know what you are. You wouldn't be in this rotten room if you weren't too lazy to work. The trouble is you want a job that will pay you big money and you don't have the education for that. You didn't even finish high school."

"Can I help it if they yanked me out of high and shot me into reform school?"

"You could have helped it. You didn't have to steal a car and drive off with that girl."

He frowned. "It's hurt me getting work," he admitted. "The reform school bit, and not having a diploma."

"You ought to know by now that there are some things you have to live down. You have to have the guts to fight them and lick them."

He grinned at her and she glanced away from him. There was something about that grin that upset her and almost seemed to justify their affair as a natural and wonderful relationship, and not just the blind, driving fury of the flesh.

"Come back to bed," he said.

"No. I have to open the place."

"Nuts. I've known days when you didn't get there until ten."

"Well, this isn't one of them." She put on her shoes. "And I was serious about tonight. This can't go on between us. It's just a nothing. It's worse than that."

"You sure weren't worth much last night."

"Sorry." Her voice was snappish.

"Lots of times you're no good. Why is that?"

She left the room without answering him. He was right about her being a poor lover, and she didn't understand the reason for it. Maybe that was why she kept going back to him, hoping to find in him something real that would make her come alive. Look at Lucy. She lived as a woman. She talked about what she did, comparing the men who had been with her and describing the fun she had with most of those who shared her bed.

It was already hot outside, good beer weather, and since she had left her car parked on Bently Street before the bar, she walked on past the shoe factory. The shadow of a frown crossed her forehead. She had heard that the loss of the company would force more than five hundred men out of work, and at least half those men were good customers.

Men were on their way to work, some carrying their lunch pails, and she was aware of their prolonged and admiring looks at her. She couldn't help that. She had a natural sway to her body, and when she moved she moved all over. During her junior high school year she had entered and won a local beauty contest. Perhaps she could have gone on to the state finals, but the man in charge had wanted his price and she hadn't been willing to pay it. At that time, all she had known about sex had come from the stories she had heard in school, and she had thought that one relationship gave a girl a baby.

The next year she had found out that this wasn't always so. And she had found out in a terrible way.

She still remembered the afternoon. Her mother and father had been busy in the bar and she had been alone in the apartment upstairs. It had been a hot day and since she had been alone, she had stretched out nude on the bed. So she had slept, sprawled out in the heat, oblivious to the juke box's blare from downstairs ...

It was when she opened her eyes that she saw, with a sudden cold stab of terror, the half-dressed man standing over her, looking down at her nakedness.

"They can't hear you if you scream," he grinned. "And if you fight me I'll kill you. I know what I want, and so do you."

She recognized him then as a bar customer, and she screamed her head off, trying to cover herself with the sheet, but he tore it from her. As he had said, nobody heard her, and when at last he took her she was helpless to prevent it. The pain was horrible as his weight crushed the breath from her, and in that second she wanted to die. A half hour later he had left her broken body twisting on the bed, the terror of what she had known making her shake all over ...

Most girls, she guessed, would have told their parents, but she did not feel free to do so, for she had never been very close to them. When she had most needed love and understanding they had been busy in the bar, and therefore much of her childhood had been lonely. So she said nothing, and had lived alone with her fears for the next month, but in the end she had been all right; nothing wrong with her body, but the scar of the attack was deep in her mind.

Strangely, after this she delighted in dating boys, in leading them on to a certain point and then figuratively slamming the door in their faces. Soon they started calling her a teaser, but no matter what they called her, she still got dates. Every fellow thought he was going to score where the others had failed.

But it was not until after both her parents had died, a week after her twenty-first birthday, that Sharon first met Jimmy Slade when he visited the bar and she had been an easy mark for him. In the beginning he had elaborated to her about the good job he had, but by the time she had realized that his important-seeming job was only a lie, she had belonged to him, seeking from him the thrill of love, yet never quite finding it. And when at last she had learned the truth about him, what he really was hadn't seemed to matter. She had approached him as a challenge, one that she tried desperately to meet.

The sun was hot as she crossed Fourth Street and her head ached. She guessed she deserved the headache. Drinking so much wasn't any good and she had to cut it out. Perhaps, she thought, she was trying to escape from herself, from her own strange desires, but a person couldn't do that. You met things as they came, good or bad, and you made the best of them.

Her mind went back to Jimmy, and she compared him to Carl Evans—Carl stood for the best of everything. He had a good job, he was ambitious, he was working hard for a promotion, and he didn't live like some animal in the city dump. The only way Jimmy Slade could ever get any money would be by playing it on the shady side of the law—and how long would that last? It would last only until Bert Robinson was finished with him, then he'd be finished, in jail, maybe "mysteriously" killed. Other men had worked for Robinson and had been kicked aside after they had served his purpose. Jimmy needn't think that he was any different.

The name of the bar was The Club Forty, and she liked that. It sounded better than just calling the place a bar. When her father had named his place he had thought of going in for nightly entertainment. Nothing had come of the idea, but with the right kind of talent she might be able to pull trade from uptown. Considering the situation at the shoe factory, she guessed she'd better do some real hard thinking on the subject.

Sharon unlocked the door and went inside the bar, into its cool, beer-and-whiskey-smelling dimness.

Lucy, as was her custom after closing the night before, had put yesterday's receipts in the safe, and now Sharon got out sufficient bills and silver to make change. If Lucy came down early that afternoon, Sharon would make up a deposit for the bank. Still, the safe was big and strong, and she could wait. Her bank account was healthy and she could write a check for anything she owed.

There were some dirty glasses behind the bar, and she supposed that Lucy had closed up in a hurry the night before. Lucy had a habit of rushing out and leaving a sloppy bar; a habit that Sharon didn't like.

At eleven the bar was empty. She yawned and tugged at a bra strap. Maybe owning a bar wasn't a bad life, but the business kept her tied down. She couldn't trust Lucy more than a day at a time, but there wasn't anybody else she wanted to get. More than once she had strongly suspected that Lucy had sticky fingers, but she could never prove that.

She was still alone at the bar when the door opened and Bert Robinson came in. He was dressed in a sharp Continental-style suit, the way he usually dressed, and the odor of shaving lotion floated around him. She had never seen Robinson when he wasn't freshly shaven, dressed immaculately, and smiling. She didn't care for the smile. It was both smug and cruel; the feral smile of a man who knows much, none of it good, but who will use that knowledge for his own ruthlessly selfish ends.

"Gin," he said as he climbed up onto a stool. "Gin and orange. No ice."

She fixed the drink and gave him change from his ten. Whenever he stopped in for a drink he paid with a ten or a larger bill.

"You smell like a wedding or a funeral," she said. "Which is it?"

He toyed with the drink. "It's going to be a funeral for this bar, Sharon."

"Tell me more."

"The factory. This is its last week. I got it straight. They're moving upstate to get away from the union wages. Where do you get business after that? Out of thin air?"

"I'll get by."

He nodded and drank some of his drink. "You could do that on your looks, honey, but I don't think you're that kind."

"I'm sure not."

He waved in the direction of his now empty glass. "You like living on Park Place?" he asked.

"It's comfortable."

"And it costs money?"

"Enough. You usually get what you pay for."

Robinson was a cigar-smoker and he rolled one around in his mouth. She looked at him speculatively, wondering what he was leading up to. He often came into the bar, had his drink and didn't say more than two words.

"Some of the girls in the factory are going to be looking for a fast buck when the plant closes," he said as he held the lighter flame to his cigar. "In that apartment you've got upstairs you could set three or four of them up in business without any trouble at all. You might even use the girl who works for you. Some of the trade we get are ten- or twenty-dollar deals, and I could use another house without thinking about it. You wouldn't get rich, but it's a steady racket. And you could make up for the drop in business you'll have with the shoe factory gone. And you'd be helping out the girls at the same time. Everybody wins."

She didn't want a drink, but she took one anyway—a short one that burned as it went down.

"Thanks for nothing," she said and rinsed out the glass.

"I'm only trying to help."

"Trying to help? Which one of us?"

"Both. You'd be protected, and I could expand that part of my operation. What say we have dinner tonight and talk about it?"

He had asked her out to dinner before, but she had always refused. To begin with he was too old for her, and on top of that she didn't trust him. She had gone far enough down the sewer with Jimmy Slade, but that didn't mean she was going to do it a second time with another man. Still, she didn't have to be told that there was money to be made in sex. And if he was right about the factory, she was going to be hurt and hurt badly. The money she had saved wouldn't last long, and good jobs were hard to come by.

"I'm busy tonight," she said.

"Then we'll make it some other night."

"I don't promise anything."

He got up from the stool. "You'll go for the idea when you get hungry enough, Sharon. Hungry people are people on the move. Feed a pig twice a day and he doesn't notice you, but feed him once a week and you're a big deal."

"Thanks for comparing me to a pig."

He picked up his change. "I wasn't comparing you to a pig, beautiful. I was only saying how it is with most of us. Money we have to have and money we get. Some of us get our money the slow way, like a dumb slob who works for day wages, but the smart ones clean up every night of the week."

"I might consider selling the business," she told him.

"So who wants it when there won't be any business? You're about three months late. Your chances to sell have slipped past you."

He walked to the door and went on outside.

She sighed and wiped down the bar. She simply didn't like that man, and she couldn't help it. He was the living embodiment of calculating evil, and whenever he looked at her she felt half-naked and soiled.

At noon she began to get busy and she forgot about him, except for what he said about the closing of the factory. It was true, all right. The employees had been informed that morning and the men sitting at the bar looked unhappy and depressed.

"It's going to change a lot of things," one man told her.

Sharon shrugged and drew a beer with a good head.

Maybe the man was right.

Maybe it would change her world. But for better or for worse?

Who could say?

2

Jimmy Slade slept until early afternoon, and then got up. Yawning lazily, he went into the hall and headed down toward the shower.

"Hello, honey," a girl said from the first open door.

He paused, looking at her. She was young, maybe nineteen, and all she had over her was a sheet.

"Don't you ever work?" he wanted to know.

"I could ask you the same thing, but it wouldn't be any of my business. And why should I work when I can make money without getting up?"

"You won't make any money from me."

The girl's teeth were lipstick-stained behind her smile. "Listen, you big, beautiful hunk of man-meat, who said I wanted any money from you? Honey, some of the best things in life are free."

He made a gesture of dismissal with his hand and moved on. She swore at him bitterly. He didn't care if she swore and he didn't care what she thought. A girl like that was bad news, and he'd had enough of that during his life. From now on the news had to get better.

The water in the shower was cold and he liked that. When he had been growing up at home he had hated cold water but reform school had made him get used to it. He guessed, as he looked back, that the reform school stretch had been a real kick in the tail. It had changed his whole future, but he knew without being told that he had only himself to blame.

After he finished his shower, he dried himself with a towel that someone else had used and stepped into his shorts. Until now he had just been a small noise in a big barrel, but if he could line up with Bert Robinson, running numbers or something, he'd be on the way up. Robinson had started out flat broke, and now look where he was. Even the mayor smiled when he met Robinson, and the mayor didn't often smile. Jimmy couldn't see why he couldn't do the same thing, starting out small and growing big. Two years before he'd tried hustling for a couple of girls on their own. Robinson had had him picked up and beaten soundly, but Robinson seemed to bear him no grudge. Since that time he'd been trying to line up with the boss and he was still trying. Afternoons he went up to the Palace Bar on King Street from where Robinson directed most of his operations, and if business had been good that day he'd buy anybody a drink.

Jimmy left the bathroom and moved down the hall. The girl said nothing as he passed her door, and if he had felt like it he could have put her next to some smart information. She must be too new in town to know that everybody paid off Robinson, whether it was a girl who was selling herself, or some dumb kid who had a hot car that had to be taken care of.

Back in his bedroom, he dressed and shined his shoes with a piece of newspaper. At twenty-six he was so close to being a failure that he couldn't find any humor in the thought but he kept telling himself that he'd get a break and things would be all right. Robinson always had something going and it was just a question of hitting the guy at the right time. Robinson didn't hire fast, but when he hired a man, that man was set solid. He saw the fellows who came into the Palace getting orders from Robinson, and they were loaded with cash. No five-dollar room for them. No going hungry so you could drink or walking your legs off to save cab fare.

He checked his money and fished out a bill. A twenty. For a second he wondered where he'd gotten it, and then he remembered that he'd taken it from Sharon's pocketbook the night before. He grinned and replaced it in his wallet. Now he was getting so he didn't even ask. He got her drunk and then he took what he wanted from her. The night before, feeling the cold terror of being flat broke, he'd taken the money first and the girl last. Laying her, as he had told her that morning, hadn't been much fun. She'd moaned once, almost responding, and then she'd been like a sack of beans. If he had been paying for what she gave him, he'd have demanded his money back.

Walking over to the window, he stood looking out, watching a couple of boys playing catch in the back yard. Sometimes, like now, he didn't understand Sharon. She was about the best stacked girl he'd ever seen—she was really built—and to look at her you'd think she was all sex. But that was as far as it went. She had to be walking on one leg before she'd be willing to go to bed, and then she turned out to be a false alarm. He guessed that the only reason he bothered with her was because she was a soft touch, and when he needed money he needed it, Anything else that he had to have from a girl he could get along West Avenue. For the price of a few beers and a little talk in one of the local bars, a guy could spend the rest of the night with almost any girl he wanted. He grinned, thinking of the number of girls who played for free. Robinson was having plenty of competition for his girls uptown. But, of course, that was a different deal, and a lot of his trade came from the city or the high-class resort hotels nearby that catered to the well-to-do family trade, except poppa had to have his bowling night once a week—at one of Robinson's joints.

He turned from the window and lit a cigarette as he left the room. Sharon had said that she was finished with him, but she'd said the same thing before and hadn't made it stick. Saturday nights she dated that jerk of a salesman, but as soon as he cleared town for another business trip, she was willing to forget about her fancy apartment on Park Place and trade it for a night with Jimmy on West Avenue.

It was a long walk up to the Palace Bar on King Street, but a cab cost a buck, and besides he didn't have anything else to do. Robinson reached the bar about four and lined up the business of the coming night for his men. After that he drank and talked. Lately he had been talking a lot to Jimmy, and that must be a good sign. Talk could lead to a connection, and a connection meant money, the kind of money that bought cars and dames and the big stuff in life. Guys who worked for wages or a salary were suckers. Either you had a business of your own or you dipped into the rackets. Not being able to open his own business, there was only one thing left for Jimmy—get in with Bert Robinson.

The street followed the river uptown and he liked the brackish smell of the water. A number of men were fishing from the near bank, and it was a good bet that most of them weren't fishing for fun; they were fishing for food. Jimmy had overheard businessmen say that the city was in a desperate economic situation, with all the factories moving upstate or down south, and more and more people out of jobs and going on relief. Yet, as he looked around, there seemed to be plenty of money for vice. The auto dealers couldn't sell their cars, but a girl with a figure could get from twenty to fifty dollars for ten minutes of her time.

At the bridge he cut away from the street and made his way through the park. It wasn't much of a park, perhaps five acres of undergrowth with some paths, but at night it was popular with the younger set. Before his trouble with the law, he had hung around the park a lot.

There was that soft April night a couple of years ago—a night he could never forget....

"You're chicken," the little blonde told him as they strolled through the shadows. "If you weren't chicken you wouldn't be broke."

"What do you mean?"

"People come through the park. Some of them are loaded. Friday's payday. So Friday night you take it away from one of them and we have ourselves a ball. A pad in a hotel doesn't cost much. We'd get a bottle, and I'd be good to you."

Jimmy had broken the law before this, but only in minor things. That Friday night, however, he became a savage, waiting near the park entrance while the girl hid in the shadows. He picked a well-dressed old guy who looked flush. He worked fast. Two blows from his right fist—one would have been enough—and then he and the girl ran with the wallet. Not until they were four blocks away did they stop to count their take and it came to almost seventy dollars. The girl kissed him eagerly on the mouth and he threw the empty wallet down the sewer.

An hour later they were in a cheap hotel room, a bottle on the dresser, and the girl's soft young body twisting in his arms as he fought with her clothing. They had stayed the night, drinking and making love, and the next day the girl had wanted a car.

"We'll get the hell out of here," she had said. "With a car we can head south. Miami—Palm Beach, maybe."

"And then what?"

"There's money down there. Don't you want money?"

It was easy. That night he found a blue Caddy convertible with the ignition keys still in the lock, in the station parking space. He wasn't a very good driver and he was nervous, so scraped a couple of fenders getting out onto the street. Then his nervousness left him, with that little blonde chick cuddling beside him, and he felt like a big operator. This was living, man, living big! The trouble was that he hadn't known the car had been missed a few minutes after he'd taken it, and even as he was nursing the Caddy through town the cops were blocking off the main routes and checking cars. When he was stopped and he realized what was going on he tried to make a break, but it was too late. The cops nailed him, and the little blonde chick was sobbing that he had forced her to come along, and that she wasn't that kind of a girl at all. When they checked her record, however, she got a suspended sentence that required her to be home at nine every night. But nothing had helped him. He got the school . . . .

Now as he crossed the park he guessed that he wasn't any good. Getting right down to it, he'd never been much good. Well, the past was finished and it had about as much value as a used postage stamp. A guy should live for today and plan for the days ahead—or the nights. Nights were better. Days were for squares, the jerks who held down steady jobs, but the big, fast money came out of the night.

As he neared the Palace Bar on King Street he began to swagger. Nobody knew much about him at the bar and he always acted mysterious. Sometimes he kidded the girls, like he could do something for them, and they got a charge out of that. So did he, but he didn't let on.

Inside the place, Robinson was at his usual table—some called it his office—and he was chewing a guy out, but good.

Jimmy caught Robinson's glance and grinned. If Robinson was sore at one of his men, that might mean the guy would get kicked out, leaving an opening for him to fill. Still Robinson had been sore plenty of times before and it hadn't amounted to anything. You just couldn't tell, could you?

He moved up to the bar and he sat on the opposite end from the girls. There were five of them, all looking pretty much the same, probably all smelling the same, but just then he didn't have any desire for them.

"Beer," he said and slapped the twenty down on the bar. "And don't give me all head."

He smiled inwardly. That was the way to be—tough and hard. Even if there was no reason for it, you put up a strong front. Act weak, and you were licked before you started.

The beer was cold, hardly any head at all, and as he drank he turned so that he could watch Bert Robinson. Robinson was after another guy now and he was pounding the table with his fist. The guy just stood there and said nothing, his shoulders sloped forward, his face worried.

Jimmy was on his third beer when Robinson got up from the table and came over to him. He hadn't expected that, but now Robinson coming to him gave him a lift. Mostly Robinson held court at the table and people took turns coming to him.

"Some of these jerks don't appreciate what you do for them," Robinson said as he sat down.

Jimmy shook his head sympathetically. "No, I guess they don't."

Robinson ordered a gin and orange. "I can't have that, Slade. I put money in a guy's pocket and I got a right to some return for it. He's got to play square with me."

"Sure," Jimmy said. "That's only fair."

"Ten years ago I'd have worked these punks over myself, but I'm getting too old for that now. I get excited and my heart starts beating like a hammer. I've got too much to do to wind up in a hospital bed with a nurse holding my hand."

Jimmy nodded and pretended to study the situation. Obviously, Robinson needed a man with a strong arm, and that he had. He had the power, and he knew how to use it.

"If I wasn't so busy I might be able to help you out," Jimmy said, trying not to appear too anxious.

"Too busy doing what?"

"Things."

"Like taking care of Sharon Doyle?"

"I grab what I can get. If she happens to give me a tumble, I don't stop her none."

"Maybe you could fix it up for me."

"She makes her own deals."

"So what? You're close to her. I'm not. I go down there once or twice a week but she doesn't act as though I'm alive. There's something about her that I like. I could have a different dame every night but none of them have what she's got, that's for sure. Then that shoe factory's closing down this week. She'll be hurting for business, and I need a spot for three or four more girls. She's got the perfect setup with that apartment upstairs over her bar. Throw that Lucy out, or let her in on the deal. She needs to be slapped around anyway. Girls in this town pay off Bert Robinson, or they don't work."

"She'd never go for it," Jimmy said. "Not Sharon Doyle."

"I'm leaving that part up to you. You get her to go along with me and I've got a job for you. You're big and you can ride herd on these clowns who work for me. Or I tell you to get a guy, and you get him. And the girls—some of them are cheating on me and I want to know who they are. I don't care if each one of them gives it away to a dozen men a night, but, by God, they better come through with my cut!"

Jimmy took a deep breath. Here was the offer he had been waiting for and he didn't know what to do about it. He knew what Sharon thought of the girls who sold their bodies for a living; he guessed she'd rather close down than have anything to do with that. But it would bring business to the bar. And she didn't have to become one of them.

"I'll see what I can do," he said to Robinson.

"And set up a date with her for me."

"That may be impossible."

Robinson downed his drink. "Nothing's impossible," he declared. "I've got the dough and she's got the looks. We could make one hell of a team if she'd only settle down to it. You always need new girls in this racket and she could line them up."

Even to Jimmy it was a rotten business, but who was he to sit in judgment? He couldn't continue living off his looks for the rest of his life, and if he wanted to get inside with Robinson he'd have to do as he was asked.

"I'll take a stab at it," he said.

"The girl must like you."

"Maybe."

"And you like her?"

"Not enough to matter. She's just a dame. There's millions of 'em."

"She's one in a million."

"Ahh, they're all the same. If one says No another says Yes. And those who say No don't mean it half of the time. They want a guy to crawl on his belly."

"I'd crawl for her," Robinson said.

"You may get that chance."

Robinson had another gin and orange and then returned to the table to take up his business where he left off. It was a girl this time, and she was crying and rubbing her hands together. The reason for her crying was obvious; she was at least five months pregnant. Robinson listened, nodded, then slipped her a bill and she drifted outside.

Jimmy sat at the bar drinking beer. He felt good. Of course, he didn't have a spot with Robinson just yet, but if he used his head he'd be set. And—if Sharon would play ball, he'd be really in.

At six he left and retraced his steps through the park. He had things to do and he couldn't fool around. He felt about eight feet tall.

Somebody was going to get hurt.

3

Lucy Forbes drew a short beer for herself and looked down the empty bar. Not in the three months that she had worked for Sharon had she ever seen the bar entirely empty, but it was empty now. As a matter of fact, she hadn't had a customer for over half an hour and she was getting bored.

She finished the beer, rinsed out the glass, and then turned to look at herself in the mirror. When she had first come on duty Sharon had told her that even her nipples showed right through the blouse, and they did. That didn't bother Lucy; too many men had seen her naked, and there was nothing at all wrong with her breasts. So what difference?

She shrugged and turned from the mirror. During the twenty-one years since her birth she had seen the rotten side of life and she guessed that a little more wouldn't hurt. The only thing she couldn't take was getting herself pregnant again, and she always made sure that the men she entertained wouldn't get her that way. The time before had been a mistake. She had been going by that crazy chart, and you sure couldn't depend on those things. Anyhow, she reflected, not being married wasn't playing fair with the baby. Better to be single than married to one of the dumb Johns who came into the bar—these married guys, these cheats and liars who spent money that should have gone for food and clothes for their wives and kids.

She had seen them all, the good and the bad, but no matter what they were, they were only after one thing. A few would pay, but most of them wanted it for free. If she went to bed with a man, the man ought to be willing to pay, even a little something. After all, she wasn't getting rich at her job here, and the way things looked now, the job wasn't going to last for long, anyhow.

There wasn't much else to do and she scrubbed off the bar top. Probably even that was a waste of time. People came in to drink and not to admire a scrubbed bar. Only tonight they weren't coming in to drink. The shoe factory was closing and everybody was hanging onto what money they had. Guys who had been seeing her almost every week would now be hauling their freight at home. She threw the cloth under the bar. Well, maybe their wives would get a break. She laughed. Or would they?

There was a stool behind the bar and she sat down on that, pulling her feet up to the top rung and letting the hem of her skirt ride above her knees. Her knees were smoother under the nylons and she had good legs, just as good as Sharon's, and the men admired them. But beyond that she couldn't compare herself to Sharon Doyle. Of course, she had a nice thirty-eight bust, but her tiny stomach had put on a couple of inches during the time she had been expecting the baby and she hadn't been able to lose it. Perhaps she could trim to twenty-four again if she cut out the beer, but she enjoyed beer and she wasn't about to give it up.

A few people moved along the street, but nobody came in. Without any business she couldn't clip the cash register for a few bucks or pick up a date. On the sixty dollars a week Sharon paid her, she hadn't been able to go very far, but what she got from the men counted up. Her room upstairs was for free and all she had to do was to keep it clean. As for her meals, she didn't eat much and what she did eat came out of cans. About once a week she had something decent to eat with Carl Evans but that was always after closing, and then she was never very hungry.

She thought about Carl Evans, and she was quite sure that she didn't understand him—or herself. On weekends he came in off the road and Saturday night he dated Sharon, sometimes taking her dancing but never keeping her out late. After he told Sharon good night he came down to the bar and hung around, not really asking Lucy for her time, but letting her know in various ways that he was interested in her. On Sunday morning, after closing, they went uptown to eat. Then he took her to a bottle club for a few drinks—he had a key, and his own bottle, and you could buy cold beer there—and about dawn they checked into a hotel, since he was afraid to use the room over the bar. Sometimes he made it with her all day Sunday, but usually, he just talked about his job and Sharon.

"You're regular," he had said to Lucy last Sunday.

"I'm a fool."

"A fool? But why?"

"Very simple. What's in this for me? You treat Sharon like a lady, but you have your fun with me. She gets you all excited and I put out the fire. I'm not that hard up, so where's the percentage for me?"

But she liked him, anyway . . . .

She got up to draw another beer and made up her mind that she wouldn't see him again. He was in love with Sharon and she didn't stand a chance in that direction. Of course she could have told him the truth about Sharon and Jimmy Slade, but she needed her job and she was afraid of Jimmy. All Jimmy had to do was to look at her and she felt herself shake inside. He was so big, so sort of all-American male and she sensed the violence in him. She doubted if there was anything that he wouldn't do. But he was Sharon's, and she liked Sharon enough to keep off. Anyhow, he was always costing Sharon money and when he drank at the bar he never paid.

It was quiet in the bar and Lucy thought about the three

thousand dollars in the safe. She knew the combination. All she had to do was to pick it up and get out of town, real quick. Three thousand dollars meant new clothes, a different city, and a fresh start. If she went far enough and fast enough they'd never find her. They could check her home in the Pennsylvania coal-mining country, but she hadn't been home in over three years and her folks didn't know anything about her. For all she knew, half of them were dead.

The money in the safe bothered her, but she knew that she couldn't touch it. Sharon had been too good to her and Sharon would need that money now. As for her own job, Lucy wasn't too worried. A pretty girl could always make a living, and men were willing to pay for her company. Even if she had to go to work for Bert Robinson in one of his houses she'd make out. A prostitute had maybe ten or fifteen good years and if she was smart and saved some of her money she could bust out of the racket and get into something legal. Or get married.

She was on her fourth or fifth beer when the door opened and Jimmy Slade came in.

"Nice blouse," he said as he sat down at the bar.

"Thanks."

"And you've got some pair inside it."

She drew him a beer. "Shut up," she said. "Shut up, Jimmy."

He sipped the beer and, although she didn't expect it, he put a dollar on top of the bar.

"Where's Sharon?" he wanted to know.

"Probably home."

"I tried her there and drew a blank."

"Then I can't help you. I came on and she went off."

"Maybe that salesman showed up."

She shrugged. "He's a nice guy."

Jimmy drained his glass. "So what's the matter with me?"

"Nothing much that getting a job wouldn't fix." She ran a beer with a short head. "If you could hold down a job, that is."

"I've got bucks coming my way," he said.

She made change from the one, taking out for both beers. "Yeah, I've heard that before, Jimmy. You'll be saying that when they bury you."

"And what will they say when they bury you, Lucy? That a hot little number got herself chilled?"

"Drop dead, will you?"

He leaned across the bar, grabbing for the front of her blouse, but she backed away from him.

"You're nobody to talk," he said. "You're nobody at all, baby. Any guy who's got the price gets the fun, huh? Well, don't let it fool you. You work this town and you pay the right people. That way you don't have no worries and you keep busy. You follow me?"

"Don't try to shoot off big to me," she told him. "You pull about as much weight in this town as a dead fly. What if you do sniff around Bert Robinson? What does it prove? Call him up, and he wouldn't even recognize your name."

He stared at her, real hard and tough. "You ought to be paying Robinson off," he said. "Bert doesn't mind none if he gets his, but the way you do it, you don't pay nobody."

"I run my own life."

Jimmy sneered. "You just think you do, baby. No dame runs her own life and you know it. Maybe a guy does but not a dame, especially a dame who sells herself. You sell yourself and you have to follow the crowd. Say you get ten from a guy and you split fifty-fifty with Robinson. What's the harm?"

The way he was looking at her made her wish that she had a bra on under the blouse. Most men didn't bother her, but he did. When Jimmy looked at a girl, she thought it was dirty, almost animal.

"Don't tell me you're beating the drum for Robinson," she said.

"I only know he's been watching you and that ain't good. The guys who have parties with you would be going uptown otherwise. That means he's losing dough. Bert Robinson hurts real bad when he loses dough that way."

"Let him line up the girls on West Avenue, then I'll talk to him."

She knew no man could organize the amateurs on West Avenue. No more than anyone could organize the girl she had shared an apartment with when she had first come to town. The first week had been good, but during the weekend she had drunk too much and the girl had made love to her, a tender and wonderful kind of love that had left Lucy shaken and satisfied. A month after that, feeling disgusted and ashamed, she had moved out while the other girl had been at work. Since then she had often been tempted to enter the twilight zone again, but something had always held her back. She tried to lose herself in the men who knew her. Often she failed to achieve her goal, but she felt rather decent because of her efforts. Man was for woman and woman was for man. As long as she kept it that way, she felt she'd be all right . . . .

"Beer," Jimmy said.

She reached for his glass, her thoughts still astray and this time when he made a grab for her he didn't miss. His hand found her rising fullness, his fingers twisting.

"Damn you, cut it out!" she yelled, and tore herself loose.

"You aren't too busy to close up for a few minutes so we could go upstairs. Let's do that. Then I'll tell Robinson that he's got you pegged all wrong; that you're on the square and just playing because you like to play. As long as he thinks you don't charge, he can't do nothing."

She rubbed herself where she hurt and then drew the beer. She was very careful as she put it down in front of him.

"I wouldn't go upstairs with you if you had a million dollars," she said. "Or two million."

"You'll talk another way when I get big. You'll be the one asking me, and I'll tell you to go to hell." He lifted his glass, hesitating. "You're too wise, baby. Somebody should cut you down to size, and maybe I'm the guy to do it. Maybe I should give you the business. Some dames go for the rough treatment."

"I'm not one of them," she said, afraid to be alone in the bar with him. "You keep your hands to yourself, Jimmy. I don't want to have anything to do with you, now or ever. If you're lonely, look for Sharon or find some girl on West Avenue. Just leave me alone."

While she was talking he had finished his beer. Now he slid from the stool and swaggered along the bar. Something inside her turned cold as she saw him round the end of the bar and start toward her. Once a man had beaten her terribly, cutting her lips and breaking a rib, and she'd never gotten over it. Why men wanted to beat girls she didn't know, but some of them did. She guessed they were sadists, the way Jimmy Slade was a sadist.

"You stay out from behind this bar," she shouted. "You've got no right back here!"

But he came on, stalking her, laughing at her.

"Yell if you want," he said. "Nobody's going to hear you and nobody'd care if they did. Dames like you need to be taught a lesson. Talk to you and you don't understand, but give you a fist in the mouth and everything gets real clear."

There was no way for her to get away from him and she began to shake. Until the week before there had been a club under the bar but Sharon had thrown the club out with some junk. Lucy was sorry now that she didn't have the club. Jimmy might get it away from her, but at least she could put up a fight. That would be better than just standing there and taking it.

He was coming toward her slowly, and she knew that she had to stop him. That one beating had been enough for her and she didn't want another. Besides, Jimmy's twisted mind might not let him stop before he had done some real damage.

"I'm warning you," she said tightly.

He laughed at her again. "A lot you've got to say about it. You look down your nose at me, and you're nobody. You think I'm a bum, but you're a bigger bum."

She waited until he was just a few feet away, then she made her move. With a swift, sudden motion she grabbed a filled whiskey bottle from the back bar and hurled it straight into his face. He had no time to grab it, no time to duck, and she heard the sound of the bottle as it struck bone and flesh, then the heavier sound as it fell to the floor. He let out a groan, backing uncertainly away from her and pawing at his face, She grabbed up another bottle, ready for him again, and she felt a little faint as she saw the blood begin to run down his chin. She had hurt him, hurt him badly, and it was hard to tell what he might do now. Men had killed for less and she didn't want to die. She just wanted to be left alone.

"You nailed me," he said as he took his hands away from his face. "Damn you."

"Well, you pushed me into it."

He saw the other bottle that she was holding and he backed away from her. There was a great deal of blood coming from his nose and he seemed to have difficulty breathing. For a few seconds he leaned against the bar, shaking his head and gasping.

"I'll get you for this," he promised.

"Don't blame me. When the day comes that I let somebody knock me around, I'll be out of my mind. If you want to fight, find a man and get it out of your system. Or haven't you got the guts?"

He used the bar cloth to clean off his face. It did no good; the blood kept on running.

"You'll find out what guts I've got, baby. No dame lays a bottle into my face and gets away with it."

"Try it again and you'll get another one in the same place."

He threw the bar cloth down and turned away from her, walking down the space behind the bar toward the door. He didn't swagger now and she heard him cursing in his thick voice, calling her names that had been born in the gutter.

When he had left she sighed but it wasn't exactly a sigh of relief. She had won this time, but the next time might be his turn. There were so many ways that he could get her that the thought of it made her shudder.

She was relieved when the door opened and a big guy came in. He wasn't dressed fancy, but he didn't look like a factory worker. She had never seen him before. He had a sunburned, weathered face and nice-looking, blunt features.

"Ginger," he said as he sat down at the bar. Then, when she started to reach behind her for a bottle, "No, not that Ginger ale."

"Gee," she said. "Big deal."

He made no comment, but as she got the ice and ginger ale she could feel him watching her. She glanced up quickly, thinking about a fast twenty dollars, hoping to see the usual hunger in his eyes. She was disappointed. All she saw was a normal, healthy interest.

"Dime," she said and rang it up. "Ought to be worth that much just for the ice."

He grinned, and casually asked her what time she got finished. She shrugged, letting her front bounce, but she didn't say. As he began talking about himself, the way some men did at the bar, she stared past him into the empty street. She decided that the guy who ordered ginger ale and paid for it with a lone dime couldn't have much more than five bucks in his pocket. Making up to him wasn't worth the trouble. She wasn't sleeping with any man for five bucks, drunk or sober.

"I live out there along the river," he was saying. "It's better than in town and nobody bothers you. I catch bait and some fish and do a little handy work."

"How thrilling," she said dully and decided further that he didn't even have five bucks. Probably a glass of soda pop was a big deal for him, a real night on the town.

He sat there silently and she found her glance wandering back to him, her mind thoughtful for a moment. Maybe he wasn't dressed sharp and maybe he didn't have any money, but he seemed to be the kind of a man who would be strong enough for a girl to lean on.

"Guess there's nothing around here for me," he said and slid down from the stool.

She became very practical again. "You sure guessed right that time, mister," she agreed.

He went out, his big shoulders sloping a little, and she rinsed the glass in the sink. She guessed that he was some clod, coming in there and thinking that he could pick up somebody for nothing. A dumb guy like that sure belonged outside of town along the river.

It might have been thirty minutes later when the next man came in. He was young, fairly handsome but with too-sharp features, and she didn't think she had ever seen him before. As he crossed to the bar she noticed that he walked with a slight limp.

"You cash checks?" he wanted to know.

"Not personal ones."

"Why not? It's good."

"Sorry. That's the rule. Pay checks are okay, but the others are out." Lucy tucked her blouse inside her skirt and gave him a good show while she was doing it. "What'll it be, mister?"

She was too busy looking at his face to know where the gun came from. One second he was just another customer, perhaps a date for the night, and the next second he was pointing that gun at her.

"The safe," he said shortly. "Open it, honey. You open it fast, and I'll take care of the dough."

She wet her lips with her tongue. "But I don't know the combination."

"Like hell you don't! People have seen you carrying the take back there and putting it away for the night." He waved the gun. "Let's go, baby. You want a bullet, or are you going to do like I say?"

There wasn't anything else that she could do. To argue with

a man who had a gun was stupid.

Five minutes later he was out of the bar, carrying the money in a paper bag.

She leaned weakly against the safe and began to sob. She realized that she ought to call the police and report the robbery, but somehow she was afraid to do it. She'd never had much luck with cops, and most of those she had had any contact with either had their hands out, or took for free what other men gladly paid for. Besides, there was only her unsupported word for what had happened. No reason to think that they'd believe her story.

A short time afterward she closed the bar for the night, locking the front door, then climbing upstairs to her room. She didn't know where she was going but she did know that she was moving as soon as possible.

She'd had enough—more than enough.

4

After the shoe factory had closed, Sharon made a desperate effort to bolster her sagging business. She hired a small combo for Friday and Saturday nights but the band only played part of Friday night.

"It's a shame to take your money," the leader said. "We play for money, but we don't want to play to four walls. You just haven't got any customers."

By eleven the band was gone and she was alone. She didn't think she had ever been quite so lonely. She was just too far downtown to pick up any trade. Staying open, she concluded, was about the most foolish thing she could do. She wouldn't take in enough to pay for the lights, and yet she had to stay open, hoping, or she was lost. She shook her head, fluffing out her blonde hair and reached for a bottle of rye. Maybe she was lost anyway. A lot of bad things had happened in the last couple of days, bad enough to make her forget her previous rule of not drinking on duty.

She poured a long jolt of rye and downed it straight, gasping for breath as the last of it went down. She thought of the morning—could she ever forget it—when she had found the safe empty. That had been a crusher. Of course, she had dashed upstairs, looking for Lucy, but when she had discovered that

Lucy had gone, Sharon had called the police. Headquarters had sent a couple of men down and it hadn't taken them long to make up their minds what had happened. Lucy had lifted the money and taken off. They said it was obvious.

Sharon had another drink and told herself that she would stay sober. She didn't believe that about Lucy. She had been too good to Lucy to have the girl pay her off like that, and Sharon couldn't believe that Lucy would have turned into a crook for a few thousand dollars. Not that the money wasn't important just then. It was. That morning she had tried borrowing from the bank, and they would only lend against her savings account. As for giving a mortgage on any building along Bently Street, the bank was against it. She had been advised to sell for what she could get and move on. The trick now was to find somebody to buy at a decent price, but that was almost out of the question. She doubted if she could get enough out of it to start again in another spot.

There were probably other things she could do, but running a bar was the only work she knew. When things were going all right she liked it and there was a good living in it. She didn't pay her rent on Park Place with her looks, that was for sure. She had to have the old money coming in or she'd have to give up what she had, and she dreaded the thought of having to do that. People who lived on Park Place were respected and the address stood for something. The man at the bank had been impressed, but it hadn't helped her get a loan. In fact, the man at the bank had suggested that she could cut down on her expenses and move in over the bar until she could work up some trade. The thing the man didn't tell her was just how she could work up a new trade. Like this band thing—what a bomb! She had advertised the band on the radio and in the newspapers but all she had accomplished had been to throw that money down the rat hole, and that kind of dough she sure didn't have. If she had sold ten glasses of beer during the evening she had been lucky. Two or three weeks of this and she'd be broke, really down. What would she do then? Take a job for fifty a week and forget the whole mess? She had that wonderful apartment filled with just the furniture she wanted—mostly custom-made pieces—and giving it up would be like losing a gallon of blood. And what could she do on fifty a week? My God, she spent more than five dollars a week on stockings alone.

She poured another drink and drank it slowly. She was hurt, hurt bad. While the Chamber of Commerce made pretty speeches about getting new industry into the city, local taxes kept going up—the new schools were to blame for some of that—and industry looked elsewhere. She couldn't see anything but poverty for half of the city, a poverty that would soon be eating into the guts of almost every man, woman and child. Where do you go from there? You were caught in a web that grew tighter and tighter, the strands of the web choking you to death. Finally you lost what you had, or sold your holdings for a fraction of their value, and then you joined the others. You were real, low-down broke, and you became a member of the club. Lucky, lucky you!

Agitated, upset, she walked the length of the bar, her hips rolling under the tight skirt and her breasts rising and falling easily in a new bra. Her back was to the door as it opened and she turned slowly, her hopes of a sale dying. She hadn't seen Jimmy Slade in several days and she hadn't even thought much about him, only to hate herself for ever having gone to his room. She had promised herself that she never would again, that nothing could make her do it.

"Where's Lucy?" he wanted to know as he sat down at the bar.

"I don't know. She left without notice."

She drew a beer for him and she knew that she wouldn't get paid for it. As she put the glass in front of him she noticed the swelling of his face, especially around his mouth and nose.

"Somebody clobbered you?" she said.

He rubbed his face thoughtfully. "A little accident, but I'll square that one of these days. Nobody lays it into Jimmy Slade and gets away with it. Somebody gets me once, so I get them twice for kicks."

She yawned and reached for a cigarette. He always talked big but she guessed he couldn't help it. Some people couldn't admit that they'd been taken and let it go at that. They had to plot revenge or they weren't happy.

"That factory closing killed me," she said, drawing a short beer for herself.

"I told you it would. You should have unloaded when I said. You could have picked up a bundle and had a ball."

"Now I'm stuck. I admit it."

He motioned for a refill. "You don't have to be stuck," he said. "There are ways."

She drew the beer. "Such as?"

"Robinson. Bert Robinson. He likes you and he'd steer things in your direction. Your bar business would pick up and the upstairs would pay off. Give it a couple of months and you'd be loaded."

"Thanks. I'm not earning money that way."

"So what's the harm? A guy needs a little love and he pays for it. Robinson is big and nobody would bother you."

"No," she said firmly.

"And you could gain more by being nice to him. He's nuts over you and he told me that. He'd give his right arm just to date you. How far you went with him would be your business, but I don't think it would have to be all the way. He wants a doll on his arm when he drifts around, and you're the doll."

She laughed at him. "You trying to set me up, Jimmy?"

"I promised him I'd do what I could."

"So that you can get in solid with him?"

His swollen lips parted in a smile. "I won't lie to you. I want in on his deal and I'm going to make it. Give me five years at just one of his rackets and I can retire for keeps. But I need your help to get started. All you have to do is to be nice to the guy."

"That would be tough in itself."

"Maybe, but it would be worth it. What are you going to get from that hardware salesman? Marriage and a couple of kids and your shape all shot to hell? This way we can pick up a fortune if we work it right. Guys come up from the city to play and money doesn't mean anything to them. We wouldn't have to worry if a factory was working or if it wasn't. This bar would be jumping, and you could double your prices."

She had another short beer and thought about it. She knew that some girls sold their favors—who didn't, one way or another?—but it seemed like a dirty way to make a buck. Any man who came along and had the price was accepted. It had nothing to do with love or being decent. Even her own trips to Jimmy's room hadn't been that bad. At least, she had been looking for something, a strange and wonderful something, and the fact that she hadn't found it wasn't anybody's fault. Some girls went through their whole lives and never knew the beauty of love.

"Don't try to drag me into your mess," she said. "If you had any ambition, you'd look for a job and quit worrying about the rackets."

"I want something big for both of us."

"No, you don't. You only care about me for one purpose. The last time you said I wasn't any good, and I'm willing to let it go at that. I'm not any good and you need somebody else who is. Well, go find them and don't bother. You've cost me money and free drinks and I'm just lucky I didn't have your baby. That would have been something, wouldn't it? Me getting big with your child, and you on the way to becoming a father? Some father you'd make! You can't even support yourself."

"Give me six months and I'll be able to buy and sell that hardware salesman."

"You leave him out of this."

"Leave him out? Why should I? I've seen him in here, waiting for you, and I don't think much of a guy like that. Somebody tells him to drive a hundred miles and make so many stops and the poor jerk does it. You need a brain the size of a pimple to do that kind of work. Me, I'm shooting for the big stuff. I'll work the girls over when they get out of line and all the time I'm beating my brains out I'm getting ready to cut in on Robinson, comes the right moment." He got down from the stool. "Guys get over a lot of things, but not a bullet in the belly. Remember that, honey. A bullet in the belly means a hole in the ground. Nobody comes back from that."

She felt a chill race up and down her spine. Jimmy was weak in a lot of ways, but he was a dreamer, and she didn't doubt that he would kill in an effort to make his big dream come true.

"No more on the house," she said, and rinsed out his glass.

He rolled his shoulders around, brought his fists up into fighting position, and swung his right at thin air.

"If anybody can do less than nothing, you're doing it," he said. "Lock up, grab a bottle and we'll go down to my room."

"No."

"How come?"

"That's the craziest thing I could do. I'd rather sit here alone and burn up electricity than go down there with you." She shrugged. "It was all a mistake, Jimmy, just as I told you.

You're headed for some very large trouble and I don't want any part of it."

He punched at the air again. "Have to get the old right in shape," he said.

"You should have had it in shape before you picked up that face."

He frowned and fumbled for a cigarette. She was surprised that he had one. Generally she had to give him money for the machine.

"Make it easy for me and date up old man Robinson," he said through the smoke. "And think it over about using the upstairs. You can knock down some real dough and be clean at the same time." He inhaled deeply. "Lucy worked the men and you didn't say anything to her."

"I felt sorry for Lucy."

"And she left you, after all your trouble."

"Well, the money was gone from the safe and the police think she took it. I don't. There was another reason, something that scared her. I don't know what it was, but it must have been terrible."

Jimmy put on his swagger as he walked to the door and she hated him when he did that. He acted like a big shot and he wasn't anybody at all. Maybe Robinson would take him on for a couple of hundred a week, get him to do some rotten work and then kick him out. It had happened to others. Why did Jimmy think that he was any tougher or smarter?

"If you need some exercise you know where I sleep," Jimmy said from the door. "In case I'm not there just flop down on the bed and be patient."

As he went out, she wondered if she hated him. Or was it something else? Right from the start she had known that he wasn't any good, yet she had gone to him. As early as their second date she had belonged to him in that cheap room and the next morning she had given him money for rent and booze. And she had kept on doling it out. How much she had given him she didn't know, but it must amount to quite a lot.

Now that she had started drinking on the job she didn't stop. There wasn't anything else to do and she was terribly depressed. Strangely, she was worried about Lucy. Maybe the police were right about Lucy taking the money, but she couldn't see it. She didn't know why, but the picture just wouldn't come into focus. She closed her eyes and she saw again that lovely naked body as she had once seen it upstairs. At once she felt a strange tightening in her throat, the same kind of feeling she experienced just before she was with a man, then this feeling was usually lost in a rushing tide of guilt and self-disgust. Possibly the reason went back to her first time, to the rape, and it would take a strong love to overcome it. All she had to do was find that love, and she would be all right. Perhaps she had found it with Carl Evans without realizing it. But, she asked herself, could she tell from his simple good-night kiss? It would take the fury of passion to bring the truth to the surface.

She was still thinking about Carl when the door opened and he came in. He wasn't as big as Jimmy Slade, but he had an honest face and a ready grin. His slacks and sports shirt were, as usual, clean and freshly pressed. He always looked so crisp and cool, even in this hot, muggy weather. A nice, solid-citizen type of guy.

"I didn't know where else to look for you," he said and sat down at the bar. "I knew you shouldn't be working, but you weren't at the apartment."

He seldom drank anything except beer and she drew one for him.

"Lucy left me."

"For a better job?"

"I don't know. She just walked out without saying anything."

"Funny."

"Yes, it is."

They talked about his trip that week, and she told him about the loss of the money. Like Sharon, he didn't believe Lucy had taken it; he was sure that the girl was incapable of doing such a thing.

"I read about the shoe factory moving," he said.

"I didn't read about it, but I know that it ruined me in one clean sweep. I wouldn't have thought that so many people would stop drinking all at once."

"Food comes first. Or it should. A man who's working feels secure, but put that same man out of a job and he's scared. In this town he's got a right to be scared. He's one of hundreds, and there's a line-up for every job. I think I'm lucky. Sure I find places where business is bad, but in other places it's good and I try to make it average out. I may not sell in one area, but in the next section I'll double my orders. That's why my income doesn't vary ten dollars a week."

She knew that she shouldn't keep switching her drinks, but she continued to do so, not caring how high she got or where the night ended—as long as it didn't finish in Jimmy's room. She blinked her eyes and stared at Carl. She'd like to spend the night with him, to find out if he was the man he ought to be, to help her chase the rainbow of love across the sky and catch it in her hands. Jimmy or the others hadn't done anything for her, but that didn't mean that it couldn't be done, that the sleeping fires of desire couldn't be fanned into a wild, all-consuming flame.

"You're drinking too much," Carl told her after a silence.

"Well, I'm discouraged. I've been here since eight this morning and I haven't taken in enough to buy a bus ticket out of town."

"Time to sell."

"Who'd buy?"

"I don't know. But if you can't find anybody, just lock the door and forget about the place."

"And what would I do then?"

"Very simple—marry me."

She had a quick drink and said nothing. Marriage to him might be okay, but she would be lonely as a stray cat during the week. He would be on the road and she would be stuck in a stuffy apartment. If the ties between them weren't strong enough, they'd eventually drift apart and the love nest would become a nest of bitterness. Then there was the other part, the physical part, and she wanted to be sure of that. A girl could fake it for one night, not for a whole marriage. If she did fake it she was a fool. Marriage was meant to be a happy union, honestly shared. Dishonesty, faking any part of it, would destroy its very purpose.

"Marry me," he said again. "Dear Sharon."

"Saying yes is pretty final, isn't it?"

"Why wait, darling? I'm doing well and I can support a wife and family. This isn't any business for a girl. It takes a man to run a bar. You've done a fine job, and it makes me respect you more than ever, but now is the best time to get out of it. We could build a wonderful life together. We could go to the city weekends, see good plays, hear concerts, symphonies. I'll join the country club, too, and you'd have a chance to meet some of the best people in town. We'll have two kids—I don't believe in big families—and we'll get a house in that new, split-level development, Beachcrest Manor. How does that sound?"

She was silent.

"What's the matter?"

"I'm just thinking. I—I can't give you any definite answer right now, Carl. But I will—soon. That's a promise."

Sharon made another switch in her drink, and this time she had a pink lady. By the time she closed she'd be looping, but it didn't matter. If she was going to think about marrying Carl she had to know it was right before she made up her mind—and there was only one way she could know for certain.

Maybe he could arouse her where other men had failed, and if this was true it could be fine for them. But how could she get him to act? She smiled to herself and finished her drink. The best approach, as far as she could see, was to get him into her apartment and then show him something he had never seen before.

She closed up early—what was the use of staying open?—and they went outside. He had walked down from Park Place and they got into her car. At first she had trouble with the key, but she knew what she was doing, or she thought she did, and once clear of the deserted factory section, she drove carefully.

It took about ten minutes to get up to Park Place and he talked about marriage some more. She blinked her eyes against the tired feeling of the booze and she listened to him. Maybe she was a sucker not to jump into it with him, but she was determined not to marry a man and spend the rest of her life being frigid. She had seen that kind of women come into the bar and they were desperate, drinking heavily and always lost.

After they got to the apartment he hesitated about coming in for a last drink but she finally talked him into it.

"You make the drinks," she said as she flipped on the living room light. "I'm going to slip into something comfy."

"Sure." He left for the kitchen, and she entered the bedroom, unbuttoning her blouse as she did so. If she had her wish he'd spend the night with her and she'd drive him wild. He'd go wild and perhaps she would, too. The pleasures of the flesh would be hers to enjoy, and for the first time in her life she'd be all woman.

She was breathing heavily as she undressed. Like the first time with Jimmy, she wasn't able to wait and she didn't want to wait. For a second she blamed the booze, but she knew that it went deeper than that. The booze only made it easier for her to seek out what she felt she must find, to search for the complete satisfaction which was every girl's right.

"All ready," he called from the living room.

She picked up the robe and then threw it down. She was ready, too. Ready and willing and hungry for love, for the kind of love that she had never experienced. She glanced at herself in the mirror and she smiled. Her curves were rich and full, her thrusting breasts lifting and falling, and no man would be able to refuse her.

Naked and confident she left the bedroom, hiding nothing, any shame that she might have felt completely forgotten. Here was a man who loved her and she was offering all that she had, all that any girl could ever give.

"Well!" he gasped and dropped both drinks to the floor. Only one glass broke.

She tossed her head and swayed toward him. "Am I not beautiful?" she demanded softly. "Wouldn't you like to know what I'm like before we go any further?"

Standing before him she waited for his kiss but as she looked into his eyes she saw that the eagerness and the love she was sure she had seen there was gone. In its place was an expression of pain and shock.

"Good night," he said stiffly, and walked to the door. He turned, his face pale. "I didn't think you were this kind, but I was wrong. You're just another Lucy—another damn whore!"

The door opened and closed behind him and she began to cry. She didn't even notice when she stepped on a shard of the shattered glass and cut her foot as she started for the kitchen. The bottle was out there.

At dawn she was still drinking and crying.

She felt terrible.

5

For two days it had rained hard and Jimmy stayed in his room, sometimes sleeping—how could a man sleep so much?—and sometimes standing at the window. When the roof began to leak and the water started coming in, just missing the bed, he went to the top of the stairs and shouted at the woman about it.

"Maybe I need a boat," he yelled. "Give it another day, and the fishing ought to be pretty good."

"For anybody who doesn't pay their rent, you sure want a lot of service," the woman shouted back.

He grunted and returned to his room, staring for a second at the growing puddle, then lighting a cigarette. There had been no good reason for him to yell at the woman like that—he could have told her about it decently. But if he was going to be hard, he had to be hard all the way. The trouble was he had been thinking about it a lot since he had been waiting for the rain to stop, and he knew deep down inside—knew more clearly than he had ever known anything—that the hardness was only a shallow veneer and that it could never become a true part of him. He was big enough, and he would fight if he was pushed into it, but even in school he had never been one to pick a scrap. He guessed he was a real prize phony.

As he crossed the room he put on the swagger that he had developed, but he quit it before he reached the window. The swagger was to impress men like Bert Robinson, but when he was alone Jimmy knew that it was nothing but a fraud. He had seen some of the men who worked for Robinson doing it, their pockets loaded with money, their clothes sharp, their self-confidence unlimited, and he had adopted the trait for his own use. But like the hardness that he kept shoving out in front of himself, it really didn't belong to him. It was like wearing another man's suit that didn't fit.

There was nothing to see outside, except the mess that the rain had made of the back yard, and he turned to look at his face in the mirror. Some swelling was still noticeable around one eye and when he moved his upper lip it was stiff and sore, but if anybody didn't know that he had been clobbered they probably wouldn't guess it from his appearance. Anyway if he went up to the Palace Bar to see Robinson he wouldn't have to answer a lot of fool questions. If he went up there. The way he felt about it right now, he didn't know what he was going to do. All he knew was that he was broke and he had to do something about it.

The pool of rain water by the bed was growing fast and he stepped around it and sat down on the edge of the mattress. Maybe he could get some money from Sharon, putting on the poverty act and crying all over the place, but he hated to do it.

Nobody had to tell him that he had treated Sharon lousy. He had hung onto her like a leech, even stealing from her pocketbook when she'd been drunk, and he'd used her countless times for his own pleasure. Not once had he thought of the possible consequences. Maybe she hadn't thought of them either, but that last morning she had left him it was easy to see that she had been worried. He couldn't blame her for that, any more than he could blame Robinson for wanting her. She wasn't a passion queen like some girls, but she had that terrific body. A man only had to have a pint of blood in his veins to make up his mind what to do with it. And he hadn't been sold on the idea of trying to set her up for Robinson. If a girl didn't like a man, that was her right, and there wasn't much that you could do about it. Robinson shouldn't have made that one of the conditions of employment. Big as he was, he ought to be able to manage his own romances.

Since Jimmy had confined himself to the room, he had thought a lot about Sharon and of how he had twisted her to his own advantage, but he had thought a lot about Lucy Forbes, too. After she had smashed him in the face with the bottle he had promised to get her, but he hadn't really meant that. He had been thinking of Robinson at the time, of what he might have to do to some of the girls to put them in line, and he had only been trying the pitch on Lucy. But she hadn't whimpered or screamed for help; instead of that she had picked up the bottle and whammed him. He couldn't hold that against her. He had bought what she had given him, and he had been lucky that she hadn't broken his nose. That would have been all that he needed.

Stretching out on the bed he closed his eyes, but even closing his eyes didn't wipe out the terror that he had seen in Lucy's face. He was sorry about that. Maybe she had taken men upstairs over the bar for a few dollars but from the things

Sharon had said, Lucy hadn't ever had much of a chance. She had been raised in poverty and she was fighting against it in the only way she knew. Like anybody else with an ounce of guts.

Hunger pains pulled at his stomach, but he didn't have any money for food. Too much of the twenty he had taken from Sharon had gone for cigarettes and beer, and now he was broke. Of course, being broke wasn't anything new to him, but whenever it happened it made him feel weak and helpless.

He was almost asleep when the landlady came slamming in through the door and banged a pan down on the floor under the leak. The drops began making a loud, tinny noise as they started dripping on the metal.

"It's coming through downstairs," she said—which told him why she had even bothered to bring him a pan. "I wouldn't mind any, except that I just had that ceiling painted."

"That's more than you've done to your rooms. They haven't been painted since this old dump was built."

The woman brushed a strand of loose hair away from her face. "For the rent I get I shouldn't give you heat in the winter," she said. The strand of hair fell down in front of her face again but she didn't fight with it. "Which reminds me, Mr. Slade. Your rent was due day before yesterday."

"I'll get it to you as soon as I can."

She walked to the door. "No. Not as soon as you can. I'll give you two days. Two days, and then if you don't have it, you get out. Seems to me as though a healthy man like you could get some work and pay his honest debts. I rent cheap and I ain't waiting until my social security begins to get my money."

The door slammed shut as she went out.

For several minutes he refused to do anything about the dripping noise but pretty soon he couldn't stand it any longer. Getting out of bed, he found a dirty T-shirt and threw that in the pan. The noise stopped immediately. With a sigh of relief he lay down again, but he didn't go to sleep right away. There was too much on his mind, but he wasn't any closer to reaching any decision than he had been when he had first determined to find out where he was going and how he was going to get there. He could stall Bert Robinson with some excuse for not being able to do anything with Sharon, and perhaps he would be able to wangle a deal that would put some bucks in his pocket and a nice new car under the seat of his pants. On top of that he'd get himself a fancy apartment and plenty of dames who lived faster than the car could run. Yes, from a distance it looked good, almost too good to refuse, but the bottle in the face that Lucy had handed him had shook him up real hard. Part of it had been the taste of his own blood filling his mouth, and if he was in the rackets there would be more violence like that. Not that he was afraid—at least, he didn't think he was afraid—unless he was afraid of being poor. And if he was afraid of being poor, then he had millions of people to keep him company . . . .

He didn't know if it hit him before midnight or afterward, but he did know—as if he already had had the decision made for him—that as soon as the rain stopped he would make an honest effort to look for a steady job. Once he was tied up with Bert Robinson—if he could tie up with him—it would be too late to change. All he had to do was make one mistake then, and he'd end up in a place a lot more rugged and a lot worse than reform school. He could make book on that and win every time.

Sleep finally came to him, but it was a troubled sleep, a sleep punctured by a dream. In the dream he was looking for Lucy but the difficulty was that he had no idea of where to look with any assurance of success. The lights of a dozen bars drifted across the surface of his mind and countless faces paraded before him. All the faces were of girls, but none of them was Lucy. Lucy, frightened and desperate, had vanished into the unknown.

The sun was out when he got up the next morning, and he picked out his best clothes. He dressed carefully. Checking his cigarettes, he saw that he had four but after hesitating a moment he lit one, and that left three. As for money, it wasn't necessary to look. He didn't have any.

It was a good day to walk and although he couldn't afford a cup of coffee he felt better than he had in a long while. At least, he was starting out in an attempt to do the right thing. No man could do more than that.

The old man who owned the used furniture store on the corner was dragging stuff out onto the sidewalk in an effort to set up a display. Jimmy had watched the store for Pop Gilson a couple of times and his pay had been ten percent of any sales that he made. Of course Jimmy wasn't the only one who had helped Pop. Lots of guys had done it on the same basis when Pop had had a woman upstairs who required his attention. More than one wife along the avenue had furnished her railroad flat by going to bed with Pop. On these deals Pop increased, his sale price and he kept the woman coming back until she was sick of him.

"I know how you could make some money, maybe," Pop said as Jimmy came up to him. "Ten percent you get, and after all that rain the people ought to be out."

Jimmy regarded an old ice box that wasn't worth five dollars. "Kind of early in the day for you to be busy upstairs," Jimmy said.

Pop grinned, his buck teeth uneven and yellow. "She's the youngest in a long time," he said. "Nineteen, and she just hit the avenue. Came in from upstate and she's trying to set up a flat for her husband by next week. So she comes in here with hardly any money and we get to talking. I make the connections for a flat, she picks out the stuff she needs and we settle the details upstairs. That was the day it started to rain and we've been working things out ever since."

"You'll get your neck busted one of these days."

"Not the way I work, boy. I know when a dame is safe and when she ain't."

Jimmy left Pop and moved on. If he tended the shop for ten per cent commission and he sold nothing he wouldn't be able to raise a thin dime toward his room rent or food. Pop could get somebody else, or see to things himself and leave the girl alone.

As he neared the river he saw that it was running high and swift. That would kill the fishing for a week or ten days and the people who had been depending on the fish for food would have to look elsewhere. Nobody in his right mind would go out into that current, no matter what kind of a boat a man had. Farther downstream the river narrowed, and after it rushed between high rock walls it tumbled over a falls. A lot of people stopped to look at the falls, and almost every year one or two fools lost their lives there.

Most of the offices were open by the time he got uptown and he tried the state employment agency first. It was a poor choice. Long lines of sad-faced workers waited to put in claims or seek jobs. He didn't linger more than a few minutes. The lines were moving slowly and it would be hours before he got to talk to anybody.

There were a couple of private agencies nearby and he tried them next. The woman in the first office was cleaning papers out of her desk.

"You're wasting your time," she told him after he had explained that he was looking for a job. "Take it from me, mister, there aren't any jobs to be had in Sanderstown. I've placed people for fifteen years and I've never seen anything like it. If you ask me, the city died and it's just lying on top of the ground until somebody buries it. I'm closing up this office and getting out. If you hear of anybody who needs a typist let me know, and I'll pay you the regular fee."

Jimmy was discouraged when he left the woman but he went up to the next floor to try his luck again. Somehow, somewhere, there had to be a job.

In the next office he had to fill out a form before being interviewed. He didn't lie about anything, either the reform school or his lack of education, and he knew that it was stupid to try and jazz up his past work history. By the time he finished with the form he was disgusted with himself. At the age of twenty-six he presented the clear picture of being completely worthless to any employer.

"You haven't got much in your favor," the man said after looking over the form. "The reform school business doesn't help you, although some people would overlook it. The thing that really hurts is that you didn't finish your education. In boom times you might get away with that, but unfortunately these aren't boom times. A man who does any hiring at all is in a position to be very selective. I've got good men who finished college, men with experience, and every door is closed to them."

Jimmy lit a cigarette, and now he was down to two. Maybe he should have watched the store for Pop. The way things were going he was getting nowhere fast.

"Then I guess that lets me out," Jimmy said, nervously inhaling.

"Oh, I didn't say that. There are some jobs that nobody wants and they're always kicking around. I've got one in a little factory across the river that requires a strong back and no brains. You move crates from one end of the building to the other and you sweep up after the shift is done. The job pays forty a week. If you put in more than eight hours on any day you just forget about it."

Jimmy thought about the job. Forty a week was a lousy wage—how did the factory get away with not paying for extra hours?—and after deductions he wouldn't draw anywhere near that much. Still it was money and nobody could stop him from looking for something better.

"I guess I don't have any choice," Jimmy said. He crossed his legs. "You figure the guy over there would advance me something?"

The man smiled. "My guess is he wouldn't even advance his wife a dime toward his breakfast tomorrow morning. He'd refuse on the theory that he might die during the night and not be able to eat it."

"Sounds like a real character."

"Exactly. The kind you grow to hate."

The interviewer explained the placement fee to Jimmy— that was a week's salary—and made out a card of introduction.

"You'll get the job," the man said as Jimmy left the office. "Nobody else wants it."

For a couple of blocks he followed a girl with a bouncing shape, but after she turned he continued on toward the bridge and the river, thinking about the forty a week. Trying to live on that kind of money would mean cutting down on his normal beer intake and watching the number of cigarettes that he smoked. If a job was worth being done it ought to be worth a decent wage.

Before he reached the bridge he almost turned back and gave up on the whole thing. But maybe if he did a good job he'd get a raise, or break the owner down to pay for overtime, after forty hours. There was a law about a thing like that, wasn't there?

The bridge traffic wasn't heavy at that time of day. Most of the people who lived across the river worked in the city proper and there weren't many cars until around five in the afternoon. Then a cop came down to govern the number of cars that used the bridge at any one time. Lots of people said that the bridge was too old and that it wasn't safe, but a deal with the state to help build a new one had fallen through. The way Jimmy figured, the other side of the river was no place for a factory.

Trucks coming to it had to use the bridge and couldn't be loaded to capacity, and that probably cost extra money.

When he was about a third the way across the bridge he glanced upstream toward an island where he had once spent a night with a girl. Suddenly he stopped as he noticed a metal boat plunging down the flooded, angry waters at terrific speed. There was somebody in the boat, standing up. It looked like a kid, and he was waving his arms, and trying to yell, but the roar of the water smashing against the bridge piers drowned his cries.

Jimmy began fighting to get out of his clothes. It was only a mile to the falls, and there wasn't anyone who could manage a boat in that wild current, let alone a kid. He would go over the falls, and that would be the end of him.

As Jimmy peeled out of his clothes and kicked off his shoes he glanced around for help, but no one was around. Stripped to his shorts, he climbed over the railing and turned his attention to the boat. The boat was coming too fast to give him much time to think, but he couldn't help wonder if he'd ever reach the shore alive and with the kid. When he had been going to school he'd been a pretty fair swimmer, seldom tiring, but he hadn't done any of it lately and he'd grown soft.

It was about twenty feet from the bridge to the water, but the length of the drop never entered his mind. His chief concern was meeting that boat and catching it before it got past him. If it got past him, the kid was done.

Ten seconds ...

Twenty seconds ...

And then he was jumping down feet first, jumping because a dive might throw him off, his eyes focused steadily on the boat as the water rushed up to meet him.

He lost his view of the boat for a few moments as the cold water closed around him, but with tremendous power he fought his way to the surface and blinked his eyes clear. In spite of his tension he grinned and locked his fingers on the side of the boat. Instantly his legs were swept beneath it and he struggled to free them. The roar of the water against the bridge piers began to fade into the distance.

"Hi, kid," he said, looking up into the anxious face of a boy of about twelve. "Kid, can you swim?"

The boy shook his head and started to cry. "I lost the oars," the boy gasped. "I couldn't do nothing."

Jimmy thought fast and he talked fast. There was no way of saving the boat—it looked like an expensive one—but with just the boy he had a good chance of reaching shore. He told the boy how to climb over the side, to put his arms around his neck and ride his back.

"And don't get scared," he said to the boy. "You just keep calm and we haven't got any worry. Make believe you've got an inner tube under you and let me do the swimming."

The boy was obviously frightened, but he controlled himself and did as he was told. It wasn't easy. One mistake, and the boy could have been lost to the rushing water.

As soon as the boy was on Jimmy's back, holding fast, Jimmy let go the boat and plunged into the desperate fight to gain the shore. For a terrible moment he had the feeling that the effort would be useless, that the river would conquer him, that they would both die. Then, putting everything he had into his arms and legs, he sensed that the distance to safety was being shortened inch by inch.

He couldn't remember reaching land, of hanging onto a bush with one hand, or of the boy trying to help him onto solid ground with the other. He knew only that it was almost impossible to breathe, that his lungs burned with every rush of air. By the time his mind cleared he was still half in the water and still hanging onto the bush.

"We made it," he gasped as he struggled to his feet. "We made it, kid!"

Five feet beyond that he fell face down on the little patch of sand. He had done what he had set out to do.

And it had just about killed him.

6

Even though it was Saturday morning there was nothing doing at the bar and, bored to the point where she could have screamed, Sharon dug out the cleaning supplies, ran some water in a pail, and propped open the door of the men's room. When business had been good she had hired a flunky to do this job, but with sales off more than ninety percent she couldn't afford it.

The wall in the room was a mess, covered with dirty words

and filthy drawings, and she wondered why men did things like that. What did it prove? That man could be so low that he couldn't even reach up high enough to chin himself on the curb along the gutter? And the telephone numbers, some of the numbers complete with a brief description of the girl's talents? Were they real numbers, or just fakes?

After she finished she felt crummy and she washed up in one of the sinks behind the bar, yawning as she did so. She had closed early the night before, just after midnight, but after she'd reached the apartment she'd stayed up for a long time. Carl Evans was in from the road and she hoped that he would forgive and visit her. Her hope had been for nothing. At three she had heard him come in with some girl who couldn't stop laughing and she had given up and gone to bed. But she hadn't gone to bed to sleep. The last few nights she hadn't been sleeping much but she had done a lot of thinking.

Every afternoon Bert Robinson came down to the bar after he had taken care of his men uptown and even if he had spent a fortune every trip—which he didn't—she dreaded to see him come. He kept hammering away at her, trying to make her forget running the bar and move in with him. She couldn't recall all the things that he had promised her but one had been a car as big as any in the city and the other was that she didn't have to be a woman to him until she wanted it that way. She believed it about the car, but not the rest of it. Bert wasn't the kind of man to stay in the same house with a girl and not get what he was after. And a man who was nice to a girl probably had it coming to him, ring or no ring. The bad part was that once you belonged to a man you were never free, any more than she was completely free of Jimmy Slade.

She hadn't seen him since he had rescued the boy from the river but that hadn't stopped her from thinking about him. A man could be good or worthless, but after a year of surrendering to him the scars of the illicit love remained. Only time erased the past, or came close to it, but to erase it the present and the future had to be better than what had gone before.

She drew a short beer and tried to decide just how much longer she could continue under present circumstances. She didn't think that it would be any great length of time. When her statement had arrived from the bank she had discovered a two hundred dollar error in her check book, and that had cut into her dwindling balance. The same day she had tried to borrow from the other three banks in town and had gotten a big fat NO in every one. With the local economy plunging madly toward some sort of disaster the banks were being more selective about loans than they ever had been. On top of this, they didn't look on the bar business in a happy light. Determined to do something, she had seen a couple of real-estate men but they hadn't given her much encouragement. Everybody, they said, wanted to sell and nobody wanted to buy. So the day had been wasted, and when she had reopened the bar about five that afternoon she had ripped into a bottle of ninety proof and had stuck with it until it had made her sick.

The beer in the glass was nearly flat by the time she drank it and she made a face, not just because of the taste but because she felt so low and she didn't know what to do about it. Her rent was paid on the apartment for the next month, but after that she'd have to get out. The furniture had cost her plenty, but if she tried to sell it she would only get a fraction of its value. The same held true for her car. By the time she was done with everything all her possessions would be gone and she'd still be broke. For this reason alone she continued to think about Bert Robinson. Maybe he was a racketeer, as well as being too old for her, but the road he held open for her was paved with the luxury of financial security. More than one girl had prostituted herself to enjoy the finer things in life. Love didn't enter into it. She had the body that he wanted and he could pay for the right to own her. Her choice came down to getting everything that she wanted, or having nothing at all.

She drew another beer, more out of habit than anything else, but before she tasted it she threw it out and got a bottle of coke from the cooler. Lately she had been drinking too much beer and both her dresses and skirts were getting tight around the middle. Either the beer had done it, or she could blame Jimmy Slade. Still it was too early for anything to be showing up from Jimmy, therefore it must be the beer. Put two more inches of curves inside her blouse and the strain on the material was almost more than it could stand. Had she been working behind a bar where sex sold drinks, she'd have loaded the cash register with bills. But in this hole she could have pranced around naked and even the No Sale sign wouldn't have moved.

Nobody entered the bar for the next couple of hours and she switched from coke to beer and back to coke and then she had a double shot that left her gasping. She shoved the shot glass and the bottle aside, holding onto the edge of the bar with her hands, her head down, and coughed so hard that she thought she'd never stop.

"Arizona is good for that," somebody said. "Or maybe you just need another belt from the bottle. Why leave a job half finished?"

She straightened as she recognized the voice and wiped the tears from her eyes. "That's rotten stuff," she said and reached under the bar for a beer glass. "There ought to be a law against it."

"Show me a law that says you have to drink."

She said nothing and drew the beer. As she put the glass in front of him she looked at Jimmy Slade. He was wearing work clothes and he didn't look as sharp as he had in the past. There was a smudge of dirt on the back of one hand, and he had always been very particular about the condition of his hands. Even when she had been in that cheap room with him, half drunk and nearly hating herself, she had known that his hands would be clean.

"For a change I'm buying," he said and put a bill on top of the bar. "Have one yourself."

"Thanks, but I think I've had enough." Just seeing him again made her nervous and she toyed with the top button on her blouse. Old desires began to awaken, desires that slept deep within the flesh. "I read in the paper that the boy's father was going to give you a job."

"You read straight. I got the job, all right."

"I wouldn't say that you sounded too happy about it."

He drained his glass. "You wouldn't either if you were me. The pay could be worse—I get a buck seventy-five an hour, plus half again as much for today—but I was put with this guy who's got a grudge against the world and he's using me as his own personal football. When I hired out I was told that I was to be taught trade, but I've learned nothing."

She changed her mind about having a drink, but she had no intention of charging him for it. And the beer she set up was a salute to what they had known together, the twisted nights when she had sought to live as a woman and had failed in her attempts.

"Bert Robinson has been asking about you," she said slowly.

"That follows."

"He wanted your address but I wouldn't give it to him. He said you were a chump to do what you did."

"Maybe, but I didn't have any time to think about it just then. The kid was there in that boat and I was the only one who could help him. I had a lead to a job on the other side of the river, but things like that don't enter your mind when somebody needs help. And the kid was regular. He did what I said. The thing that burned me was somebody stealing my clothes or throwing them off the bridge. The first person who got to us along the shore was a girl, maybe of twenty or so, and her face got all red when she found me in just my shorts."

Sharon leaned against the bar, her breasts high up over the edge, and she decided this was a Jimmy Slade she hadn't known. The Jimmy she had known had gone into that swagger when he had been trying to impress somebody. Most of the things he had said, the way he had said them, had been tough. In a sense he had been like a little boy who had been wearing a tissue paper mask that would blow away with the first gust of wind.

"I wish I was clearing a dollar seventy-five an hour," she said. "If I got that much for every hour I put in around here I might not hate to open up the bills that I get in the mail. Once you go over the tenth of the month they put you on a list, then you can't get anything without paying cash."

"You won't find any jobs in this town," Jimmy said. "The people who owned the house we were working on today are moving out. They've come down on the sale price of the house three times and they can't even get anybody to look at it."

"Bert Robinson is about the only person who's got any money," she said.

"And he'll keep on making it, jobs or no jobs. Right now, most guys are discouraged, so when they get a little money they go out and tie one on. That means a bar, and a bar means dames hanging around for the kill. The guys get loaded and the rest is easy. The dames get the money that's left, and the guys go home broke."

She drew another beer for him, poured a drink for herself,

and stared out at the empty street.

"I've been thinking about Lucy," Jimmy said suddenly. "She seemed regular, and I don't think she took any money from you."

"I don't either, but the police feel she's their only lead. They were down here again yesterday and they searched the apartment upstairs. They found a snapshot of her and they're going to plaster the papers with it. Probably they found out from some of my old customers what she did after she closed the bar, taking men upstairs, and a girl with that kind of a reputation, according to the police, isn't the sort of a girl to be trusted."

"There are plenty of other girls in this town who do the same thing."

"And somehow they get away with it," she agreed.

He had a few more beers, paying for them, but she stayed away from the liquor. Anyway, she would lock the front door early and cruise the bars. Saturday night ought to be a good night to look for Lucy and she wanted to see the girl again. The money didn't enter into it. Losing the money had her pinned to the wall, but something else had hurt more. She missed Lucy's beauty and the girl's wild and lovely body that had been so utterly female. It was a little silly when she thought about it, but that's the way it was. Now that the girl was gone she longed for her with a strange and powerful longing that she didn't understand.

"I got paid a little today," Jimmy said. "Give me an hour to change and we can go out for dinner. You're only wasting electric lights by staying open."

"No," she said firmly.

"Why not?"

"Because you know how it would end. In the morning I'd wake up in that horrible room and I'd hate myself."

"At least you wouldn't have to pay my rent."

She pushed back away from the bar and her bra settled, the soft cups holding her breasts firm and tight.

"Forget it, Jimmy. I made some mistakes with you but I'm not going to make another one."

"Bert Robinson must be treating you all right."

"You leave him out of this. He has nothing to do with it."

Jimmy kept after her, promising that he wouldn't do

anything, that he wouldn't touch her no matter what condition she was in, helpless or willing, but she didn't really believe him. Of course, she admired him for having taken a job, but she couldn't honestly say that it went beyond that. She had fought for a year to find love with him and it hadn't arrived. There was no reason to hope that she would discover it at this late date.

Any other time she would have shuddered when Bert Robinson entered the bar, but that afternoon she welcomed his arrival. It killed off Jimmy's attempts to sway her, and she let out a long sigh of relief as she fixed a gin and orange.

"Well, if it isn't the world's biggest sucker, himself," Robinson said as he joined Jimmy at the bar.

"Have it your way," Jimmy said. "I'm eating regular and nobody is chasing me."

"Maybe I should change that statement." Robinson tasted his drink. "You're next to the biggest sucker. The sucker of all suckers the cops picked up last night."

"I wouldn't know about that."

"Hell, it's been on the radio and in the papers. Seems like a kid worked in one of the banks, and he got to playing the horses. He took a few thousand, but he was too dumb to keep running. He came back to his house to get his car and the cops jumped him. Before he could blink he was in jail and crying all over the place."

"All of which doesn't affect you."

"You're wrong, Jimmy. It's a kick right in my belly. The kid names his bookie and the cops haul the bookie in. But the worst part is that the old guy was the best bookie I had. Only, he was greedy. I told him a hundred times that he should only take what a chump can afford to bet and lose. But, no, he has to have it all. So, knowing that the kid works in the bank, he gives the kid credit and the kid winds up in the hole. Then the old guy, thinking that he's smart, puts the screws on the kid and the dumb slob has to do something. So he dips into the bank, sure that he would square himself, and when that blew up, he dipped again."

"I still don't see where you fit into it," Jimmy said.

Robinson sipped his drink. "I didn't think you were so stupid, Jimmy. When a bookie folds some of my income drops, and I don't like that. Right now the numbers are on the lean side and I was counting on the ponies to brighten the picture. In addition to that, I have to do what I can for the bookie or the others lose confidence in me. What stings is that the old guy was caught with enough evidence to convict a dozen men.”

“If you pay off the police, why did they even bother him?”

“Once again you’re wrong. I don’t pay off the police. People say I do, but I don’t. Most cops are honest; they’re paid fairly well, they’ve got families to think about and they’re working for that early retirement. Try to bribe one of them and you’ve got a fair chance of being thrown into pokey. That means you have to work higher up, not stopping the routine arrests that are bound to come along, but making sure that any punishment doesn’t hurt anybody too much. If a girl gets fined twenty-five bucks it doesn’t mean any more than charging her double for a meal. Then on her next date she works five or ten minutes for the city, and it’s forgotten. When the sentences are light the cops become discouraged and they don’t make as many arrests as they would under normal conditions. A good cop has to have the full force of the law behind him.”

“Which leaves only the judge.”

“You tell me, Jimmy. I’ve already talked too much.” Robinson’s eyes traveled approvingly over the fullness of Sharon’s blouse. “But I can’t help the kid in the bank. Taking money from a bank is a federal charge and nobody reaches that high up. If he had stolen a million they’d give him from five to ten years, but since it was only a few thousand they’ll hit him over the head with the book. The more you take the better you’re treated. The same goes for me. The more people I step on the quicker people get out of my way. If you’d wake up, Jimmy, you’d do some of the stepping for me. Why spend the rest of your life fooling around with stopped-up sinks?”

“My hands are clean,” Jimmy said, getting down from his stool.

“Clean hands and empty pockets.”

Jimmy said something as he went out, but Sharon didn’t hear it. The door closed behind him and Robinson hunched his shoulders forward. “That guy could amount to something,” Robinson said.

“He seems happy.”

“Yeah, happy and half out of his mind. What’s he get for crawling under buildings and busting his back? A few bucks a week so that he can end up broke before he gets paid again? That's about it, and why I should even think about him I don't know. Or maybe I do know."

"Leave him alone," Sharon said.

"You're damned right I know," Robinson declared, ignoring her. "That swagger and half of what he used to say was an act, all bluff, but on him it looked good. He's big and he's strong and he makes you think he means business. I'll go for that pitch any day. Some guys haven't got any guts and other guys don't know when to stop being hard. A guy has to fit somewhere in the middle and Jimmy fills up the hole. All he has to do is wake up and go after the big dough."

Robinson was dry, and she took care of that. "You asked me about the girls and the upstairs again yesterday," she said. "I told you I'd think about it. The answer is still no."

He nodded and tasted the drink. "It's okay, so don't worry about it. I was only trying to help you out, but when I talked with a few of the girls they didn't like the idea. What I'd like to do is to line up the girls who are cutting prices and eating into my business. I've got a guy working on it now but it's a slow process. One thing I'm sure of, and that's when he gets done with them they know which direction the sun comes up in the morning."

"I don't know how you can sleep at night," she said.

"Sleep? I sleep okay, but if I had somebody like you to keep me awake I wouldn't waste my time on a lot of useless dreams."

A customer drifted in for a beer, swallowed it quickly and drifted outside again.

"I know a place where we could spend tonight and tomorrow in the country," Robinson said.

"Thanks, but you're wasting your time."

"I never waste my time. I always get what I want."

"This is one time you won't."

"Let's wait and see if you can say the same thing a month from now."

He left after he finished the orange and gin and she had a shot to steady her nerves. It was getting so that she couldn't look at Robinson or think about him that it didn't upset her. Why didn't he forget about her? Of course the curves she had and which she couldn't hide might have something to do with it, but there were any number of girls with nice shapes.

Sometimes it seemed to her that almost every man who saw a girl in full bloom lost all normal human emotion and became some sort of savage. Yet, being honest about it, these desires might be normal enough, desires which, in one degree or another, belonged to just about all living things.

She kept the bar open until nine that evening, but she could have done more business if she'd been selling pencils on a street corner. The wait and the lack of anything to do worked against her. She drank too much, and when she fixed her face, using the mirror behind the bar, she had a terrible time with the lipstick that she didn't really need to make her lips red and inviting.

Before turning out the lights and leaving the building she thought for a second and had another drink. She needed that drink like she needed a second pair of ears, but she tossed it off and picked up her pocketbook. Maybe if she drank enough she'd forget about looking for Lucy and if she could forget Lucy it was possible that she would forget Bert Robinson. Somehow she could see violence ahead of her if Bert didn't stay away from the bar. He had made his boast that he got what he wanted, and he hadn't been fooling. Maybe he tried to gain his objective by being nice at first, but if being nice didn't bring him his reward there were numerous other ways he could use to force the issue.

Her car was in front of the bar, the only car on the block, and she stumbled inside, bumping her head and feeling a garter snap. Thoughtfully she slammed the door and rubbed her thigh. That was the second garter to break in as many weeks and she was getting tired of it.

She had some trouble locating the ignition key but she finally got the car started. Of course there was nothing wrong about prowling the bars in a skirt and blouse but she thought she would feel better if she made a change and a dress would look better anyway.

There wasn't much traffic in that part of the city, but she drove very carefully. All she needed was some kid to dash out into the street and two lives would be ruined—her own and the life of the kid. The kid would lie broken and crushed under the wheels of the car and the memory of it would never leave her.

At one point, in spite of her slow speed, the car left the street and wandered up onto the curb. She jerked the wheel, wondering how she had done that, and got the car back onto the street. She shook her head and guessed that she should have been satisfied with a couple of drinks and let it go at that. During the past few days she had been going at the bottle too heavily and she hadn't been eating anything. That was probably the trouble. Almost everybody agreed that you ought to eat if you are going to drink.

It wasn't any great distance up to Park Place but she had an awful time getting there. Just before she reached the apartment house the car jumped the curb again, and this time she barely missed a tree. That shook her and she felt like crying. She was the next thing to being broke and she was in no condition to go out. All that awaited her was a beautiful apartment that could be as lonely as a midnight prison yard in the dead of winter.

She wasn't clear about leaving the car, but she was aware of having difficulty climbing the cement steps and of fighting a losing battle with the front door. Then she remembered that the front door was always kept locked. With a groan of disgust she began looking through her pocketbook for her key, but nothing seemed to be very real to her and she couldn't find it. After the second search—why did she carry so much junk around with her?—she gave up and sat down on the top step.

A few minutes later she fell off the top step and landed in the shrubbery.

"You little fool," somebody said to her a long time afterward. "If I had any sense I'd have left you out there."

She knew that she was being carried and she knew that the man was Carl Evans, but she was too stunned and helpless really to care.

She also knew that he was crying the way a man cries when he meets bitter defeat.

But beyond these things she knew nothing.

Perhaps it was just as well.

7

Jimmy managed to plod through until Wednesday, learning nothing, and there were plenty of times when he had to struggle with himself so that he didn't have real trouble with Benny.

"You could show me how to thread a pipe," he said to

Benny. "All you do is set the gadget for the right size and use plenty of oil. I don't see where it's so hard."

"You're in my way," Benny said. "Stand aside, chum. I can do it faster myself."

Benny was in his forties and he had been brought up in the plumbing business. He knew the trade like the back of his hand, but he wasn't willing to share his knowledge with anybody else. Still Benny had taught others so Jimmy had come to the conclusion that Benny didn't like him. There wasn't much he could do about that. He had met people he hadn't liked, sometimes for hardly any reason at all, and if that's the way it was with Benny he might as well make up his mind that they'd never get along.

"I started out in this racket for peanuts," Benny said on Tuesday. "I could do anything that any plumber could do, but when I hired out the guy thought he did me a favor when he gave me a buck and a half an hour. Now you come along and get a quarter more and you're so dumb it makes me sick."

"That's no way to look at it. Things have gone up since then, and so have wages."

"Yeah? Well, I don't care what things have done. If they were going to put on another man they should have grabbed a guy who's got a home and family to support. The boss could have given you fifty bucks for saving his kid and you could have used it to blow the town. You've got nothing to hold you here. A married man has ties and he can't just pack up and move."

"Okay, okay," Jimmy sighed. "Just give me something to do and I can make believe that I'm earning my money."

But Benny didn't give him anything to do, so he just stood around. They were finishing a new house and there wasn't much left to be done, anyway. Jimmy walked around in the cellar and looked at the supports under the house. Somebody was going to get burned when they bought this thing and get burned good. He could peer up through the flooring and see daylight, and a lot of the stringers under the floors were cracked.

"Let's get out of here," Benny said at quitting time. "And don't go out to the truck with empty hands."

About all Jimmy did was to carry the tools and he carried them outside to the truck. Benny was a lousy driver and he was scared to ride with him, but Benny wouldn't let anybody else drive. Even Benny's wife, it was said, wouldn't ride with him and she wouldn't allow their children to do so. To make matters worse, Benny was a heavy drinker, seldom getting home from work until nine or ten, and fellows who knew Benny claimed he was in debt up to his ears.

For once Benny took it easy going out of the driveway but at the corner he disregarded the stop sign and a station wagon almost plowed into them from the side. Jimmy took a deep breath and lit a cigarette while Benny cursed the driver of the wagon.

"We don't have to go back to the shop," Benny said.

"All right."

"I had a flat on the car this morning so I'm taking the truck home with me."

"You can let me out wherever you feel like it. I haven't worked so hard that I can't walk."

"Don't get wise," Benny said, getting sore. "I'm going by West Avenue and you ride that far, huh?" Benny just missed another car that was pulling from the curb. "Some guy calls me at the house last night and I'm meeting him in a bar near West Avenue. He said he wants his plumbing fixed on Sunday. I do that when I get the chance. I figure if a cluck like you is worth the money the boss pays you, I've got a right to promote a dollar on my own."

"Who's stopping you? I'm not."

Jimmy got off at the corner of West Avenue and the truck snarled away from the curb. He flipped the remains of the cigarette into the gutter and felt some of the tension begin to leave him. Every day that he worked with Benny he was tense and nervous. Of course he could have gone to the boss with his complaints, but Benny was an experienced man and he didn't think that the boss would believe him.

He walked down the street and he saw Pop Gilson out in front of his store. Pop was obviously trying to sell an old chair to some woman and the woman was shaking her head. Most likely Pop needed the sale. He hadn't been open much lately. The girl's husband hadn't shown up and she was still living with Pop. A gossip who lived next door said the two of them drank all night long and raised hell.

When Jimmy reached his room he examined his wallet and threw it on top of the dresser. On Sunday, as soon as the bars had opened, he had wandered around looking for Lucy and he had spent more than he should on a lost cause. None of the bartenders he had talked with had seen her and when he had tumbled into bed about midnight he wondered why he was even worried about her. She was anybody's girl, and if he wanted somebody like that they were a dime a dozen along the avenue. Still, he knew that it wasn't the mere promise of the physical that fired his interest in her. No matter how he looked at it he saw himself and Lucy as two of a kind, both of them wrong in what they had done and confused about where they were going. That was the chief reason he felt sorry for her. Even when he had been going up to the bar to meet Sharon he had liked her looks, her breasts showing naked under a thin blouse, and he wanted her to know that he understood about her belting him with the bottle. He'd been at fault, and had gotten what was coming to him. Somehow it would make him feel better if she knew.

He picked up Monday's paper and her picture was right there for him to see. The police wanted to question her about the robbery at Sharon's bar. Jimmy threw the paper aside and began getting out of his work clothes. If Lucy hadn't left the city already there wasn't much chance of her leaving it. She couldn't hide that beautiful face and somebody would recognize her. Granted that she was still in the city, Bert Robinson was about the only person who could help her. If she went to Bert there would be a price for whatever he did. The price would be a bed in a house or a room where men could come to her. Robinson would use her and she'd never stop paying. Maybe he should be worrying as much about Sharon, but he wasn't. For the year he had known her he had been aware that there was in that girl an edge of coldness that never seemed to melt, an inner resistance that he had never been able to break down.

He stripped naked and found a big towel that he tied around his middle. He didn't know why he should bother to clean up. He wasn't going out and he didn't feel dirty. The night before he had gone up to the Palace to see Bert Robinson, but when he had asked about Lucy, trying to act casual about it, he had drawn a great big nothing.

"I'm looking for her myself," Robinson had said.

"Why?"

"If I told you, you'd know as much as I do. If you were working for me maybe I'd give you the job of digging her up. A job like that ought to be fun. They tell me she never learned how to say no."

Jimmy didn't know whether or not he should believe Robinson, and he couldn't understand why the man should be interested in Lucy. She was just a girl and she hadn't done anything to harm him. Of course, she had been entertaining men, but there were any number of girls like that in the city. The girl down the hall was a good example of that. For a few bucks she offered the same merchandise that cost twenty-five or fifty dollars uptown. Uptown you paid for the atmosphere, but who looked at the walls or the ceiling at a time like that?

Before leaving the room he considered Robinson's offer again. It had been a solid offer, backed up by a pile of bills on top of the table in front of him, but he had turned it down. Robinson had been angry with him, calling him a fool, predicting that he would come crawling back to him, begging for a break. Jimmy had shouted that he wouldn't, and that had been the end of their conversation.

Now as he turned it over in his mind he wasn't sure that he hadn't made a mistake. Had he gone in with Robinson he would have been free to look for Lucy and once he found her he could help her out of the city. Crossing Robinson would present certain dangers, but accepting the dangers was better than having a helpless girl kicked around. However, there were other things to think about. His present job wasn't satisfactory, but it was honest and he wasn't breaking any laws. Just a short time before he would have given half of one arm to be in with Robinson, to pull down the big money, legal or not. Maybe he had grown up in a hurry and he was now seeing the facts differently.

The hall was empty when he stepped into it and he didn't think anything of just wearing a towel.

"Hello, honey," the girl said as he passed her door.

He didn't look in at her and he continued on to the bathroom. He started the water for his shower, removing the towel and stepping in under the spray. He stayed under it for five minutes and then toweled briskly. The towel was wet as he wrapped it around himself.

The girl was waiting for him in the hall, and if she had been wearing any less she would have been nude. Even the girls who loved for a fee were generally more modest. When they got down to where they couldn't go further without displaying their wares they had the money in their hands. A guy might be able to love them up a little bit in a bar but he didn't get so much as a look until he parted with the cash.

"It's around the house that you're working?" the girl said, moving directly in front of him.

"Well, I've got a job, but so far I haven't worked at it very much,"

"Only suckers work."

"Maybe."

"But I guess a guy has to work to have any money. Or be born rich." With one hand she tugged at the top of her bra. "You got any money, big boy? Say a five that you don't know what to do with? Some of the guys down here only have a couple of bucks to spend on a girl and it's hardly worth my time. Up in the hills where I come from they said almost any girl could get ten bucks, but I haven't seen that much on one guy since I've been here."

He pushed her out of his way and she kicked at him. The kick missed and it made her furious.

"I hope you drop dead," she yelled at him. "Tomorrow or sooner."

There was nothing for him to do after he returned to the room and he had a cigarette. He had no excuse for being tired but as soon as he finished the cigarette he stretched out on the bed. He wished he knew where to look for Lucy, just to talk to her and square himself if nothing else, only now he was stuck and he couldn't arrive at any plan of action. Since her picture had been in the paper she'd keep close to wherever it was she was hiding out and she wouldn't dare to visit the bars.

The next morning he was five minutes late for work, but Benny didn't say anything, and that surprised him. In fact, Benny didn't say much of anything as they drove away from the shop except to tell Jimmy where they were going.

"One of those service calls," Benny said. "The hot-water heater is out and I'll start that. You can use the plunger to unplug the bathroom sink."

Ten minutes later they stopped in front of a neat little house with a nice lawn.

"You sure move slow," Benny said to him as they started up the walk. "I could go faster standing on my head and using my hands."

Jimmy almost clipped Benny with the plunger, but he didn't. He simply followed Benny up to the front door and waited for somebody to answer the bell.

The girl who opened the door was young and she didn't appear to be quite ready for early callers. Although she wore a robe, it clung to her, outlining a ripe figure, and anything a man couldn't imagine didn't belong to her or any other woman.

"This is what I call service," she said as she let them in. "The last time I called for a plumber he took two days to get here."

"Not us," Benny said. "When you call us you just ask for Benny, and you can have any kind of service you want."

Benny was obviously a little more than slightly interested in looking at her further, but she told him how to get down to the cellar and the hot water heater and he left to take care of that.

"You come with me," she said to Jimmy. "But don't look at the house. Things got a little wild here last night and I didn't get around to picking up."

The living room smelled of stale smoke and old booze and there were glasses sitting on anything that would hold a glass. A woman's bra lay on the floor and the girl kicked it aside. Jimmy grinned and watched her shake from behind. Her party must have just about torn the roof off the building.

"I wash my hair in the sink," she said as she led him into the bathroom. "Maybe I lose some hair and that stops up the drain."

There was no water in the bowl and he turned on the hot-water faucet. The water ran down the drain all right and pretty soon the water was hot. He couldn't understand it and he told her so.

"It must have cleared up by itself," she said. "And probably the heater only needs an adjustment." She smiled at Jimmy. "But you could do something for me while you're waiting for your partner. I want to switch the bed in the bedroom and I can't manage it by myself. All I need is a strong back to do the lifting."

"Okay," he said. "You might as well get something for your money. They'll charge you for this trip even though there's nothing wrong.”

He left the plunger on the floor near the bathroom door and followed her down to the end of the hall and the bedroom. The bedroom wasn't very big, and since the bed was a double there wasn't much room. On the far wall there was a nude painting of a man and a woman, different from most nudes he had seen. Nothing had been left out or hidden.

“I don't know where you're going to put the bed,” he said. “If you turn it the other way you won't be able to stand in front of the dresser.”

“You take this end,” she said. “I'll show you how to do it.”

He went around the bed and over to the other side. She brushed past him, smelling of perfume, and stopped just short of the door, her back to him. As she turned, rather slowly at first, he saw that she had untied the robe and that it hung open down the front. Something told him that she knew what she was doing, because even as she came to a stop at the end of the turn she let the robe slide down off her arms and fall in a pile on the floor.

“Hey,” he said. “Hey, now.”

He was going to tell her to cover up, but already she was screaming like a wounded cat. He had never heard a scream with so much terror in it, and it banged against his ear drums. Wondering what he should do, he glanced toward the windows and he saw that they were closed. That was a break. The chances were that she wouldn't be heard outside, and maybe he could quiet her down.

“Shut up,” he hollered, moving toward her, but afraid to touch her. “Shut up, will you?”

She lunged for him, still screaming, and tore at his shirt. He felt a couple of buttons rip loose and, suddenly desperate, he shoved against her, trying for her, trying for her shoulders but missing them and getting his hands full of the two things that proved she was a woman. He let her go immediately and she spun away from him, throwing herself on the bed. She stopped screaming as quickly as she had started, but then she began yelling the one word that would scare any man.

“Don't, please!” Her voice filled the house. “Don't rape me. Please don't rape me. Anything but that—don't rape me please!”

He knew that he should run, that he should get out of there, but when he tried, his legs refused to respond. He stood there, the sweat pouring down his skin, that single word bringing cold terror into his life.

Moments later the strength poured back into his legs and he stepped to the side of the bed, leaning over and cursing. He hadn't intended to slap her, but his open hand cracked against the side of her face and her head snapped violently. She twisted away, rolling across the bed, a giant sob escaping her.

"That's enough of that," a man's voice said.

Benny was standing in the doorway. He wasn't smiling and he had a big wrench in his hand, one that he must have gotten from the truck. The girl let out a long, choked sob and lay still.

"I didn't do anything," Jimmy said. "I just came in here to help her move a bed and she blew her roof."

"Oh, yeah? I know what I saw and I heard the girl. You figured I was down in the cellar and you could make it with her. Well, fellow, we don't work that way in our outfit." Benny hefted the wrench. "Right now we're going back to the shop and square this away with the boss. As for the girl, you'd just better hope that she doesn't charge you with what you tried to do."

Jimmy left the bedroom without looking at the naked body on the bed and he picked up the plunger on the way to the front door. Outside he walked in a daze to the truck, threw the plunger in back, and got in beside Benny.

Nobody had to tell him that he had something to worry about. Attempted rape was just about as bad as the real thing, and most people would believe the girl if she filed a complaint against him. Benny would support the girl, repeating what he had heard and telling what he had seen, and the possibility of a jury believing the right side of the whole thing was frighteningly remote. A conviction for rape wrecked a man's whole future. Nobody wanted him after that. Next to murder, Jimmy guessed there wasn't a worse crime.

"There wasn't anything wrong with the sink," Jimmy said.

Benny said nothing.

"Or the hot water."

Benny swore savagely and narrowly missed a car.

"I didn't touch the girl, only to slap her. She was going nuts and I couldn't get her to stop."

"You had her down on the bed," Benny said. "If I hadn't

shown up when I did, she wouldn't have had a chance."

"You've got me all wrong, Benny. I wish you'd listen. She asked me about moving the bed and I was only doing her a favor."

Benny swung the truck sharply to the left.

"No, I haven't got you wrong, fellow. Lots of dames don't get dressed in the morning. They show what they shouldn't show, and maybe they give a guy ideas. But they're just ideas and you don't carry it beyond that. Just because you see a girl you like—I'll admit the girl up there was pretty—it doesn't mean that you can have your way with her. Some girls are man-crazy, but not that one. It all adds up to the biggest mistake you've ever made. You'd have to rescue ten kids from the river to make up for that damn fool stunt you put on in that house."

When they got to the shop Jimmy sat outside and waited while Benny went into the office. He didn't have any hope of keeping his job. He was washed up now, all right. Pulling the kid out of the river had tagged him as a hero, but that girl had dropped him in two minutes into the slob division. She was the only one who could square him, but if he went back to the house to try to talk to her, most likely he'd make matters worse.

After Benny came out he had to go inside and they didn't waste any time with him. He didn't see the boss, just a girl in the outer office, and they were in so much hurry to get rid of him that they didn't even take time to write out a check. They paid him off in cash.

"And don't come back," the girl said to him coldly.

"You think I'm nuts or something?"

He left the building and walked down the street. A couple of times he thought about looking for another job but things were getting worse in the city day by day and there weren't any jobs, not even for forty a week.

The first bar he came to gained a customer and he ordered a beer. He lit a cigarette and made rings on the bar with the bottom of the glass. He had tried doing things the right way and he had caught it in the face, almost as hard as Lucy had pegged him with the bottle. All that had to happen now was for that girl to go to the police with her lie and they'd pull him in like a dead fish on the end of a line. It seemed to him that the more he tried to be honest the less luck he had. When he had been promoting money from Sharon and trying to get in with Robinson he hadn't had any real worries. Now, through no fault of his own, he had a worry on his mind that was enough to turn his hair gray. He had lost his job unjustly and that crazy girl held all his future in her hands.

Over the third or fourth beer he thought of leaving town, and he might have considered it seriously if it hadn't been for Lucy. He didn't quite know what he would do with Lucy if he found her, but if he didn't do anything else with her he could do what the other men had done. Still it wasn't the physical side of her that he was thinking about so much. He was thinking of a number of things in relation to Lucy but when he tried to form some kind of picture out of the pieces he couldn't get them to fit. He just knew that strange inner forces, forces that he didn't understand, seemed to be driving him in one direction.

After leaving the bar he played with the desire to stop off and see Sharon at her place but finally decided against it. No man who was any man at all could look at Sharon and not want her as a woman, but he'd had his moments with her and they were finished. What she needed was a man like Robinson who could give her the money she liked to spend—money that she wasn't earning now. On the other hand, she possibly deserved somebody better than Robinson. Robinson would treat her like a queen until he had no further use for her, then she'd either be swallowed up by the organization or he'd kick her out of town. But, Jimmy told himself, this was none of his business. Sharon was old enough to take care of herself. If she didn't have an affair with Robinson, she had that salesman who had been chasing her and most salesmen made good money. She wouldn't be the first girl who had forgotten all about love and settled for the old bucks.

He stopped off at a few bars on his way to West Avenue, having one or two beers in each place. In the dump north of the avenue the women who sought drinks from anybody were tired-looking and crummy but as he neared the avenue the faces became younger, some of them barely legal age, and their figures were better. By the time they became old enough to vote most of them would have kids and only a few of them would have husbands.

He stopped at a deli and bought a couple of six-packs and continued on toward his rooming house. He carried one of the packs in his right hand, being careful not to swing it too much, and the other pack under his arm. Carrying the pack under his arm proved a mistake and although he heard the kid running up behind him he didn't get out of the way fast enough. The kid, shouting a gutter curse, shoved the six-pack and it went flying out from his grasp, thumping as it hit the sidewalk. The kid jumped into an alley and disappeared as Jimmy stopped and picked up the six-pack. He wouldn't be able to drink that beer for a while, that was sure. Once he put the opener to a can he'd have the ceiling soaking wet.

Pop Gilson was in front of his store, messing with a canary in a cage that had lost most of its feathers, and Jimmy walked down there. He didn't have anything to do and if Pop wanted the place watched he could do that.

"I should ought to let this thing go," Pop said. "It won't sing and who wants a canary that won't sing? It's like having a woman who won't go to bed with you."

There was an old rocking chair in front of Pop's store and Jimmy sat down. He held the beer on his lap and tried to rock. It was one of those platform things, and something was stuck so that it wouldn't move.

"I'll tend shop," Jimmy said.

"For why?"

"Maybe you've got something you'd rather do."

Pop shook his head. "Not now I haven't. This morning when I woke up the girl was gone and she hasn't come back yet." Pop shook the cage violently and the bird jumped around. It flapped its wings but it didn't make a sound. "There was a guy here looking for you," Pop said, "only a little while ago."

"What kind of a guy?"

"Just a guy. Dressed nice and all that." The bird leaped over from its perch to cling to the side of the cage and Pop snapped at the tiny claws with a heavy finger. "I made him buy a chair from me for five bucks before I told him where you lived and then he told me to keep the chair."

Jimmy got up from the chair. All of a sudden he didn't feel so good.

"You think he was a cop?"

"A cop? Naw, he wasn't no cop. I can smell a cop a mile away and I don't bother with them none. If a cop asks me anything I turn into the dumbest guy in the world. I couldn't even spell my own name for a cop and do it right."

"I'd have given you five to keep your mouth shut."

"Maybe, but how was I to know that? You never had no money before you started working and I've got it in my head that a fellow like you doesn't work steady for very long."

Jimmy gave Pop a hard look and started back up the avenue. Pop was no different from the others who lived in the slums. He'd sell out his own mother for a five-dollar bill and then kick her in the face because she didn't appreciate it. They said you were safe on West Avenue but you were only safe as long as somebody who had money to throw away didn't come looking for you. Even sex wasn't as strong along the avenue as the lure of easy money.

He didn't have to go into the rooming house, but he did. If somebody was waiting for him there was no sense of putting it off. Pop had claimed that he could smell a cop, but Pop could be wrong and he just hoped it wasn't a cop. Anyhow, if the girl had made any charges against him his address was available at the shop where he had worked.

At this time of the day there was hardly anybody in the house, and his steps sounded hollow as he mounted the stairs. In front of his door he paused for a second and then shoved it open. Bert Robinson looked up from where he sat on the edge of the bed. Jimmy shrugged and entered, kicked the door shut and carried the beer over to the dresser.

"This is some dump," Robinson said.

"So what do you expect for five dollars a week? A fancy pad with a private bath and a dame thrown in?"

"Tough," Robinson said thoughtfully. "That's what I like about you. Maybe you don't mean it about acting tough, but nobody can tell. It rides well on you, and when you swing into that walk you really put the hard business over."

Jimmy punched a couple of holes in a can of beer, but he didn't offer one to Robinson. "So what do you want from me?" He turned to the man.

"Finding you cost me five bucks."

"You just wasted five bucks."

"I wouldn't say so, and it was cheaper than trying to get it out of Sharon. She'll take my money for drinks but even a fifty wouldn't buy the information about you that I was after. If she keeps up the distant act I guess I'll have to bend her arm a little.

Nine girls out of ten in her position would lock the door of that miserable bar and have some fun in a slick apartment. Hell, I'm not so old and I'm not so bad. As a man, I'm better now than I was when I was twenty."

"You didn't hunt me up to boast about your bedroom skill," Jimmy said. "Anyhow, Sharon and I don't see each other any more, and what she does is her affair. I tried to swing it for you, but she put the board in the fence. If you ask me, she doesn't know what she wants."

Robinson lit a cigar and got up from the bed. "I know what she's going to get," Robinson said. "I can play it straight for a while, trying to sell myself to a dame, but when that doesn't work I get impatient. Once I've lost my patience things start to move in a hurry. With a girl like Sharon I'd rather have it halfway decent, but she's calling the shots; she's making her own future."

Jimmy opened another can of beer, although the first can wasn't empty. Sharon, or any other girl, he decided, ought to have the chance to pick her own man. Force would bring nothing but hate, a strong hate that could explode in tragedy.

"Well, let's forget about her," Jimmy said. "Right now I'm curious about why you bothered looking me up. You must have more important things to do with your time."

Robinson helped himself to a beer. He took one of the cans that had been dropped and when he opened it the stuff shot all over. He swore softly and banged the can down on top of the dresser.

"I saved your neck this morning," Robinson said as he wiped off the front of his suit.

"I don't know how."

"Look," Robinson said impatiently. "Don't hand me the innocent act. You made a service call this morning, and you went too far with some girl."

"How would you know that?"

"I make it my business to know what's going on. I don't sit in some corner and let the world pass me by. Like with this girl, Jimmy. I can use you, but if you're locked up you can't do me any good. So I go up to see the girl and she's willing to take five hundred to forget about it. Now the question is, do you have the five hundred?"

"That's a stupid question. You know I can't get my hands

on that kind of money. And I didn't molest the girl, or try to. She cracked up or something and I got caught in the middle."

"Can you prove that?"

"It's my word against hers."

Robinson tried another beer from the other six pack. "You know who a jury would believe, don't you?" Robinson asked. "There was a witness, and you can't deny the girl was naked. You couldn't even get a character witness to testify for you. You'd be up there on the stand all alone, defended by some court-appointed lawyer, and when you're all done they'll lock you up for a few years. Once you get out you can beg for work and nobody will hire you. You could bury yourself alive in a hole in the ground and everybody would be glad that you did. You could be anything but a rapist and you'd have a chance. It's the one thing that destroys you. People figure that if you blew your cork once you'll blow it again."

Jimmy began to sweat. He had thought of most of this before and it made sense, too much sense. "If you saved my neck you must have paid the girl," Jimmy said. He shook his head. "But I guess not. You wouldn't have asked me about the money if you had."

"Why should I pay for a horse that might not be willing to work for me? What the girl does is up to you. She'll take the five hundred and let the matter drop, but if she doesn't get the money, she'll shout her lungs out. It all depends on whether or not you come to work for me. You give me your word on that and she gets the dough. Keep on the way you've been going and you'll meet trouble."

The beer had lost its taste and Jimmy put the can down. If he refused Robinson the law would beat him silly, and the years that lay ahead of him would be as empty as most of the pockets along the avenue. Going in with Robinson would make it safe for him with the girl, but within days he would break other laws. Still Robinson was solid and that shouldn't cause any worry.

"What would I have to do?" he asked.

"You're smart, Jimmy. You see the light that shines."

"I only asked what I had to do. I didn't say that I'd do it."

Robinson blew a smoke ring. "Well, I thought of having you straighten out some of the girls, but I've put Willie onto that, and that's better. You're too handsome and you might have too much fun with the girls, keeping them from their work. Willie don't look so hot with that limp, and he hates the girls, anyway. He wouldn't sleep with a queen unless he beat her stupid first."

"None of that tells me what I have to do," Jimmy said. "Maybe I'm dumb but I want to know which road turns left."

"You'd have two jobs. One is to find Lucy Forbes if she's still in town."

"And the other?"

"That'll develop as we go along. But it'll be big when it breaks, very big. You do what you're told and you'll be in line for a bonus."

In the end Jimmy accepted the offer, mostly because he was in a corner and it was the only way he could get out.

"Here's a couple of hundred so you can get some clothes," Robinson said.

"Thanks," Jimmy said, taking the money.

After Robinson left he sat down on the bed and finished the beer.

Somehow, a lot of things didn't seem right to him.

Only one thing made him hopeful.

Robinson was going to pay him to look for Lucy, and that wasn't so bad. Jimmy had wanted to find her anyway and now, right now, he wanted to find her worse than ever. If she still had that money from the bar—if she had taken it and she hadn't spent it—maybe, by talking nice, he could make a deal with her.

The way he looked at the situation, the time was ripe for both of them to get out of town, a long distance out. After six months people would stop looking for them and the money would help while they waited. Sure, it was running, but sometimes you had to run. And if she didn't have the money she had something else that could keep a guy real busy.

He guessed maybe it would work out all right.

Money wasn't everything . . . .

8

It had been a miserable ten days for Lucy, ending up in this horrible shack along the river. After three days living here she was more than sick of it. Not only was there nothing to do, not even a radio to listen to, there was nothing to eat except canned sardines and crackers. The sardines she hated and the crackers were stale. Once she thought about making coffee, but the old stove in the corner that sat up high on four skinny legs was fired by oil and she was afraid of it. Back home they'd had oil lamps to use whenever the lights went out—the oil was really kerosene, but everybody called it oil—and she knew from experience that the stuff couldn't be trusted. And with just one window in the shack, the only exit she could use because she couldn't get the door unlocked, she wasn't taking any chances of getting trapped and cooked alive. Her life was torn enough now without somebody having to get out the pine box. She guessed they used pine if you didn't have any money or if nobody claimed your body. She didn't think hers would be claimed. She had reached the point where she was sure nobody cared.

"A dollar a night," the woman had told her when she had inquired about a room. "You pay in advance and by the week."

"I've got just about enough for a week."

"Well, you'd better latch onto some more or you'll be out in the street."

The room had been worse than she had imagined it would be, and the only way she had been able to keep the rats out was to leave the light on. She hadn't been able to sleep much that night, afraid of the rats but more afraid of the future.

She'd have to do something—but what? She didn't dare give the bars a play, picking up men and using hotel rooms, because Jimmy Slade's threats still echoed in her mind. He wouldn't forget the bottle business and he'd find her sooner or later. The grudge would be there inside him, and if he worked her over he wouldn't show her any mercy. Then, too, there was the fear of being picked up by the police. It stood to reason that her running out just about the time the safe was robbed would make her a prime suspect. What a fool she'd been for not calling the police that night!

As for Jimmy Slade, she didn't know what to make of the

newspaper story about his dragging that kid out of the river. That seemed to make Jimmy a hero, and showed him in new and previously unsuspected light. According to his picture in the paper, the effects of the bottle had completely vanished; he was as handsome as ever—but just because he'd saved the kid from drowning wouldn't necessarily make him forget and forgive what she had done to him. He was still big and tough, and could be mean when he wanted to be. He'd hand her her lumps, all right, if he found her.

There was one thing she could do: go to Bert Robinson. He was taking on new girls, and she was pretty enough. The trouble was that Bert always started his new girls working in a house, accepting any man who had the price, and that was no good.

When she had worked at the bar she had tried to be selective, but for all of her care she had drawn some corkers. A lot of men acted all right when they were having a drink, but turn them loose in a girl's bedroom and the animal in them tore through the surface. Besides, the longer she was away from it the less she thought of that kind of life. Certainly there were any number of risks that had to be faced as occupational hazards. Being seized by the police was one, but there were others equally serious, such as picking up a disease or getting careless and having a child.

She had lost one child and she couldn't bear going through that again. The baby had been part of her—no matter what the father had been—and the day she had lost it she had lost life. Yet, for the child's sake it was probably better that way. At least, she had done nothing to prevent it, like trying pills or going to an abortionist. Not once had she considered escape. She had thought only how she could possibly be both a mother and a father to her baby, but any satisfaction that might have been attached to this had been snatched from her.

Sunday had been a lonesome day and she had stayed in her room and cried quite a lot. Sometimes she had cried because she had been within dimes of being broke and sometimes she had cried because of the rotten life that she had led and it was now the only kind of life open to her.

Suddenly she stopped crying, thinking of several girls she knew who had gone wrong and then straightened out on their own. It was true that you couldn't kill the past, that the memories of what had gone before were part of your whole being, but it didn't follow that what you had done yesterday you had to do tomorrow. If you bent a piece of wire, you could straighten it out, so why couldn't you do the same thing in your life, in what you thought and believed and did? It took courage, determination and patience, but it wasn't impossible by any means.

Early Monday morning, weary because of a sleepless night watching the rats, she had showered in the hole at the end of the hall and dressed as carefully as she could, even to a bra that had given her more support than she had needed under the yellow dress. It had been hot that morning and the bra had felt uncomfortable but she had told herself that any girl with any sense wore one. Back of the bar she had used her almost naked breasts for bait, but that wouldn't do for what she had in mind just then.

Downstairs she met the woman of the house and for the first time the woman paid some attention to her.

"You going out, honey?"

"Only for a paper and to look around. But maybe I can save a dime and look at the paper you've got in your hand."

"Wait until you come back, honey. I'm reading it and I can't settle down for the day unless I know what's going on."

She had noticed the woman start for the telephone as she walked onto the porch, but she hadn't thought anything about it at the time. She still hadn't thought anything about it after she'd purchased a paper at the corner store, but of course the first thing she had looked at had been the help-wanted ads. There hadn't been many ads, most of them gimmick things by out-of-town concerns, and not one of the type she had been searching for.

A domestic, she had reasoned, got about thirty-five dollars a week plus her room and board, and although nobody could get rich at that kind of job, it did offer some measure of security. She had thought that if she could get with a nice family she could work hard and save until she had enough money to leave town. Of course, there was more money in men, but she had reached the point where she had to turn back before she became totally lost. If she continued to sell herself to men, the night would come when she would drink too much, or like the man too much, and she would find herself carrying a child that she didn't want.

Facing it honestly, she supposed that the desire to belong to a steady man, giving herself to him when he wanted her, had been shattered by the men who had known her. Even as she had stood there in that store, glancing through the paper and feeling discouraged, she had told herself there was more beauty in women than there was in men. A man, naked and lusting, could be an ugly creature of animal desire. But a woman, her body meant to bring new life into the world, was the ultimate of wondrous desire itself, yet a desire so entirely different from the male there was no comparison.

And then suddenly, her mind trying desperately to arrive at the meaning of her strange emotions, she had seen her picture in the paper. It was the picture one of her customers had taken of her with his self-developing camera, and she had forgotten about it. Naturally the paper had used just her head, because she had been nude at the time and she had cut the picture apart herself, throwing the lower part away.

The appearance of her picture had ended a lot of things for her, including hope of getting a domestic job or anything else. She had choked up, the world around her growing smaller, and she had stumbled outside, knowing only that she had to run and run fast. In her anxiety she had almost run into the waiting arms of the police. At the last moment she had noticed the police cruiser in front of the rooming house, and then she hadn't needed anybody to tell her why the woman had kept the paper to herself, or why she had gone to the phone . . . .

Now as she walked around the shack she tried to remember what she had done that day. Without money, she hadn't been able to board the bus, and since almost everybody in town had seen her picture, she hadn't been safe on the streets or in any public place. In blind panic she had hurried across the bridge and taken the river road upstream. She only knew that she had to go and keep on going. Once a big, mean-tempered dog had come out to bark at her, showing its teeth, and the dog had scared her half to death. But the dog hadn't scared her nearly as much as the troopers' parked car about a mile farther on.

To avoid the troopers, she had taken a dirt lane off to the left that led toward the river, and at the end of the lane she had found this one-room shack. Finding the door padlocked she had thought that the shack belonged to somebody who only used it weekends. After the state police car had moved on, she had tried the window and it had gone up easily. She'd had some trouble crawling inside, but once there, at least she had had a place to hide, a place to think.

As she crossed the room she stumbled over a loose board in the floor and almost fell down. That was the second or third time she had tripped over the same board and always in the morning. Not until the afternoon when the sun was in the west did the one window let much light inside. Afraid to use one of the kerosene lamps, she had been going to bed in the old bunk with the arrival of darkness. But again she hadn't been able to sleep because the longer she stayed there the more certain she grew that the shack was being lived in. Work clothes and a suit—unpressed but in good condition—that belonged to some giant of a man hung from a couple of nails. They didn't seem the kind that a weekender would leave behind. It all added up to the fact that whoever lived there called it home. And if somebody lived there she had to get out before the owner returned. So far she had been lucky, but luck didn't last forever. About that she ought to know. She hadn't had much of it lately.

There were still some cans of sardines on the shelf over the sink, but she'd had enough of sardines for a while. That kind of food wasn't meant for morning, and besides it made her thirsty. The old pump by the side of the metal sink didn't work, so whenever she needed a drink of water she had to go down to the river. Between going to the river for water and using the nearest patch of woods for a bathroom, she was fed up with climbing in and out of the window. Coming right down to it, she was fed up with a lot of things.

The police were hunting her for something that she hadn't done. She had lost all the spare clothes she had. And after her stay in this dirty shack she needed a bath so that she could feel clean again. The things that she was wearing could do with a washing, too. There was a line out back, and her things would dry fast.

She went over to the nail in the wall from which hung some pants and a couple of shirts. Most likely there was nobody around, but some peculiar touch of modesty wouldn't permit her to walk naked to the river and back. She supposed it was silly for her to feel that way about it. More than one man had seen her nude, and she hadn't minded. The men seemed to like seeing her.

Deciding that one of the shirts on the nail would cover her if she didn't get lost in it, she began to undress, starting with her stockings first. There were a couple of old magazines around, along with a mess of cigarette butts, and she knew what was in the magazines without looking at them again. Apparently they were put out by some sun-bathing association, but she didn't see how they could get away with such pictures. The men and women who posed for them couldn't have much pride. The only man who had ever taken a photo of her had been that one customer, but she wouldn't think of posing that way for a living. Somehow it seemed worse than being with a man and surrendering to his every wish.

She piled her clothes on a broken-down chair and got into one of the shirts. It was a real tent on her. The bottom hung below her knees, and she could hardly find her arms, but after she rolled up the sleeves she was able to manage.

The window presented its usual problem, and she crawled through it. When she dropped to the ground, the sharp stones hurt her bare feet. Limping, she rounded the shack and walked toward the river.

Opposite this spot was a steep bank with lots of trees, but she didn't think that anybody was peeking at her. She tried the water with a bare foot and jumped. It was cold and her toes stirred up mud from the bottom. She could scoop up drinking water. When she waded, the water became too muddy to wash clothes in or to scrub her body clean, but she couldn't do anything about that.

She bathed first, lathering herself all over, then rinsing as well as she could. When she finished she felt better. Without drying—she had only seen one small, soiled towel in the shack—she put on the shirt, tied the tails up around her hips and did her best to scrub her clothes. Soon she was on her way back to the shack. The sun was hot overhead and the sky clear.

Twenty feet from the shack she stopped. She stood dead still, holding her breath, her eyes wide.

The front door was open and a towering young man with brown hair and tremendous shoulders leaned lazily against the door frame. He was grinning and studying her trim legs. Because of the shirt—she had untied its tails—she wasn't showing much except the calves of her legs and her face. Still staring at him, she sucked in her breath, her breasts swelling.

He was the same man who had come in the bar that night just before the robbery, the man who caught bait and fish and drank ginger ale. The big spender, who shot a dime just like that! Her breath slowly left her lungs. Of all the lousy luck, she thought to run into this jerk who had seen her before.

"You're in the habit of borrowing stuff without asking?" he grinned.

She swallowed once and forced a smile. It would have been simple for her to dash up the lane, perhaps losing herself in the woods, but after all she was wearing his shirt. It was hardly a costume for a girl to travel in, and she couldn't climb into her sopping wet clothes.

"I haven't hurt your old shirt," she said. "It was either that or nothing, and I'm not like those girls in those magazines inside your shack. Get your cheap thrills from them—not from me. And I only ate a few cans of those rotten sardines, and some of your lousy stale crackers." She made a face. "I hope I never have to eat that kind of junk again. You're welcome to it."

"Thanks, but I don't go for sardines, either. I trap in the winter and I use the sardines for bait." His grin became broad. "But I'll tell you right now that I never caught anything quite so pretty with sardines. I get skunks and 'coons, but until now no girls."

"Don't worry," she said, walking forward. "You haven't caught any girl yet, so don't get yourself excited." She held up her clothes. "I just want to dry my clothes and then I'll get out of your way."

She rounded the shack and threw the things over the line. There weren't any clothespins and she hoped that a breeze wouldn't come up and blow anything away. She was down to almost nothing, and she couldn't afford to lose any more. If she did, she'd be better off wearing his shirt.

He hadn't changed his position when she returned to the front of the shack, and although the shirt covered her she didn't feel comfortable. She supposed that was a funny way for her to feel. Lots of men had seen her stripped bare. Most men, and that one girl, had wanted her like that.

"You mentioned those magazines," he said. "Just to keep the record straight, they don't belong to me. A man who buys bait from me brought them out. He gets a charge out of them and he thought I would."

"You looked them over, didn't you?"

He frowned.

"Sure I looked. I'm just curious enough to do that much."

"And you got a cheap thrill along the way?"

"Skip it," he said, annoyance in his tone. He regarded her closely. "Aren't you the girl I saw in the bar a couple of weeks ago?"

"That's right," she admitted, wishing that he hadn't remembered her.

"How come you're out here?"

"Things happen."

He thought that one over. "You must be on the bum," he decided.

"I'm not doing so hot," she agreed.

"So you got in through the window?"

"Fat chance I had of opening the door."

"You know that's against the law?"

"Yes, I know, but I didn't think about it. Who does when they're in a hurry?" She played with the top button on the shirt. "You just come from town?"

"I came through it. Why?"

"And you didn't bring a newspaper?"

"I don't read the papers often. What's there to read? Crime and all that stuff? Out here, I'm away from it. I'll let it stay like that."

She began to feel more relaxed, her confidence slowly returning. "This is some dump," she said.

"It's a place to live, isn't it?"

"A real palace. Even the pump won't work."

"Maybe not for you, but it does for me. I keep a bucket of water under the sink to prime it with. Prime that pump in the morning and she'll give you water all day long. Good water, too. I've had it tested." He kicked the side of the shack with one heavy boot and she thought he was going to drive a hole right through the side. "How long have you been here?"

"One day more than I should have stayed."

"You must be hungry."

"Not for those damn sardines and crackers."

He laughed. "Okay, I'll fix something. There's no ice out

here so I don't keep much in the summer, but I brought stuff from town. The pork chops ought to be cooked first and there's enough for both of us."

She wondered about what he might try to do to her once they were inside the shack, but she soon discovered that she had no need to wonder. He busied himself emptying a bag on top of the table. She sank down on the old bunk and covered her legs with the tails of the shirt.

"What's your name?" she asked.

"Luke Shark. And yours?"

"It doesn't matter much."

"Whatever you say." He didn't have any trouble lighting the kerosene stove. "I guess you'll tell when you get ready."

"How many years have you lived out here, Luke?"

"Since I was sixteen," he replied. "The shack was here, and I just moved right in. Some guy in the city owns the place, but he never comes out and it's like my own. In the spring I sell bait and keep with it until the fishing season ends in the fall. I peddle frogs and fish, too, if there's a market. Once in a while I cut grass or do odd jobs to fill in. Then winters I trap and I cut firewood by the cord. I've figured it out, and I do all right. I pay more taxes than most fellows who work in factories."

The frying pan got hot in a hurry and he dropped in the pork chops to sizzle.

"What do you do when you get fed up?" Lucy asked. "Just walk off and leave the place like I found it?"

"I had my reason."

"Probably."

"Nobody was fishing on the river so I didn't lose anything." He poked at the pork chops with a fork, and seasoned them with salt and pepper and sage. "I've got an aunt in the next town and she's been wanting to have her porch painted. She's too old to do it herself, so I did it for her, for free."

He had a package of instant mashed potatoes and he whipped them up. Before they sat down to eat, he removed his T-shirt. She had never seen such a powerful chest or pair of shoulders on any man before.

"I could use a girl around here," he said as they began eating.

"Doing what?" she asked, as though she didn't know. What did any man do with a girl?

"Well, if I had a girl I could spend more time going after bait. She could sell the stuff, and I wouldn't have to bother with that. Most people come in the morning, but if I hang around that's half a day shot and sometimes I'm up all night catching crawlers. When it gets dry you have to work for crawlers and worms. I mix walnut shells with water and slop it on the ground. That brings them out right away. When the other bait-sellers are out, I take care of my customers, as well as theirs. People keep coming back to me."

"Are you sounding me out about staying here, Luke?"

"It was just a thought."

She didn't consider the suggestion seriously. The shack was no place for a girl to live. Besides, how long could she hide out here?

He pushed his plate aside and rested his elbows on the table. "You're very pretty. Did you know that?"

"Thank you."

He lit a cigarette and watched her through the smoke. "You're running away from something, aren't you?" He held up one hand. "No, you don't have to tell me. But if you'd like to stay here, you're welcome. While the weather's nice I can sleep outside."

He didn't say what he'd do when it got cold or if it stormed, but she was fairly sure that she knew. He'd be in that bunk with her, not sleeping and not caring what he did, and some night he'd give her his kid. She liked him some—maybe a whole lot—but she didn't want it to be that way.

"I'll leave when it gets dark," she said.

"That's up to you, but the next stop you make might not be so good. No matter who you are, you can only run so far. And I'm taking a chance by asking you to stay. For all I know I could wake up with a knife in my guts. Girls have done crazier things for no reason at all."

She helped him with the few dishes, and he was right about the pump working after it had been primed. The grease was hard to get off in the cold water, and the plates weren't exactly clean when she put them away, but he didn't seem to mind.

He spent the afternoon along the river and she got her clothes from the line and dressed while he was gone. The bra was still damp, but she put it on, anyway. She could have left the shack then but she didn't know where to go, and she was afraid of being recognized in daylight. She was lucky that Luke didn't read the papers, but even if he had seen her picture she had the feeling that he would have believed her. And somehow she was a trifle sorry that a rather nice guy would elect to exist the way he did. However, it wasn't any worse than the way her family lived, picking coal out of the ground, getting drunk and bragging about the new raise that was coming up and then having a strike clobber them instead.

Luke didn't return until late, and he complimented her on her yellow dress.

"That's better," he said. "You were showing too much the night I saw you in the bar. But I guess it was good for business."

"It doesn't hurt any."

"You figure it's worth it?"

"Sometimes I wonder. Honest."

"Take it from me that it isn't."

"I will. I'll remember that, Luke."

He put together a couple of sandwiches for them but she was too nervous to eat. The night was coming on and in a short time she would be walking down the road, alone and desperate, with nothing certain and nothing safe. Any escape would be only temporary, she thought, and if the police wanted her so much, they'd never stop hunting her. Trying to get away would only further indicate her guilt. What she needed more than anything else, she decided, was to face the issue squarely. Once the police looked into her past, they would be justified in discrediting anything she might say. A few lies, for a girl who sold her favors, were just nothing at all.

"You can come back if you get stuck," Luke said. "If the door is locked you know about the window."

"All right. And thanks."

She left the shack at dusk and walked to the road. The road was a dead end about ten miles up, so she would have to go through town. And perhaps she wouldn't make it through town. She had been living like a hunted animal since the night she had left the bar, and she was tired of it.

As she neared the bridge she began to walk faster. She knew what she had to do and it was something she should have done immediately following the robbery. Sharon was an understanding girl and perhaps Sharon would believe her. Lucy knew of no one else she could trust. Had it not been for that fight she had with Jimmy she would have considered him, but that was out.

There were a lot of people on the bridge, some of them police, but once she had started across she felt that she couldn't turn back without drawing attention to herself.

"She didn't jump," a man close to her said when her way was blocked by the crowd. "That phone call about some girl standing on the top strand was just a gag. And she didn't hit no pier. With her head smashed in the way it is she couldn't have crawled over the fence and got back onto the road. If you ask me, somebody flattened her skull and then tried to make it look like she killed herself."

"I recognized her face," another man said. "She was one of Bert Robinson's girls."

"Then that explains it. She must have gotten ideas of her own and he didn't like them. You've got to give him credit for doing a good job. She sure ain't going to have any ideas again."

Lucy shuddered and stared at the blanket-covered mound on the stretcher, and at the glistening, dark pool of blood near it. "Excuse me," she murmured and pushed forward.

As soon as she was across the bridge and out of sight she began to run.

She couldn't get away from there quickly enough.

9

Sharon wasted her time with the man who had been sent by the real estate agent—also, she couldn't bear that real estate man and his stares. Just like the other two prospects she had seen yesterday, all this one displayed was a mild interest and nothing more.

"I'd be starting from scratch," the man said. "About the only thing you've got is a license, and that's for this address. As for your stock, I can buy liquor and beer whenever I feel like it. I don't need to lose my shirt to do that."

She was glad to get rid of him and she hoped there wouldn't be any more. It seemed like everybody was looking for a cut-throat bargain, and just because she was near the bottom of the ladder they tried to kick her all the way down. But she had heard that a new factory might start up in the building vacated by the shoe company. It was just a rumor, of course, but she was counting heavily on that. Whether or not she could last until then was another question.

After pouring a shot for herself she looked at it and then threw it out. Since the night she had tumbled, drunk and helpless, into the shrubs in front of the apartment building she hadn't been drinking very much. The day after that she hadn't been able to open up and had been as sick as two dogs. Carl Evans had come over to see how she was, insisting that she eat, but after he had gone to the trouble of getting her bacon and eggs she had lost everything and felt worse than ever.

"You're killing yourself," Carl had told her seriously.

"I can't help it. That business is driving me nuts. First I'm taken for a bundle of cash and then the factory folds up. How much can a person take?"

"Most people can take a great deal. Sure I drink, but I don't do it to kill whatever it is inside me. And when I'm on the road I don't touch a drop. You can't sit at some bar until two or three in the morning and feel like yourself the next day. The company has had to let a lot of men go because of too much booze. That's why I've got a fine chance for a promotion. They know I won't make a call half soused or hung over and blow a liquor breath in a prospect's face."

He had spent the day with her, and although she had welcomed his company his constant preaching about how she should cut down on the bottle had gotten on her nerves. Of course he had been right, but she had been too stubborn to admit it.

"You must have had a real ball for yourself," she had said.

"In what way?"

"Last night. Undressing me."

"I didn't even look at you."

"Oh, come off it, Carl. Now I've heard everything."

"Well, I didn't, and that's the truth. There wasn't anything new for me to see. You made sure of that the other time."

"What's the matter with you?" she had challenged. "Aren't you a man?"

But he hadn't become angry with her, as she had intended him to be.

"I like to think of myself as being a man, but I also like to think that there's more to being a man than taking advantage of somebody I care a great deal for."

"Don't tell me there haven't been other girls. I won't swallow that."

"I wouldn't lie to you. Of course there have been other girls, but they were merely amusing for the moment. Almost every man goes through the same thing. Then he meets the one girl that fits him, and the rest of it stops."

He hadn't left any doubt in her mind that she was the girl that he wanted, wanted in the proper way and at the proper time, but he had also made it very clear that he was somewhat disappointed in her. She guessed she could understand his attitude. He was a good, solid citizen; he held a responsible position with a reliable company. So the girl he married would have to measure up to the accepted standards of propriety. Carl Evans was headed up the success ladder, and he wouldn't want the kind of wife who would hold him back.

The next drink she didn't throw out. She drank it, made a face and shook her head. Of course he had been on the road since the beginning of the week but that didn't prevent her from thinking about him. Many men who might have found her lying in the bushes would have taken their pound of flesh. More than one girl had been given her cross to bear just because of a similar incident.

She shrugged and put the bottle away. So what if Carl was on the make for her? Lots of other fellows had wanted what she possessed, the promise of fiery passion dripping from her lushly curved body, but Carl had to go and tie a string onto it— the marriage string. Well, she decided, there was no hurry about that. Not right now, anyhow. Not with Lucy staying with her ...

Lucy had been with her for two nights now, hiding out and jumping whenever the door chimes rang or there was a noise in the building. And having Lucy there was sort of wonderful.

Lucy had been nervous at first, her words running together as she told about the robbery, the gun, and the man with the limp, and Sharon had believed her. She had reasoned that any girl who had taken that much money wouldn't be down on her luck so soon, her clothes where she couldn't get them, everything she had shot to pieces.

"You can stay with me," Sharon had said. "We'll work this out."

"What about the salesman?"

"He won't be back until Friday, and we can worry about that then."

Sharon, in spite of her promise to herself not to drink so much, reached for the bottle and poured another drink. The two nights with Lucy—she had closed up right away the first night and early the night before—had been mysterious and wonderful nights but they had been a little disturbing, too. Something had gone wrong with her air conditioner and it had only been natural for them to get as comfortable as possible and avoid the heat. The first night they hadn't gone all the way with their clothes but the next night they had—had she started it or had Lucy?—and then they had been lazing around, strip-naked and drinking and talking about the robbery, and eventually getting around to men.

"He could have had me," Lucy had said of the man who lived in the shack along the river. "He could have done it and I wouldn't have stopped him. He's a nice guy, and big—my God!"

Sharon lit a cigarette and inhaled the smoke. Maybe Lucy didn't have much moral sense, but she did have a body, and nobody could take that away from her. She hadn't been pregnant long enough to develop any stretch marks and she was flat in the tummy. She had a fine pair of breasts, closer to normal than oversized, and when she walked across the room her movements were beauty itself. After she had a few beers she talked frankly about the men who had known her, the things that some men had asked her to do, strange requests that made Sharon feel ill just to think about them. And another thought made Sharon feel equally as sick: Jimmy Slade and his cheap room and the heat of his body crushing her tight, the pulsing lust that was a part of him violently and blindly seeking to lift her to the summit that almost all girls experienced. But he had failed; she had never been a full woman with Jimmy or anybody else.

Yet when she was near Lucy, who didn't quite match her in a couple of places, she had a sensation of warmth, a feeling of need crawling through her blood, that left her a little weak and uncertain. And after they went to bed, with the lights out and the darkness around them, it was worse. Then Sharon's confusion became more intense, her need sharpened to a point almost beyond endurance.

She had another drink. And another.

It was hell—and it was beautiful. Lying there on the bed with that lovely girl beside her was both a challenge and a promise. A challenge to deny herself, to trample her desires into the dust—desires which refused to become very clear to her— and, at the same time, the promise that within her grasp existed the pleasure of the flesh beyond anything she'd ever known. Forbidden pleasures, which were only discussed in low whispers.

She put the shot glass down and walked the length of the bar. She didn't know what she was so upset about. She hadn't done anything wrong—not yet. They had drunk together and slept together and nothing had happened. When she had awakened that morning she had found her arm around Lucy and her hand resting lightly upon one sleeping breast. But that, she assured herself, didn't mean much. It had very probably been a mistake, and anybody could have done the same thing. Even when she had been sleeping with Jimmy she had often discovered in the morning that she was clinging to him. No, an incident like that wasn't important. Yet it had been exciting to wake up that way, to touch the loveliness that was woman. She had been shaking as she dressed and she had even forgotten to put on stockings. Maybe it was just as well. Stockings cost money and she didn't have any of that to throw around. She was as flat as a blown-out tire.

She saw Jimmy Slade coming across the street and she went down the bar to draw a beer. Robinson had told her about Jimmy and the trouble he'd gotten into with the plumbing firm but she hadn't talked with Jimmy since then. She had hoped that he would stay away, for seeing him opened old wounds that she wanted to forget.

"Throw the crowd out," Jimmy winked at her as he sat down at the bar. "I can't drink when I don't have room."

"If you spent more than a second thinking up that one you wasted your time."

She put the beer in front of him and she acknowledged to herself that he looked very handsome in the gray suit. And he knew how to select a tie. So many men didn't. They put on an expensive suit and then ruined the effect with the wrong tie.

"I hear you sold your car," Jimmy said. "The way you used

to have it washed and polished I thought you were married to it." He tasted the beer. "You must have gotten a nice piece of change."

She poured a drink for herself. "Are you kidding?" she demanded. "When they sell you a car they give you the works about it being an investment, but when you can't go on with the payments and you have to chuck it they sob that the market is bad, and that they're doing you a favor even to consider taking it back. So you grab what you can and swear that you'll never buy another. Then after you walk for a week you wonder when you'll ever get enough cash to make the down payment on the next car—and get swindled again. With cars, people just never learn."

"Maybe what you got will carry you over."

"I paid the money out the same day that I got it to get the roof repaired. The real estate man said I should fix it and that I'd double my money when I sold."

Jimmy smiled faintly. "You got taken, Sharon. If you sold at all it would be on the business you're doing, and not on the building. My guess is that the real estate man got a percentage of what you paid the roofer."

"So I wasn't smart?"

"Far from it. You were more than a little dumb. Most real estate agents are honest but you'll always find a crooked one around."

Her temper flared instantly. "You aren't so smart yourself," she flung at him. "I only spent money, but you'll find yourself doing a stretch one of these days. Maybe Robinson saved you once, but that's all. He won't know you next time."

Jimmy's face sobered. "So you know about the girl?"

"Yes, I know about her, and you couldn't have been more of a fool. If you had to have a girl that bad, there are plenty on West Avenue who wouldn't have fought you off."

Jimmy spread his hands. "Nobody will believe that I didn't try anything with her," he said. "But the truth is that I didn't. There was something wrong at that house that morning, something that I don't know about yet, and if it takes a year off my life I'm going to find out what it was."

"Do you know anything about the girl who was killed on the bridge?"

"I wasn't there," Jimmy said.

"The police are trying to check out her movements for that night."

"Somebody must have seen her."

"Maybe they did. Lots of people see lots of other people, but what does it prove? Nothing. You get a great big zero."

His glass was empty and she drew him a fresh beer. Why had she been so angry with him? Most likely she had been stupid about the roof but she didn't have to dig at him because of that. He didn't mean anything to her, and she didn't care what he did.

"The beer is on me," she said. "What you spend won't make me rich."

"Thanks." He looked thoughtful. "Have you heard anything from Lucy?"

"Why is everybody so interested in that girl?" she wanted to know. "The police ask me, Robinson asks me and you ask me. With the police it's their job, but I don't see what you two have to do with it."

"All right. Forget that I said anything."

He insisted on paying for the third beer and she took his money. The bill was a five and she was so low on change she could hardly break it. Only a short time before she had been cashing pay checks and thinking nothing of it. Now a five was almost too much for her. It didn't seem right.

"Must be about time for the boss," Jimmy said. "He won't like it if he finds me here. The way his mind works, he'll think we're tearing up the lawn together again."

"Fat chance of that. I was crazy for a year, but right at the moment I'm sane. I'll stay that way, too, if he'll only get off my back. There isn't a day that he comes in here that he doesn't have a new pitch. Why can't he get it through his head that I wouldn't be seen with him if he was the last man alive?"

"He's got plans for you," Jimmy said. "He talks about them all the time. He even got prices on having a house built up in the hills and when a guy goes that far he isn't fooling around. He says he's going to have one of those big Hollywood beds with a mirror on the ceiling over it."

Sharon had to have a fresh drink. That Robinson was a real nut.

"Tell him to stop dreaming," she advised Jimmy. "He could buy me the whole town and I couldn't get out of it fast enough.”

"And if I were you that's just what I'd do. Take it from me and I'm talking as a friend. Get out and lose yourself."

"How can I, with this bar on my hands?"

"That's your problem. Even it went for taxes it's better than what you'll get if you stay here." He got down from the stool. "I'm only telling you this because of the past. You were good to me when I didn't deserve it, and the least I can do is give you a friendly tip. Robinson isn't playing games and you can be sure of that. He's rich, and I've got an idea that he's getting ready to jump out of the rackets when the opening is right. Most of the big ones do, and Robinson's no exception. He's fastened his eyes on you. And if he wasn't thinking of quitting he'd probably do it if you insisted. It's funny, the power a girl has over a man. Men kill and steal for the women they love."

She wiped off the bar after he left, completely missing the spot where his glass had rested, and fired the cloth back under the bar. Turning to look at herself in the mirror, she wished that she had worn something with a higher neckline. Robinson was always staring at that spot, and she often wondered if he knew whether her face was pretty or just average. That was the difficulty of a girl being too big in one area. Men didn't pay any attention to anything else. You went out on a date with a man and he wanted to put his hands there. If the girl wouldn't let him he acted like a little boy who had been kicked in the stomach. Maybe that was why the men were attracted to the pros. With the pros it didn't matter, and almost everything went. A man was a man and a pro could perform her services just as well in the back of a car as in a bedroom.

Bert Robinson arrived later than usual and he had his customary gin and orange. She could smell the shaving lotion and it reminded her of a rose garden. Only he wasn't a rose. He was a thorn in her side, and he lost no time in twisting the thorn.

"You get larger every day," he said.

"Not at my age I don't. I started early and quit fast."

"Good thing you quit when you did. If you'd kept it up you'd need a special harness to hold things in place."

"Cut it out," she said. "You know I don't go for that kind of talk. Maybe your girls think your cracks are funny, but I don't appreciate them."

He tried to reach for her hand, but she pulled it away.

"Hell, you know me better than that, Sharon. Can't a guy kid with you? And you know what my feelings are. I haven't hidden anything and I'm not hiding anything now, when it comes to you. I've offered you everything but my bank account. What is it you want?"

"Nothing," she said. That was a lie. There were so many things that she wanted. She wanted to be sure of staying in that nice apartment and to have her car back, or a car as good. "I don't want anything. What's the use of wanting? You never get it, anyway."

"You do if you want hard enough. You can't just say that you'd like to have something and then forget about it. You make your choice and then you ride with it to the end. If it takes only a week or a month you're lucky, but if it takes a year or more that's just part of the price."

She debated with herself about having a drink. The debate came to a stop as she poured one. If she kept this up she'd be stoned blind by the time she got out of the place. And she didn't want to be that way. There was too much to enjoy in the apartment.

"All I want to do is sell this dump," she said. "Let somebody throw down the cash, and I'll handle things from there on out."

Robinson got out a cigar, bit off the end and lighted it. She guessed he smoked a good brand, but she hated the smell of them, anyway.

"I'm about done with horsing around," Robinson said through his smoke cloud. "The way you treat me I feel like some leper that just escaped from a colony. Why don't you face the facts of life and see the bright side? With you in it a Caddy would look good—hell, even an old Model T would look good—and you'll be in bills up to your fanny, and not the kind of bills you're going to be collecting if you stay here. And a maid. I'll get you a maid to comb out your hair. You name it and you can have it. I don't ask anything from you, not at first or before you're ready. You have your room and I have mine. Days belong to you, doing whatever comes along, but after five we hitch up as a team and take in all of the bright spots that we can find. If nothing suits us here we breeze into New York, take in a stage show or something and top it off with one hell of a night."

"You've got the wrong girl," she said and almost sneezed because of the smoke. "You haven't got a dollar to your name that isn't dirty, and I don't want that kind of money. Give away what you've made from the mistakes of other people and you'd find yourself with less than I have in that cash register."

He thought about that for a moment. "If I hadn't done what I did somebody else would have done it."

"Which still doesn't make it right."

He leaned forward, his stare fastened on the swollen thrust of her breasts. "I suppose you'd say something different if the money I have had been come by honestly?"

She shook her head. She was afraid of him, but her fear wasn't so great that she couldn't speak the truth. Besides the liquor in her helped.

"My answer would still be no," she said. "I had one rotten affair and there isn't going to be another. I want to wake up in the morning and feel decent, not ashamed of what I did and not scared that I might be pregnant. Some girls can go through that every morning of the week and hardly think anything of it, but I'm not one of them. The next time has to be right—if there is a next time—otherwise I don't want any part of it."

"Well, that's one way of telling me that I'm on the outside looking in, isn't it?"

She was showing too much front and she adjusted the dress. "It's one way of telling you how I feel. You've known that right along, but you've kept coming down here afternoons, trying to push in where you aren't wanted. The whole thing is making me a nervous wreck and you're getting nowhere." She took a deep, unsteady breath. "Why don't you leave me alone? Can you answer that for me?"

"Because you've got what I want." He was standing now and he had discarded the cigar in an ashtray. "It's really very simple. A man sees a girl he has to have, regardless of cost, and he goes after her. If the girl is willing that's fine. But if she isn't willing the man generally gets her, anyway. Remember that, Sharon. Remember when you get hurt that it could have been the other way around." His smile flashed briefly. "And it can still be that way if you're reasonable, but I'm not going to my grave before I know what kind of woman you are."

She watched him go and she shuddered inwardly, then she

began to shake all over. Fooling around with Bert Robinson wasn't like fooling with an ordinary man. An ordinary man, even a man like Jimmy Slade, had a certain limit as to what he would do, but Robinson was playing a no-limit game. If Robinson saw a car that appealed to him, he bought it. If he saw a girl he liked, he took her, with or without her permission.

At five she closed the bar and carried some beer and a bottle up the street toward the apartment. Staying open would have been a useless gesture—she could have put on a nude show to attract customers, but that wouldn't have sold more than a few beers—and she didn't think that she should be out after dark. She had cut all hope from under Robinson and it was difficult to tell what he might do. It would be a simple matter for him to have a couple of men pick her up and cart her off. Nobody would miss her except Lucy, and Lucy couldn't go to the police. Lucy couldn't go anywhere.

It was a long walk up to the apartment and it was too hot to hurry. By the time she got home it would be too late to get in touch with the real estate man, but in the morning she'd call him and slash the price on the building and the business. With a little good fortune the real estate man would be able to move it in a hurry. Even if she took a beating on what she received— hadn't she taken one on the car?—it would be more than enough to get them out of town and make a fresh start. Lucy was as bad as she was, knowing only the bar business, but there were jobs in cocktail lounges. It would be a living.

A couple of boys whistled at her on a street corner and in that instant she hated her body. If she was constructed like some girls, flat in the chest and ugly, Robinson wouldn't have given her a second glance. But her body had been given to her and she excited men. After one look they were ready to go to bed. There was little doubt that Carl Evans felt the same way about her but he placed her in some special class, a class where she didn't belong, and he was too moral to surrender to his normal desires. Perhaps that was as it should be.

If you loved somebody, she reflected, maybe it was better to have the ring come first. And after the ceremony wasn't there usually a reception for a few friends and some drinks to help you get in the mood? And after the reception you started to drive to the hotel where you had a reservation, only you never got there because the first motel you came to had a vacancy and you couldn't wait. Maybe, she decided, that was how it was with a lot of couples. But it wasn't that way with her. She could wait to get to the hotel. In fact, she could wait forever. She had tried finding herself physically and she was lost.

It was hot in the apartment when she entered—opening the windows just added to the heat—but Lucy appeared to be comfortable enough. She was spread out on the davenport, stripped all the way down, the television on and some kid's crazy cartoon racing across the screen.

"The telephone rang," Lucy said, sitting up. "But, like you told me, I didn't answer it."

"And we won't answer it tonight."

Lucy frowned. "That's funny. You're here."

"I don't want anybody to know it. Robinson was bothering me again today and we didn't part on friendly terms. If he calls and finds me in he might try something, but if he thinks I'm out what can he do? Sit and bite his nails."

She took the beer and liquor out to the kitchen and piled everything on the table. Lucy followed her, offering to put the beer away, and Sharon tried not to be too aware of Lucy. She knew that would come later, the tidal wave of an unknown passion hammering at every nerve center, the sane part of her mind reaching out desperately to hang onto some measure of sanity. Beyond sanity lay the forbidden love of sheer lust.

Once in the bedroom she undressed, her naked body reflected in the mirror, the fullness of her breasts free of all restraint. Thoughtfully she pressed her hands against her tiny stomach, trying to find loose flesh of which there was none, and she wondered how a girl could get so big down there. Yet lots of them did. In school there had been a joke about a girl eating too many dried apples and then drinking water afterward. For a while she had almost believed it when she had seen one of these unfortunate creatures on the street, some of them so heavy that they could barely walk. But it wasn't dried apples that did it. Only some man was responsible.

They weren't hungry and they didn't eat anything that night except some potato chips. And they drank slowly and talked about things, spending a long time discussing the comparative opportunities to be found in New York as against those they might find in Florida. Twice the phone rang, going unanswered, and about eleven o'clock the fire whistle blasted through the night. Half an hour later the phone rang again, ringing the full ten times until the automatic switch cut it off.

"I don't know what makes me tired," Lucy said, stretching her wonderful body. "It isn't from doing anything." She yawned and lay down on the davenport. "I hope you don't mind if I spend the night here. It's too hot for two people to sleep together."

Sharon was disappointed, but she didn't try to discourage Lucy. With Lucy out of the bed all temptation was removed, and in the morning Sharon would be glad that Lucy hadn't been there. She had read of girls who had crossed the frontier of accepted love and they were the freaks of their own sex.

Strangely enough she slept rather well that night and in the morning she felt pretty good. After a brisk shower she felt even better for a few moments, but as she dressed she remembered that she was almost broke, and then she didn't feel good at all.

She glanced at the nude body on the davenport as she left the apartment, wished that she could touch her mouth to those lovely lips, and then hurried on. Whatever she had lost the night before would come to her another night.

When she reached Bently Street and turned the corner she stopped suddenly and let out a long sob.

She hadn't even thought about the fire the night before but now she knew where it had been.

The bar was a shambles of smoldering, charred wood and smoking brick.

She was cleaned out.

10

Jimmy tried to pay his rent with a twenty but the woman threw up her hands when she couldn't make change. "Anybody with a twenty doesn't belong on West Avenue," the woman said. Then she brightened. "But that don't stop you from paying in advance."

"I may not be here that long," he said, returning the bill to his pocket. "Why give out money for something that I may not use?"

A cat came from the rear of the house lugging a hunk of meat and the woman dove for the animal, screaming and cursing. Even after Jimmy reached the sidewalk he could still hear the woman screaming. If the cat had nine lives it would have only a couple left when she got done with it. The fact that the cat had the meat wouldn't stop the woman from eating it. She'd wash it off and she'd cook it, anyway.

Pop's store was closed, the interior as gloomy as the inside of a casket, and that meant Pop had made a connection with some female who, at the moment, was more important to him than trying to earn a living. And just then there was a living to be made. People were selling what they had and buying replacements cheap so that they could raise money to buy food and keep the electricity turned on. Pop didn't do business with everybody, but if the woman pleased him he made a deal. Part of the deal was transacted in the store and the rest upstairs. Already Pop was bragging up and down the avenue that he was going to create enough children to start a whole new town.

Toward the end of the avenue Jimmy met a young girl with the hip movement of a carnival dancer, and the girl gave him a big smile. He returned the smile without slowing his stride. He was too well-dressed for the avenue and the girls who were hunting for something better liked that. What could a girl look forward to on the avenue? A flock of kids and more poverty? And in later years a pregnant daughter before the daughter became seventeen? That was about it. There wasn't much more.

At the corner he swung right and headed uptown. His feet hurt, but he supposed it was from doing so much walking. Since he had gone to work for Robinson he had covered every bar in the city. He had looked for Lucy but he hadn't seen her and when he had asked questions he had been given a blank stare or a shrug of the shoulders. In addition to the bars, he visited the rooming houses where she had last stayed, but the woman there could tell him nothing. It began to appear that Lucy had either left town or she was well hidden. If she had left town he'd probably never see her again but if she was hiding out she couldn't stay that way forever. He still didn't know exactly why he was so interested in her or why Robinson was bugged on running her down. He just knew that Robinson would lead her into a life of hell if he got the chance, and he wasn't going to give the boss that chance.

Robinson was a beast when it came to women. More than one girl in these bad times would go a whole night without a customer, and Robinson would have Willie, the lame guy, beat her up for not producing. Of the several men who worked for Robinson, Willie was the most viciously sadistic. If there was anything he wouldn't do for a buck it hadn't been discovered as yet. One girl who had tried to fight back against him had received three broken ribs for her trouble. And Willie had bragged that while she lay moaning in pain he had assaulted her several times. When he had finished with her he had ripped out her phone so that she couldn't call a doctor. Now she was strapped up, unable to work, and Robinson wouldn't advance her a dime to help her along.

A girl came out of one of the stores and walked ahead of him, her thin dress displaying an even better movement than the girl he had met on the avenue. But he hardly noticed because just then he was thinking of something else and he didn't have any yen to meet some strange female.

In the short time he had been with Robinson, plus the rumors that he had heard, he had reached the conclusion that the rackets in Sanderstown were in a bad way. The people who played the numbers and the ponies were, in the majority, out of work, they couldn't gamble with money that they didn't have. About the only thing that had half a chance was sex, and that was suffering along with the rest of the operation. Only a couple of Robinson's girls had steady customers, real dolls with terrific shapes, and they catered to executives who were tired of their wives. Most of this was afternoon stuff, when the men were supposed to be on the golf course. At night these same girls pursued their own romantic interests and acted like ladies.

There was one girl he didn't want to think about, but he couldn't help remembering her. A small, neat brunette and a real knockout. He had met her in the quiet little north side bar and the draft beer had tasted warm and flat. He had gone there because Robinson had sent him to promise the girl money.

She had been cool to Jimmy at first, but after he had told her who his boss was, she had listened to him trying to sell her on the idea that five thousand dollars was all the money she'd need for a while.

"No," she had said when he had finished. "No, I won't take it, mister. Bert Robinson offered me that before and I told him I didn't want it. What I want is a husband and a name for my child. He brought me up here to work the bars, but in a couple of months he said he didn't want to share me with any other man, and after he moved me into that room there wasn't another man. Just him, almost every night of the week. And now I'm going to have his baby."

"He said you could have an abortion for five hundred, maybe less, and the rest of the five thousand would leave you comfortable."

"I know what he said. That's the easy way out, the wrong way, and I'm not having any. Either he does the right thing and marries me, or I'm going all the way up to the state's attorney general to tell my story. They say you can't get justice against Robinson on a thing like this, but I'll get it. I wasn't a prostitute when he met me and he turned me into one. That's against the law, isn't it? And there are other things I know, like the names of the men who used to stop up to the room to see him when he was there. It's up to him, mister. Pass the word to him that he could be choking on money, and I wouldn't go out of my way to slap his back."

The girl had left the bar then, walking out into the late afternoon sun, the glare of it revealing the trim lines of her legs through the thin dress. He had called Robinson, reporting that he'd made the pitch but that he'd missed the plate. Cursing, Robinson had slammed down the receiver, and the next day Jimmy had learned that the girl had been killed on the bridge. The police were still searching for anybody who might have been seen with her. This had upset Jimmy. He had been with the girl in the bar and he'd been seen; perhaps even their conversation had been overheard. His own picture in the paper for saving that boy came back to haunt him.

What if he had been recognized and the police picked him up? He had visited too many bars to recall all his movements that night and he didn't have the kind of background that would help him. Robinson had told him not to worry, that his big chance was coming, but he worried. The girl had been murdered and somebody had done it.

One thing about her he had remembered had been the gold locket around her neck, but the paper hadn't mentioned it as being on her when she'd been found. The locket had looked like the kind that might contain a picture, and perhaps the killer had removed it. Jimmy didn't know. He only knew that he didn't like the mess that he was walking through.

He glanced up at a clock on the corner and began to hurry. Robinson was acting nervous and irritable these days and didn't like it if a man was late. Of course the money wasn't coming in as it had been, and perhaps that had something to do with his grouch.

He walked into the Palace, passing the table where Robinson was talking, and swaggered up to the bar. He slammed down a half dollar and yelled for a beer. A man who worked the numbers, about five feet from him, jumped and glanced at him. Inside himself, Jimmy grinned. So far, he hadn't had much to do with the other men and he pushed the girls away if they came around, but when Robinson's toughest hangers-on looked at him, he thought he could see respect in their eyes.

A month before he would have been happy with his role, but now, somehow, he had changed. Maybe he had changed there on that bridge when he had risked his life for a helpless boy, or perhaps that last twenty he had stolen from Sharon had shown him with merciless clarity just what he had become. He couldn't be sure. He just knew that he had been pretty low-down, but now in some way he wanted to be better.

The man with the limp took his turn with Robinson and Jimmy was next. He slid down from his stool, taking his unfinished beer with him, and he took his time about getting over there, making Robinson wait. The wait was for the benefit of the men at the bar, and Robinson knew it.

"Have you learned anything about Lucy?" Robinson asked as Jimmy sat down.

"The only place I haven't looked is under rocks."

"Give it another whirl tonight."

"All right."

Robinson lit a fresh cigar. "That Sharon did herself up proper," he said.

"I wouldn't know about that."

"Her bar burned down last night."

"Well, I haven't heard the news or seen a paper." Jimmy finished his beer. "It could turn out to be a piece of luck for her. She must have had it insured, and nobody in their right mind would have bought it, anyway."

"Yeah, and that's just the trouble. Lots of people who are on the skids arrange for a convenient fire. The insurance companies and the fire department are wise to that dodge, so they looked around Sharon's bar to see how the fire had started. Do you know what they found? They found an empty oil can in back of the building and a pile of soaked rags that hadn't completely burned."

"She wouldn't be so stupid as to try arson," Jimmy said.

"Don't be too sure. Just listen to this—when the firemen found out that she owned the building they phoned her at her apartment. No answer. When they took her downtown to question her, she claimed that she hadn't been out of her apartment all evening, but she can't prove that. They didn't hold her, but they're still working on the case. She could be headed for bad trouble."

"Which gives you a chance to help her—to get yourself in solid."

Robinson muttered a curse. "I played that card, Jimmy. I waited for her outside city hall and I offered to alibi her, but she told me to go to hell. What do you do with a dame like that? I've tried everything I can think of, but she won't bend an inch." Robinson puffed furiously on the cigar. "I'm going to get her and get her good. When I get done with her she'll wish she'd never been born. A guy can be nuts over a girl, but at the same time he can only take so much."

The men at the bar began drifting outside as a couple of the girls came in. Willie, limping more than usual, went after one of the girls with his hands and she swore at him. He laughed and slapped her across the face. The girl swore again and tried to kick him where it would hurt. She missed, and Willie slapped her a second time, then went out.

"That gimpy guy's nuts," Jimmy said.

"And dangerous," Robinson nodded. He pushed aside his gin and orange. "But we should care. While there's nobody around to horn in, we'll have a conference."

Jimmy felt uneasy. Usually, whenever Robinson had a conference, the conferee got it in the neck.

"If it's about Lucy, I'm doing all I can. She isn't landing in any of the bars, and where else would you look?"

Robinson waved the thought aside. "It's not about Lucy. The point is that, in spite of everything you hear about this town being busted, there's still a bundle to be taken out. I figure on cutting down on the girls, using only the best at fancy prices, and moving into the dope and Shylock operations. There's just one thing that stands in my way, and the big deal I mentioned to you is the thing that's blocking me. You help me get moving, and I'll pay you five grand, and cut you in on some more heavy sugar."

"I'm listening," Jimmy said.

"You remember I told you about that bookie who was pulled in?"

"Sure. I hear they're still holding him."

"He'll come up for a hearing in a day or so. I told you he was greedy for money, and as fast as he got it he blows it on a dame with a shape." Robinson let out a heavy breath. "Anyway, he hasn't got money enough to pay his lawyer or get bail. So who has to stand the shot? I do, that's who."

"Anyhow, you're not letting him down."

"Hell, I couldn't do that if I wanted to. He was making book when I came to this town, and we got to be friendly. Frank helped me get started—Frank Globe's his name—and for a while I worked out of his candy store. I started with the girls first and I framed a judge with one of them.

"Now, Jimmy, you'll learn in a minute why I'm telling you all this . . . . So after that, I owned this judge. He couldn't move from under my thumb, unless he was willing to lose his rich wife. She's a semi-invalid and ought to die before he does. But while the judge is waiting for her to do it, he's had to steal securities from his wife. Frank fenced the securities for the judge who promptly lost his shirt on the horses.

"You can see where that leaves me. There's too much evidence against Frank for the judge to let him go, much as the judge would like to do it for his own sake, and Frank will have to be bound over for trial."

Robinson reached for a fresh cigar, but didn't light it. "If Frank had the guts he could ride it out, only he hasn't got the guts, except where his girl is concerned." Robinson put the cigar down and rubbed a hand across his forehead. "I've got at juries before—there's always somebody who needs money—and I could get at almost any jury they drew for Frank. You follow me, Jimmy?"

"Partly."

"All right. Now, the trouble is that Frank won't trust me and he's scared of a jury. He sees a trip behind bars that would take him away from his dame, and—no matter what kind of a tramp she is—he can't stand that. He's a sucker." Robinson picked up the cigar again and began nervously turning it in his fingers. "So much for that, Jimmy. The fact is Frank can't go on trial, because if he does he's going to pull into the open every dirty piece of laundry in town. The judge will be disqualified and probably pinched for taking his wife's securities—can you see what that means? The district attorney will move to have the case tried before a new judge in county court. And I just can't reach that far, Jimmy. Frank will expose the rackets, trying to save his own neck, and he'll pull me into the hole and suck me down with him." Robinson belched and leaned forward. "It's your job to see that Frank Globe never goes to trial, Jimmy. That's your five grand, and all that goes with it. I'll even furnish a gun that's clean, with its numbers filed off."

Jimmy's mouth was dry. "Why not somebody else? Why not Willie?"

"Because the man who takes over for me after I quit this town is the man who does it. None of those guys are capable of holding the organization together. And you've got nothing to worry about. Even if the cops get close to you afterward, I'll alibi you. I can get a couple of girls and say we were making fun together."

Jimmy wished that he had a beer, anything to kill his thirst, but he didn't get up to get one. He didn't seem able to move at all.

"What if this bookie starts talking at the pre-trial hearing?" he wanted to know.

"He won't. He wants to sell his candy store. Busted as he is, he needs the dough to get squared away with his girl. He's counting on acquittal or at most a minimum sentence at his trial, and then having a happy life afterward. But he knows that if he talks too soon he'll never live to make it. So he'll pretend to go along with me, getting out on bail and having a chance to straighten up his affairs. That gives me the one break I need to cool him. He can do his talking in hell."

Jimmy locked his fingers together and snapped his knuckles. What Robinson said had shaken him. "I don't think I'm your man," Jimmy said, frowning.

"I thought you'd say that," Robinson nodded slowly, staring at him, "but, kid, I'm not buying it. You will do the job and you'll do it neat. Mess it up or refuse me and I'll have you in court with that girl. She took money to keep her mouth shut, but she'd be only too happy to sting you good. She might even say you made it with her before the other guy showed up. Who's to prove different? It's too late for a doc to tell whether you did or you didn't."

Jimmy managed to get up from the table and walk to the bar for a beer. Actually he didn't any longer want the beer, but it gave him time to think. One of the girls at the bar said something to him, but he made no reply. At that moment girls were the furthest thing from his mind—except for that one slut there at that house who had lied and thrown the rope around his neck! Now Robinson was pulling the noose so tight he couldn't breathe. He tried to swallow the beer and couldn't get it down the first time. Leaving the glass on the bar he returned to the table. The beer seemed to stick in his throat.

"Where's the gun?" he asked, and remained standing.

"I'll give it to you just before you get him. If the cops picked you up with it, you wouldn't do me any good."

"All right. Yeah, sure. That's smart."

He walked to the door, went outside. The sun was hot, but he didn't notice it. During the months that he had tried to get in with Robinson, the idea of killing anybody never crossed his mind. He had been after the easy money, the fancy clothes and the big car that the money would buy, but somewhere along the way, suddenly and without warning, he had lost the desire. Then had come the boy in the river, the job that had followed, the feeling of being clean and honest, and soon afterward the burn that girl had handed him that had cost him his job.

There was a bar up ahead and he went into it, sitting down on one of the stools and brooding over his beer. The nights that he had wandered through town looking for Lucy he had told himself that he was staying in Sanderstown only because of her, but he knew that this wasn't the whole truth. Robinson had him where he couldn't move, couldn't think for himself. Robinson called the tricks and he did them. Now Robinson wanted him to do murder and he knew instinctively that he couldn't do it. He had to pretend to be willing, buying time, and then find a way out. But what way? How could he find it?

After two beers he left the bar and walked to Park Place. Calling Sharon on the phone would have been easier, but he was afraid she wouldn't believe what he had to tell her unless he talked to her in person. Robinson wasn't fooling about Sharon, and her only hope of safety, possibly of her life, was to get away and stay away. Just the thought of her leaving, of possibly never seeing her again, left an empty ache inside him. Maybe he had treated her like a tramp in his room, using the ripeness of her body for his own satisfaction and not once concerned about her, but no man could share his bed with such a lovely girl and forget her overnight.

She might be in trouble about the fire, and he supposed that her leaving town would indicate her guilt to the authorities, but there was no time to think about that. Once Robinson got his hands on her he would exact a horrible price, the price of unwilling flesh being possessed until he was finished with her. The scars would be there for the rest of her life, and she didn't deserve that. No girl deserved that. Maybe he had left his mark upon her because of their cheap affair, but she had been willing, sometimes drunk, and one look at her body had driven him out of his mind with need. Often he had said horrible, rotten things to her, driving the shame deep, but he realized now that he had only been trying to defend his own animal acts of passion. There was no excuse. Love between two people, either expressed physically or otherwise, should be supported on a foundation of mutual respect. To take less was to be cheated.

When he reached the apartment, he rang the bell several times and waited for the sound of the buzzer releasing the front door, but nothing happened. Worried, he finally gave up and looked for a bar where he could kill time. He found one eventually, a real hole in the wall for such a nice neighborhood, that smelled of smoke and sweat.

He knew that he should be out looking for Lucy, but it was almost as though she had never existed and he didn't know where to look. And he wondered if perhaps his interest in her hadn't been a little foolish. What did he expect from her when and if he found her—the same thing that she had given or sold to other men? Still, if his own search had happened to coincide with the job Robinson had given him, he couldn't help that. Of course, if he found her they could run for it together, forgetting the past and the people who might hunt them. And with Lucy there would be sex, the wild and yet beautiful sex of nature. But sex alone, Jimmy reflected, wasn't enough to build a lasting relationship. Sex was only one important part of the puzzle of life; a puzzle he was trying to put together, but one which left him constantly confused.

It was almost dark when he left the bar and he was hungry, but he didn't stop to eat. The only one who could help him was that girl who had lied. He had to talk to her. If she was at all human, she would hear him out. Possibly she would be reasonable. He hadn't tried anything with her, and nobody knew it better than the girl herself. All he would ask of her was the decency and fairness to take the noose from around his neck.

No lights shone from the house when he arrived, and he waited in the shadow of a giant tree.

At midnight, he was still waiting.

And at dawn, he left to walk down to West Avenue.

And then he became violently sick at his stomach, leaning against a street lamp until he gained the strength to drag himself to his room . . . .

11

Lucy twisted on the bed, feeling the anxious arms around her, desperately reaching out with her own arms to bring Sharon's wonderful body closer. A sob tore at her throat as the morning sun crept through the window and washed over them, the heat of the sun lost in the heat of her own naked flesh.

"Oh, no!" she whispered thickly but she didn't mean it, not then, not even as she remembered the other girl or the promises that she had made to herself, promises that had said she would never do such a thing again. "Please," she heard herself begging—and this she meant. "Please, honey!"

With a shuddering thrill she looked into bright, seeking eyes, saw the lovely blonde hair, the lips that were so perfect and moist. Her fingers felt the smooth skin and a terrible pounding started in her head.

"It's all right," Sharon murmured. "I guess it has to be."

And then, with only the silent walls their witness, they belonged to each other as only two girls seeking forbidden love can belong. Gone from that room were the conventions of society, a society which would have frowned and condemned them. Into the room came the strange passions of the ages, passions inflamed by a need to love and be loved, wild passions which rushed beyond the limits of the human mind. But when the last of the passion was ended, Lucy felt Sharon move away from her, heard the long intake of breath that she thought would never reach bottom. For a second the bed shook violently and then the girl beside her lay still.

"It's going to be a nice day," Sharon said weakly. There was no point to the remark at all.

"Yes, I think it will." That statement was just about as pointless.

Sharon breathed deeply. "I—oh, why try to avoid it? It was my fault. You were asleep, and I started the whole thing. I—"

"It's okay," Lucy said, knowing that such a relationship was almost never all right. "It's okay," she insisted.

"I'm—ashamed."

"I understand, Sharon. I understand more than you think."

"That's kind of you, but I guess I've always wanted to know what—it was like."

"You aren't alone. Many girls do. And then often it stops there, as it should."

"Have you ever wanted to know?"

"Yes. I—but we don't like to talk about it."

Sharon sighed deeply. "I think we should."

"That's up to you."

"You must hate me, Lucy. I feel as though I hate myself. When I wanted to do what I did, it seemed so right, so necessary, and then suddenly it was all wrong, horribly wrong, worse than any one thing I've ever done. You must hate me for being a fool."

"No, I don't hate you. We made a mistake—yes, an honest mistake—but everybody makes one once in a while. I've made my share, and I guess most of mine have been worse than yours. You didn't know what I was like until you tried, and you couldn't have known what you yourself were like, either. Maybe you were looking for something that you never found, and I can understand that. Or maybe some of it was the worry, because people aren't themselves when they're worried. First you had it over business conditions, and now it's the fire, with some of those men thinking that you set it. They don't think you were here that night, and you were decent enough not to use my name."

"Well, you aren't going to be arrested for something that you didn't do," Sharon said. "And you can count on me for that. It was my money anyhow, and I believe all you told me about the man with the limp. But the police wouldn't, not now. You've waited too long, and they'd think you were lying."

A few minutes later they got up and dressed, which they hadn't done the day before. Lucy still had on the dress she had worn when she had left the rooming house. She had tried on several that belonged to Sharon, but Sharon's dresses had been too full in the bust for Lucy, not to mention the difference at the hips. But she wasn't going to get upset about it, Lucy decided. This dress wasn't too bad, and anyhow she didn't think she was going anywhere right away.

Sharon emptied the contents of her pocketbook on the dresser top and counted her money.

"Enough for a bottle and some beer," she said. "And, thank God, enough for the electric bill. I've got to pay that; there was a Late Notice on it, and this is the last day. I'll go down and pay it."

"But you ought not to go out." Lucy yawned and stretched. "You know you're afraid of Robinson, and you can't tell what he might take it in his head to do. That's why we haven't been answering the phone or the door. Can't you mail a check for the bill, and not leave the building?"

Sharon checked her stocking seams and smoothed her skirt. "It can't be helped," she said. "There isn't any money in the bank, and anyhow they won't wait. Besides, I ought to be safe enough in daylight. But at night I couldn't walk to the end of the block without dying every step of the way."

There was nothing for breakfast but instant coffee and they drank some. They didn't discuss what had taken place in the bedroom. As far as Lucy was concerned there was nothing to discuss. They had ventured into the dark, inviting jungle where so many other girls had lost themselves, but they had been wise enough to turn back while there was still time. Lucy doubted that they had to be alarmed about being sexually drawn to each other again. A perverted relationship had tried to exist in the bedroom, only to die swiftly. But from its death had sprung a new, fresh life and an outlook that was clean.

"Give me an hour," Sharon said as she got up from the table. "But no longer than that. If I'm not back by then, you get out of here real fast."

Lucy felt weak. "But where would I go?"

"Don't play dumb. You've done a lot of talking about the fellow who lives along the river. He sounds regular, you like him, and going there, even if it is only a shack, is better than sitting around in some jail. And I've got an idea that Robinson is after you as much as the police. Add it all together, and it spells a lousy mess."

Lucy walked to the hall with Sharon, then she double-locked the door and was alone. Of course, the door downstairs was also locked, but even at that she didn't feel safe. If the prize were worthwhile, all the locks in the world wouldn't stop a man.

She shrugged and walked around the apartment. There was nothing to drink, but she didn't care about that. She couldn't hide in these rooms for the rest of her life, and she couldn't live without money. She might be able to hitch out of the area easily enough, but she was the only one who could help Sharon in that business about the fire, and she wouldn't quit on the girl who had believed her story about the robbery and taken her in.

The hour slid by and she began to get nervous. She stood in the middle of the living room, frozen, waiting for the footsteps that never came. Something, she told herself, had gone wrong. Sharon had been mistaken about the daylight protecting her. A man like Robinson wouldn't let daylight scare him from whatever he wanted to do.

Ten minutes after the hour, Lucy left the building and hurried down the street, anxious to reach that awful shack. And the safety it offered her. She sighed as she finally crossed the bridge and began walking along the road. Only now did she wonder what Luke Shark might say when she returned. He had offered her his bunk, promised to sleep outside, but could she believe that? He was a man, wasn't he? And being a man, wasn't there just one thing that he wanted from a girl? Nice girls didn't break into any such shack, and any man with half a brain knew it. She was only glad that she hadn't been too free with herself. Back in the apartment she had talked about him a great deal, not as she had talked about the other men but with some degree of respect, and she guessed she liked him. She didn't know why she should. She hardly knew Luke and he lived little better than some savage in a cave. Still he worked, and he seemed to make a living. That was more than could be said for some men.

He was outside the shack when she got there, and although he smiled when he saw her he didn't act surprised.

"There's beer inside if you want some," he said. "A customer just left it, and it's cold. He always brings me beer when he picks up bait."

"No," she said slowly. "Thanks, but I don't care for any." She watched him as he punched holes in the top of empty coffee cans with an ice pick. "Maybe I could do something. I'm not lazy, but you'd have to show me."

"Sure. After lunch."

They had a lunch of cold beans, bread and warm milk and then she followed him down to the river. He tried to tell her why he was digging in the sand for lamper eels and how they were used to catch fish, but she didn't understand much of it.

"Golly," she exclaimed as she grabbed the first one and lost the thing. "They're like wet snakes. They slip right out of your hand."

He laughed and dug into the sand again. "You'll get used to it," he promised her.

She did, and they worked all afternoon. Her back ached, but she didn't say anything. By the time they finished they had a half-full bucket of the creatures and they were both covered with mud and sand.

"I'd clean up now, but there's no sense to it," he said. "I've got to get some frogs after dark for a customer in town. I'll take my swim when I'm done. But don't let that stop you from hitting the water. While I put the tampers away you can have the river to yourself." He picked up the bucket and stuck the shovel point down in the sand. "I won't bother you any, and I won't look."

Somehow she believed him. After he disappeared into the woods, she began to strip out of her clothes.

The funny part was that she wouldn't have minded if he had looked. There was something quiet and strong about him that went deep down inside of her; a strange and wonderful something that held no hint of shame attached to it.

Minutes later she was in the water.

And she felt good ...

Real good.

12

Sharon sat rigid, staring straight ahead at the trees, refusing to look at the lame, sharp-faced man in the car beside her. For hours they had been parked on a lonely road in the mountains and she had tried not to listen to his horrible curses and filthy words. But he hadn't molested her, and for that she was grateful. He still held the gun he'd used to force her into the car at the corner below the apartment. And unless a girl wanted to die, it was pretty hard to fight against a gun.

"I wish I was Robinson," he said for about the tenth time. "With the body you've got, you could kill a man and make it a pleasure to die."

She said nothing. On the way out of town, the man, who had told her that his name was Willie, had stopped at a little stand for cigarettes, selecting a place where he could watch her, and she had noticed that he walked with a limp. Lucy had said that the man who had held her up in the bar had had a limp, but she couldn't see why a man who worked for Robinson would have done such a thing. Anyway, there were a lot of men who were lame.

"Too bad Robinson was so busy this afternoon," Willie said. "He'd have made you happy by this time."

"Shut up, won't you?" She was losing control and she rocked back and forth, clenching her fists together. "Can't you shut your mouth?"

"Maybe I like to talk."

"Well, I hate it."

She let out a little cry as he reached over and slapped her across the mouth. Her lips were already swollen; it was the third time he had slapped her.

"Look," he said. "Look, baby, I told you, didn't I? After tonight I'm done here and I'm getting out. Robinson sent me to hunt for you, but he doesn't know that I made the score. I'll tell him that I pulled a blank, and when I'm done with what I have to do, we'll shag away from this town together. You won't be Robinson's woman, and I'll treat you square. I know what I have to do, and you'll ride with me. That way, you'll be in on it with me, and that will lock you in tight. You can't leave me then, and that's how it should be. If I take you to Robinson, he'll give you hell on earth. You'll get the royal treatment until you start carrying his kid. That will wind it up. There'll be another body on the bridge, but you won't read about it. You won't read nothing, 'cause you won't be breathing. Don't kid yourself on that."

"Shut up," she said again. "I wouldn't walk across the street with you if you didn't have that gun."

He slapped her once more, harder, snapping her head violently. "You're nobody!" he sneered, blowing cigarette smoke in her face. "You were giving out to that Jimmy plenty, and he's just a crumb. If he'd thought anything of you he'd have gotten you out of town at any price."

She said nothing and rubbed the side of her face, remembering, thinking, and wondering. That morning in the apartment she had, very briefly, known a real physical completion, losing all reason for a moment. But now she also knew that such a situation would never entangle her again and she regarded herself as fortunate that she had learned her lesson so quickly. Learning the lesson had brought back the memory of Jimmy—vivid and sharp—a memory that she believed to be completely honest.

It was true that she had given him her body, not to mention money, but it was equally true that she hadn't given her heart. Drunk and frequently helpless, she had belonged to him, making love cheap, a thing to be walked upon, her liquor-fogged mind only partially aware of their relationship, her deadened emotions groping for an experience she had failed to achieve. Now, perhaps understanding herself better than she ever had before, she couldn't place all of the blame upon Jimmy. She had often resented his tough and cynical attitude, but she didn't think that had been the real Jimmy, any more than the handsome, strong young man who now worked for Robinson was the real Jimmy. The real Jimmy was the man who had gone off that bridge, risking his life to save a boy.

There was something out of line about the attempted rape also, something that didn't belong there. Jimmy wouldn't ever have to resort to rape to get what he wanted, and he wouldn't have risked his future by such a stupid act. It didn't make sense, not a bit of it. Perhaps, she decided, Jimmy was caught in the jaws of a trap, just as she was caught. Most likely he hadn't helped her because he couldn't help himself. She thought it odd that she should have this new confidence in Jimmy, which almost amounted to love; to be convinced that it would be good for them if they could just have another chance. Probably it was all a happy dream, anyway, a silent hope that would never come true. Right now, the hard fact was that she was in this car with Willie, and Jimmy worked for Robinson. All you could get out of a combination like that was trouble, big trouble.

"Maybe I started you thinking about that Jimmy," Willie said. "But don't waste your time, kid. After tonight he won't be worth much to any dame."

She looked at Willie then, and his eyes, gray as death and alive with a wildness she had never seen before in anyone's eyes, frightened her.

"What do you mean by that?"

He laughed and flipped the cigarette outside. "None of your business," he said. "But he's as good as long past history right now." Willie made a quick grab for her swelling dress front, but she managed to avoid him. He cursed and lunged for her, clutching her this time, and she hurt where his fingers sank into the creamy softness of her breast. "Come on, baby." His voice was thick, unsteady. "I know what you've got, and you know what I want."

She hadn't forgotten that he had the gun, and he might use it if she pressed him enough, but she fought him anyway. A couple of her fingernails broke as she raked his face, drawing blood. The interior of the car became a sewer of four-letter words, but they stopped suddenly when she sank her teeth deep into his arm. His other hand had been at her knee, inches above the hem of her dress, but now he released it and pounded the top of her head with his fist. Still she didn't let go until she felt the blood in her mouth.

"To hell with you!" he said as he started the car. "If I've got to work that hard for something, I don't want it. Let Robinson try taming you. I'll get me a jane who never heard the word no and wouldn't know what it meant if she did."

They were about five miles from town. It was a wild ride down the mountain, but Willie kept on the road. A couple of times she glanced at his arm. He had an ugly wound where she had bitten him and dark blood was caked on his skin all the way down to the wrist.

"Where are you taking me?" she asked.

"What's it to you?" he said, the tires squealing as he made

a sharp curve. Then he grinned. "Robinson's got a pad on the other side of town, and he's got a flunkie who can watch you." Willie laughed. "The flunkie always makes the girls undress, but he don't lay a hand on them. There's something wrong with the guy, and he only wants to look. That's how he gets his kicks. What kind of crazy business is that?"

As they neared the edge of town her mind began to race. She had to get away from Willie, not only because of herself, but because of Jimmy. Willie had hinted that something terrible was going to happen to Jimmy, and he had to be warned. Not only that, but something just as bad or even worse would happen to her if she was delivered to Robinson. She could become Robinson's woman, locked up and alone. And any tomorrow she might have planned for herself would be destroyed.

Willie kept to the main drag when they entered town. She closed her eyes briefly, trying to picture the corner of First and Front Streets. At this hour the intersection would be filled with cars, the traffic snarled up as the drivers tried to get home in a hurry, and the cop there going half insane from the blasting horns. If Willie took that route he'd have to slow down, probably stop, and she would have one desperate chance to scream for the traffic cop, or jump out and run.

"Damn!" he exclaimed as he approached the corner. "Damn the stupid fools in this stinking town!"

She smiled. He apparently thought of turning into a side street to avoid the congestion up ahead, but yellow saw-horses, stretched before a deep trench, blocked the passage; the street was closed.

The air left her lungs as he slowed and started to turn, but the drivers behind him got on their horns. He had no choice but to go forward, straight into the traffic jam at the intersection. Caught in the slow-moving parade of cars and tracks, they inched along to the accompaniment of Willie's constant curses. Suddenly she felt the sharp bump from the car behind; there was the crash of breaking glass amid an uproar of shouts and blaring din of horns. Willie, his face livid with rage, turned to direct his shouted filth at the hapless driver of the rear car, and in that instant Sharon saw her chance. Swiftly yanking open the door, she threw herself out just as Willie, seeing a clear space before him, started the car with a jerk.

Almost before she landed, she heard Willie curse at her, then she was in the crowded pavement with more confused shouts and pounding din of horns, aware of the shrilling of the traffic cop's whistle ahead.

Toward that piercing sound she turned blindly, but slipped on spilled oil. Her feet flew from under her and she went down hard on her buttocks, rolling, almost hitting the cop.

Dazed and unassisted, she stumbled to her feet and pushed the hair out of her eyes. Already people were running toward her from the stalled cars and the sidewalks. She was braised, but she felt safe. Willie would think that she had reported him to the cop, and he'd be on the run.

"He shove you out of the car?" the policeman wanted to know.

"No, I did it on my own. It's my husband," she lied. "I got fed up with his yelling."

She moved off, pushing through the crowd, and nobody stopped her. It would have been simple for her to have told the truth to the policeman, but that would have meant a string of questions, and probably a visit to city hall. She didn't have time for that. If she was going to warn Jimmy, she couldn't waste a minute.

Once out of sight of the intersection she started to run. Some men stood in a doorway watching her and she knew that the one broken bra strap left her all loose and alive in front. She ran all the harder, and she supposed they got a cheap thrill.

It was a long distance down to West Avenue and she had to slow to a walk as she turned the last corner. Her legs felt like heavy sticks of wood, and her lungs were seared with the fire of her rapid breathing.

She didn't know the old man who had the used furniture place on the street but she had heard Jimmy speak of him. Just as she neared the store a policeman brought the old man outside.

"I didn't know she wasn't of age," the old man protested. "She looked eighteen, nineteen. I didn't ask."

"That's your tough luck, Pop. I only know what the complaint said. Her folks didn't like it. You've got to get wise that some people along the avenue are still decent."

Sharon passed them and walked on. She guessed the old man had gone too far this time, but he wasn't alone in that.

Lots of people went too far, wanting too much, seeking the impossible—and dying with their hands empty.

She climbed the front steps of the rooming house that she vaguely remembered having staggered up so many times, Jimmy's arm around her for support, his hand pressing against her where she was full and round. She wondered as she closed the door behind her how she could have been so rotten and cheap and wrong, making the whole thing dirty for both of them. Even the big women's magazines that she'd read at the apartment said that a girl couldn't live fully with a man if there was the slightest feeling of guilt or shame overshadowing the relationship. They said you had to want each other honestly, terribly and beautifully, all the way and forever. Only then could a girl perform the normal function of her sex. It meant that you gave yourself to a man, without reservations, without the aid of cheap booze that turned you into nothing but a living corpse. A few drinks frequently inflamed passion, but too many drinks killed it. That's what the article had said. She knew, as she climbed the stairs, that she would never make the same mistake again.

The door of Jimmy's room was closed, and she prayed a little as she pushed it open and went inside.

But Jimmy wasn't there.

The room was empty.

She threw herself upon the bed and began to sob.

She had no way of knowing how long she slept but as she came out of it she was startlingly aware of a hungry mouth over her lips, a mouth smelling of liquor, and she felt the anxious searching hands upon her body.

"You wise slut," Robinson snarled at her. "I figured you'd come here. Maybe you got away before, but you won't do it again." He kissed her, then slapped her because she wouldn't respond. "This is where you get yourself a man, baby. This is where you get what you should have gotten a long while ago."

"It'll be rape," she told him, trying to cover herself where he had exposed her.

"I don't give a damn what it is," he said, knocking her hand aside. "And down here you can scream all you want and nobody will bother. They'll just laugh and say that some other dame is getting her wagon fixed."

She knew that he spoke the truth, and she felt suddenly frightened. There was nobody to help her, nobody at ail. She was alone, and she had to fight him alone.

He howled with pain when she bit him on the arm, and she kept on, twisting her head back and forth so that it hurt him more, hanging on as he straightened up, following him, her ears ringing from his savage curses.

But suddenly she knew that she wasn't winning, that he was too much for her. His free hand rained blows upon her head and body, driving her down to her knees, forcing her to let go. Then with a snarl, he drew back his foot and drove his shoe into her stomach. The floor rushed up to meet her.

There was no place for her to go except under the bed and, gasping for breath, she made a lunge for at least temporary safety. But he caught one of her feet, holding her fast. Frantically she clawed at the bare floor beneath the bed, trying to dig her fingernails into the wood. Then her right hand came into contact with something round and hard and heavy. She blinked, said a little prayer, and clutched the object firmly.

As he dragged her out, the bottom of her dress slid all the way up to her stomach, but clutched in her fist was the piece of iron pipe. He was getting a good look at her, but before she was done with him he'd have a better look at something else.

"Strip," he yelled as he let her go and backed against the door. "Strip, or I'll kick your stomach all the way through your spine."

She stood in the middle of the room, her breasts heaving, the piece of iron heavy in her hand.

"You come near me, and I'll lay your head open with this," she promised him.

He saw the weapon in her hand and some of the desire left his face. "You could kill a man with that," he said.

"I'll kill you before I'll let you touch me."

He wasn't dumb. He reached for the door knob.

"I'll get you yet," he said. "And when I do, you'll be almighty glad to die!"

He went out and slammed the door.

For a second she remained standing there, feeling funny.

Then slowly she slumped to the floor in a dead faint.

13

Frank Globe's candy store wasn't far from the bridge, and Jimmy walked over to the river first. For the last hour, since Robinson had given him the gun, it had felt heavy in his pocket and he was glad when he dropped it into the darkness and heard it hit the water with a splash. There wasn't any sense in carrying the gun, because he wasn't going to use it. It was about the only thing that he knew for certain. Everything else was up in the air.

He turned from the bridge and moved under a street light to check his watch. Robinson had said that job was to be done at ten o'clock, because that timing would give him a chance to work up an alibi if one was needed. Now there was less than fifteen minutes left; fifteen minutes before he was supposed to kill a man.

But why any particular time to take care of Frank Globe? An alibi was a simple thing to supply for a man like Robinson. And why hadn't the boss mentioned that five thousand dollars again? Plus why had he been so short with him that afternoon, reminding him only of the girl and what she could do if he failed to get rid of Globe? It was like a threat, as if he was being forced into killing the bookie, and there wouldn't be anything for him after that.

All these things had been bothering Jimmy Slade, and he couldn't shake his worry. He smelled a bad piece of meat, but he couldn't find where it was.

Walking rapidly he hurried toward the candy store. He didn't know Frank Globe, but if the guy had any sense at all—woman or no woman—he'd be glad to leave town and sit it out until things cooled off. Even if he jumped bail, he would be far better off doing that than taking the big sleep in the cemetery. And he could still break this whole rotten business open from a safe distance, and lie low out of town until Robinson had been destroyed.

The candy store wasn't much—one of those small neighborhood joints that carried everything from penny candy to comics, but the building seemed in good repair and there was an apartment over it.

The only man in the store was a short, thin man of about fifty who looked as if he might have been born with that tired look on his face. He certainly didn't appear like the kind of guy a girl would go nuts about, but then, usually, you couldn't tell which way a girl was going to jump, could you?

"Good music," the man behind the counter said and jerked his head toward a portable radio sitting on a shelf. "Plenty of my customers bitch about the local radio station, but give me those old numbers and the sweet, smooth music every time."

Jimmy leaned against the counter. He didn't know just how he was going to handle this, but he had to be honest with the man. If he could only get the bookie to leave town, then he could tell Robinson that he'd done the job, sinking the body in the river, and that would give him a little extra time to work himself free. All he needed to do was to get that girl over to his side, if she could be sold on it, and he'd be clean.

"Are you Frank Globe?"

The man's serious eyes studied Jimmy's face. "Yeah, I'm Frank all right, but I'm not taking any bets. Not any more. I've got enough trouble already."

"Not as much as you're going to have," Jimmy said.

Frank scratched his chin. "Say, fellow, who are you?"

"Just a guy who's trying to steer you right. You stay in this town, and they'll chill you off with a bullet in your guts."

"Crap," the bookie said. "You fixing to give me a nightmare or something? Quit trying to sound like some of them punk comics."

Jimmy went after Frank then, giving it to him straight and leaving nothing out. Although the older man's earlier doubt changed to an obvious fear, he couldn't be swayed. Frank admitted, wiping the sweat from his forehead, that he was taking a big risk by staying in town but he explained that money was a big problem, and so was the girl. He was selling the business as soon as he could, and he was trying to get the girl—her name was Mae—to dispose of the house that he had bought for her.

"But she ain't about to do it," he added. "Not unless she gets all the dough for herself and I figure on needing some of it."

"Then forget about her. A girl like that isn't worth the time of day." The announcer on the radio was saying something about a girl who had found a man along the river with a broken leg, some girl who was now in a big jam, but Jimmy didn't listen. "You'd better bust out of here," he said to Frank. "I don't want to know where you go, and I won't let you down. Stay with the girl for the night and I'll go after the five thousand from Robinson for getting out of the way. You can have the money. Take the girl with you if you can't get along without her. Any way you do it, five thousand ought to hold you over."

The plan might have worked. Or it could have flopped, sucking them into a hole, but Jimmy never had the opportunity to find out. He heard the door open, saw the look of concern jump into the bookie's eyes, and he jerked his head around.

"Yeah," Willie said, sneering. "Yeah, chums. You guys so much in love you'd like to hold hands?" He laughed, stepping forward, and spit close to Jimmy's feet. "I told Robinson that you were a two-bit punk, and you didn't have the guts of a dead fly, but he was too busy, and wouldn't pay me no mind."

It was quiet in the store—the radio station went off at ten—and the gun in Willie's hand was very steady.

"I should have my head examined," Frank Globe moaned. "You led me on, fellow, you and your speeches, and all this time this Willie was getting ready to tag me."

Jimmy shook his head but he didn't say anything. He figured that he should be frightened, but for some reason he wasn't. He wasn't dead yet, nobody was dead, and it was hardly more than ten or twelve feet to where Willie stood. The difficulty was in getting there without catching a bullet first.

"I tailed you," Willie said to Jimmy. "Robinson thought you'd come through, but I didn't. When I heard the gun hit the water after you threw it from the bridge, I knew I was right. Guts you don't have and heaving the gun away makes it bad. Robinson set the time for ten so that you could cool off this creep behind the counter, and then I could get you right on top of it. With two guns it could be made to look like a double killing, and it would be nice for everybody. But now, with just one gun, it bugs the works. Instead of the five grand I was to get—the five Robinson promised you—it's going to cost him ten. When I take a risk, I collect by the yard."

Jimmy saw it then—Robinson had meant to have him killed, but he didn't understand it. He asked Willie, and the killer sneered again.

"I guess it don't do no harm to tell you before you get blasted," Willie said. He toyed with the gun, and winked at

Frank Globe. "Anyway, I've got the time to blow away, Frankie boy. That dame of yours sold the house without you knowing it, but she won't be packed before midnight so's we can blow town. If I went up there now she'd never get packed. Know what we'd be doing, Frankie boy?"

"I don't believe it," Frank said softly.

"What the hell do I care what you believe? Days when you used to be working, I was hitting homers with the bases full." Willie kicked the magazine rack, and a couple of magazines fell to the floor. "But she could have stayed put if I'd made it with another broad this afternoon." Willie looked at Jimmy. "Your dame—Sharon. She's a heller, ain't she? Look at my face and arm."

Inside Jimmy, part of him threatened to die. "What did you do with her?"

"Nothing. She jumped out of the car and beat it. Let Robinson find her if he wants. This town's blowing apart and I'm hauling my freight. I'll take the girl who's willing."

"I still don't know what this is about," Jimmy said. "Only that Sharon got away from you. And she made your face real pretty. On you, it couldn't look better."

"She's a slut," Willie declared. "And she's partly to blame for the fix you're in. When you started hanging around Robinson, he laughed it off until he wanted your girl. I never saw a guy so whacky over a dame as he was over her, and he's worse now than he was before. He still thinks there's something between the two of you, no matter what he's been told, and the way he figures is that she can't be in love with a corpse. But that won't necessarily send this twist into his arms. Not by a crock-full, it won't. The night I stuck up the bar, Robinson hoped she'd be driven to him because she lost her cash, but he guessed wrong. I made a mistake then, one of the few I've made—I didn't kill the girl in the bar who could identify me. Robinson wanted her found, and he wanted her out of the way. Looking for her was something for you to do while he was setting you up for the big pitch tonight.

"When the cops didn't go for that girl's accident on the bridge, and they turned it into a murder rap, Robinson used that, too. You were with her that day, and I put the iron pipe I used on her skull under the bed in your room. Her blood and hair is on it, and they don't need more than that. Anyway it works is good for me here. They'll think you killed the girl and then, guilty of also killing bookie, turned the gun on yourself. Neat?"

Jimmy swung around a little more and wet his lips. His Tongue was dry, thick. "Robinson had you burn the bar down," he said. "That was another way of trying to drive Sharon to the wall, wasn't it?"

"Sure, and it sounded logical. He tried calling her apartment and she didn't answer. Even better, she didn't answer when the firemen phoned. And she couldn't account for her time. It looked like she had to run to Robinson then to save her from an arson rap, but she was willing to take what was coming to her. That drove him half crazy. But he isn't near as crazy as he'll be after he tries to nail her. He'll have to club her stupid brains out before he gets what he wants from her. With all the dames he could have, he's jerky enough to want a sassy one for a steady diet. With the rackets shot to nothing, he should be worrying about his business so much that he wouldn't have time to go to bed with a movie star."

"I catch the rest of it now," Jimmy said, the missing section of the picture suddenly coming to him. "I had that job at the plumbing shop and I'd changed my mind about joining Robinson, but he wouldn't go along with that. The guy I worked with, that Benny, needed money. On top of that, he didn't like me. He could have been bought cheap, and the girl could have called in, asking for service and to have Benny take care of her. There was nothing wrong with the sink or hot water heater. She went nude in the bedroom and put on her rape act. I was Robinson's boy after that."

"You're guessing real good," Willie said. "That Benny was glad to get a hundred bucks and the girl did it for nothing." Willie leered at Frank Globe. "Your girl, Frankie boy. Your girl, and believe me, she did plenty of things for free. Even if she'd been examined by a doctor that morning he'd have found that she'd been with a man. I made sure of that."

"You rotten swine," Frank yelled. "I'll—"

And then Frank was scrambling behind the counter like a crab, upsetting a pile of candy and spilling the open boxes and chocolates over the floor. A strange, wild expression of a man dealing death swept across Willie's face as he lunged forward, cursing furiously, his attention momentarily directed away from Jimmy. But a moment was all Jimmy needed.

The unleashed power of his muscles drove his body straight into Willie, hurling Willie aside and sending them both crashing to the floor. They struggled for possession of the gun, and although Willie was wiry and strong, he lacked Jimmy's all-important motive, a desperate strength, urgency that increased his physical strength far beyond normal. Groping, he found Willie's right arm and he went to work on it, forgetting all else, listening for the gun to clatter to the floor. Willie screamed under the pressure, but he wouldn't release his grip on the gun. He realized now that it meant his life. Then there came a sharp crack, and the clatter of the weapon to the floor.

Jimmy got to his feet. Trying not to look at Willie's pain-twisted face, he reached down and picked up the gun, the snap of the broken bone still echoing in his ears.

"Thanks," Frank Globe gasped, leaning against a counter. His face was dead white. "When he said that about Mae, I fell apart. It was a dumb thing to do. I didn't have a thing back here for a weapon, and he'd have gotten me sure."

"Don't thank me," Jimmy said. "I'd have been next and I sure wasn't in the mood for that."

Willie groaned as Frank went back to call the police. Jimmy waited patiently. The police could put off taking down his story until tomorrow.

Right now he wanted to find Sharon. There was something that he had to say to her.

Only three words, but they meant a lot.

14

Lucy was tired, but she didn't mind the walk from the shack to the hospital. She went to see Luke every evening and she felt guilty for not going in the afternoon, too. But afternoons she had the farmer boy in to help her with the bait, and she was too busy with customers. She was even getting so she didn't mind handling the worms and crawlers, and she had learned how to handle the crawfish to avoid their pincers.

The hospital was nice, and the people working there treated her as if she was somebody. It was a good feeling, one that she'd never had before. And she felt even better when she sat down beside Luke's bed.

The trouble was that he hadn't been talking much, just about how she was managing with the bait and the boy, and everything inside her was crying out for something solid to hang onto. His hospital insurance paid for a private room, but either because of Luke's own shyness, or the cast on his leg, there hadn't been anything between them. When she thought about it—as she did most of the time—the physical part of her life with a man didn't seem as important as the man himself. Oh, she wanted him, as any girl might want a man she loved, but her want went beyond the brief momentary thrill that was all she had known before. With Luke, she was sure, she would have an experience that would overreach anything she had ever known. Lucy knew it would be something very special. But maybe Luke didn't want what she did. That was a worrisome thought.

The hospital room door was open and she went in smiling, trying to think only of him and not of herself. The break hadn't been a bad one, serious as it had seemed when she had found him along the river bank, and it wouldn't be long before he would be back. They could keep the boy on to do the active work, and he could sit around selling bait.

"You're late," he said but he didn't sound angry. "Almost ten minutes late."

"It's hot. I guess I walked slower than usual."

She brushed his lips with her mouth, as she always did, and sat down on the edge of the bed. He was propped up in bed and he had some paper in front of him. She noticed there were lines drawn on the paper.

"I'm no good at this sort of thing," he said and pushed the paper aside. "It comes out almost the way I want, and then I find I haven't got any closet space."

"I don't understand," she said.

He took one of her hands and held it. His hand was big and powerful, like the rest of him, but that night along the river she had been his strength. She had helped him back to the shack and then she had gone to the next house to call for an ambulance.

"I guess it's my fault," he said slowly. "I haven't told you anything, but I've been thinking about it. My insurance will take care of all of my expenses here and I've got some money put away in the bank. I can dig my own well and we can get some land away from the river so we can build a house. I couldn't ask you to live in that shack, and anyway, I was getting fed up with it. Then you have to think about having a family, and things ought to be decent."

She didn't know why she was crying, but she was. She didn't sob, but the tears rolled down her cheeks and she blinked her eyes furiously. He was talking about a home and children. While she probably wanted these things as much as he did, she couldn't hurt him. She would rather lose him than bring pain into his life.

"You don't know what you're talking about," she said weakly. "Remember while we were waiting for the ambulance? I told you what I was, what I had done—about the men and getting pregnant. I didn't leave anything out. I thought we were finished, that I wouldn't see you again, and somehow I had to let you know. I didn't want you remembering me as being somebody I wasn't."

He lifted her hand to his lips and kissed the tips of her fingers. "You didn't have to come in with me, Lucy. You could have left me there by the shack and the men in the ambulance would have found me. But you stuck, knowing that it meant being picked up by the police. Not many girls would have done that."

"I don't know," she said, and some of the tears stopped. "If you honestly want to help somebody, you don't think about the consequences. And it worked out all right. The police know who held me up, and I don't have that to worry about."

She paused and fell into a deep silence. She didn't have to go over that again. It had been in the papers, and he knew. And he knew more about her than what had appeared in the papers. She hadn't spared herself while they had been waiting for the ambulance.

"It isn't what you were," she heard him say. "It's what you are today and what you'll be tomorrow that counts. I've got some black marks against me, too, but I think I can be a good husband and a good father." He kissed the tips of her fingers again. "Maybe we aren't much, either one of us, but that doesn't say that we can't become better people if we are willing to help each other. Know what I mean, hon?"

This time she did sob as she turned to him, but now she was smiling and the look in her eyes drove deep into his, the look pulling them closer together until their lips touched, at first lightly, and then with the beautiful fury of love.

She closed her eyes and became lost in the kiss.

At last she had found a man with faith and courage.

It was up to her to match what she had found.

Sharon was humming as she finished hanging the new curtains, and then at the postman's double ring, she went downstairs to get the mail. There was an envelope from her insurance agent and a couple of ads. One ad was from an insurance company that insured people up to the age of eighty, regardless of health, and the other ad promised untold riches to anybody who was sucker enough to fill out and return the coupon. Back upstairs she threw the ads away, saving the best of the mail until last. Inside the envelope she found a check from her insurance company. It wasn't enough to cover the loss caused by the fire, but it was still pretty big.

She kissed the check, thinking of Jimmy and laughing a little as she did so, and put it away in the dish closet. Sometimes at night, after they finished doing what most married people did, they had talked about this money. Sharon had thought of using it right away, but Jimmy had insisted that it be put aside as an educational fund.

During these talks she had come to know a different Jimmy. He wanted to stand on his own two feet, earn a living for them, and she had to admit that he had gotten off to a fine start. Of course, this apartment wasn't like the one she'd had on Park Place, but it was their home and she loved every foot of it. As soon as he was firmly established they could buy new furniture and that would make it even better. The only purchase they had made since their marriage had been a new bed and mattress, plus springs, and since he didn't finish work until ten or eleven at night, they had spent most of their time in the bedroom.

The night of their marriage—there hadn't been time for a real honeymoon—she had been more than half-scared, afraid that she would be unable to find herself as a woman. She had quickly learned that her fears had been unfounded. Sober, and in love with her man, she had crept into his arms in the darkness. There she had discovered what it was like to be a whole woman. It hadn't been Jimmy who had awakened her at five in the morning. She had aroused him, her hunger beyond control, and she hadn't let him go back to sleep again.

There was a paper on the table but she didn't look at it. Both the papers were filled with details about Robinson, about the vicious organization that he had controlled, and she was tired of reading about it. She asked only to forget what had almost happened to her, and to be left alone. That way, side by side, they could help each other build a solid future. There had been enough questions by the police, and she only hoped that she wouldn't have to appear as a witness at any trial that might come up.

The apartment was warm, and she slipped out of her dress. She wore nothing underneath, but she seldom did when she was alone like this. Just before she expected Jimmy she'd slip on a robe, but that was usually a waste of time. He wouldn't eat his late dinner until afterward, the dinner getting cold while they were in the bedroom, and later they would have a couple of beers and talk about the day. She didn't keep anything to drink in the apartment, and she didn't miss it. No longer was it necessary for her to hide behind the false emotions that came from a bottle of booze.

There wasn't anything for her to do, so she went in and stretched out on the bed.

Within minutes she was asleep.

Jimmy took longer than he usually did to put things away, but customers kept stopping in and interrupting his work. He didn't mind that. Customers meant money, and some of them had become his friends.

He had tripled Frank's business and that was because he was drawing trade from all over town. Of course some of the people wanted to talk about Robinson, getting him to explain those savage seconds with Willie, but he couldn't say any more than what the papers said. What he really knew, his statements backed up by Frank, would come out at the trial and not before—the district attorney had warned him about that.

Robinson, his evil empire crumbling around him, had tried to pass the blame down the line, but it hadn't stuck. His own girls had turned against him and any number of charges could have been thrown his way. Of course, the grand jury had indicted him on each count—as well as indicting the previous judge for forgery—but the sensational and most serious thing was the murder of the girl on the bridge, and this was coming up first with both Willie and Robinson as defendants. Willie had broken, signing a complete confession of everything in the hope that the law would go easy on him, but there was little chance of that. Robinson had ordered the killing but Willie had done the job—that tied both of them up together. A conviction was almost certain, the chair within easy reach. And of course, others in the organization would serve time.

Jimmy began unpacking a carton of candy, his thoughts on the events of the past week. He had to give credit to the police. They had moved fast that night, calling in extra men for duty, and nobody had gotten away. Even Frank's unfaithful girl friend had been picked up for rolling a man, and she'd had the man's wallet in her pocketbook. She was with the rest of them, in jail where she belonged.

"You can take over the store," Frank had told Jimmy. "You can pay off my lawyer as you go along, and when I get out I'll have a stake to make a start somewhere else."

It had sounded like a good offer, and Jimmy had gone for it. The building and the furniture in the apartment upstairs had been included in the deal and his monthly payment wasn't too high. Working for himself was a lot better than learning the plumbing trade. The owner of the shop had contacted him about taking up where he had left off—Benny had been fired—but he had turned it down.

Yesterday Lucy had stopped in for a moment and she had seemed happy enough. He had wondered, talking to her, what he had ever thought he had seen in her, shape or no shape, but he guessed it had just been a normal desire to help somebody who was in trouble. But that was done with; she didn't have any trouble. She had her man, and Jimmy was glad for her.

He lit a cigarette and leaned upon the counter. Some of the customers he got surprised him. Like that salesman Sharon had been dating before her marriage. He came in for cartons of cigarettes when he was in town. Jimmy grinned. The last time he'd stopped in he'd had a red-headed number with him who looked hot enough to burn the paint off the walls. She'd sure showed off her cleavage, but when Jimmy had gone upstairs that night he'd forgotten all about it. The real thing had been waiting for him up there and nobody knew better than he did that he was married to one hell of a woman. When he had been going to bed with her on West Avenue she had been a convenience, but now she was a necessity. It was different with them from what it had been in his room, as different as night and day.

Yawning, he looked at the clock. The only bad feature about the store was the long hours, but he had arranged to take care of that. There was a woman down the street who would use a few extra bucks until her husband returned to work—a couple of new factories were moving into town, one very big. While the woman minded the store he could relax for two or three hours during the afternoon. He hadn't mentioned this to Sharon, but he knew that she would go for it.

The woman came in while he was putting out the cigarette. She had helped Frank one time when Frank had had the flu, and Jimmy didn't have to show her how to do anything.

"Don't you worry none," she said as he went out. "You just get a good rest."

There was nobody in the living room when he entered the apartment and he walked back to the bedroom. He smiled in appreciation when he saw her sprawled out on the bed, the sight of her nude body making his head pound.

Anxiously he undressed and dropped down beside her. She stirred, her eyes coming open, and he laughed as he bent down to kiss her.

The woman had been wrong about his getting a good rest.

So wrong that he was more than an hour late getting back to the store.

Some things just won't keep.

The End

Orrie Hitt Definitive Bibliography

(all paperbacks unless noted)

I'll Call Every Monday (Red Lantern HC, 1953; Beacon, 1954)

Love in the Arctic (Red Lantern HC, 1953)

Cabin Fever (Uni-Book, 1954; Beacon, 1959, as Tawny; Softcover Library UK, 1974, as Lovers at Night)

She Got What She Wanted (Beacon, 1954)

Shabby Street (Beacon, 1954)

Leased w/Jack Woodford (Signature HC, 1954; revised by Hitt & retitled Trapped)

Teaser (Woodford HC, 1956; Beacon, 1957; Lancer, 1963)

Unfaithful Wives (Beacon, 1956)

The Sucker (Beacon, 1957)

Nudist Camp (Beacon, 1957)

Pushover (Beacon, 1957)

The Promoter (Beacon, 1957)

Ladies' Man (Beacon, 1957)

Dolls and Dues (Beacon, 1957)

Trailer Tramp (Beacon, 1957)

Devil in the Flesh (Valentine HC, 1957; Kozy, 1960, as Sins of Flesh)

Ellie's Shack (Beacon, 1958)

Suburban Wife (Beacon, 1958)

Summer Hotel (Beacon, 1958)

Wild Oats (Beacon, 1958)

Affairs of a Beauty Queen (Beacon, 1958)

Call South 3300: Ask for Molly! (Beacon, 1958)

Burlesque Girl (Beacon, 1958)

Trapped (Beacon, 1958)

Girl's Dormitory (Beacon, 1958)

Woman Hunt (Beacon, 1958)

Hot Cargo (Beacon, 1958)

The Cheat (Beacon, 1958)

Rotten to the Core (Beacon, 1958)

Love Princess (Saber, 1958)

Hotel Women (Vantage HC, 1958)

Hotel Confidential (Vantage HC, 1958)

Sheba (Beacon, 1959)

The Widow (Beacon, 1959)

Add Flesh to the Fire (Beacon, 1959)

Private Club (Beacon, 1959)

Carnival Girl (Beacon, 1959)

The Peeper (Beacon, 1959; Softcover Library UK, 1973, as Twisted Passion)

Too Hot to Handle (Beacon, 1959)
Sin Doll (Beacon, 1959; Softcover Library UK, 1973, as The
    Excesses of Cherry)
Ex-Virgin (Beacon, 1959; UK Softcover Library, 1969, as Made for
    Man)
Suburban Sin (Beacon, 1959)
Pleasure Ground (Bedside, 1959; Kozy, 1961)
Affair With Lucy (Midwood, 1959; Midwood, 1961, as Married
    Mistress)
Girl of the Streets (Midwood, 1959)
Summer Romance (Midwood, 1959)
As Bad as They Come (Midwood, 1959; Midwood, 1962, as Mail
    Order Sex)
Hotel Woman (Valentine HC, 1959; Kozy, 1960, as Hotel Hostess)
Wayward Girl (Beacon, 1960)
The Torrid Teens (Beacon, 1960)
From Door to Door (Beacon, 1960)
Motel Girls (Beacon, 1960)
Tell Them Anything (Beacon, 1960)
Call Me Bad (Beacon, 1960; Softcover Library, 1970)
Untamed Lust (Beacon, 1960)
Never Cheat Alone (Beacon, 1960)
The Lady is a Lush (Beacon, 1960)
Sexurbia County (Beacon, 1960)
Tramp Wife (Chariot, 1960)
Hotel Girl (Chariot, 1960)
Lonely Flesh (Chariot, 1960; reprinted 1963 as Lola)
Suburban Interlude (Kozy, 1960)
The Cheaters (Midwood, 1960)
A Doctor and His Mistress (Midwood, 1960)
Two of a Kind (Midwood, 1960)
I Prowl by Night (Beacon, 1961)
Dirt Farm (Beacon, 1961; Softcover Library UK, 1968, as The Hired
    Man)
Summer of Sin (Beacon, 1961)
Four Women (Beacon, 1961)
The Love Season (Beacon, 1961)
Frigid Wife (Beacon, 1961)
Virgins No More (Beacon, 1961)
Party Doll (Chariot, 1961)
Strange Longing (Chariot, 1961; reprinted as Female Doctor, 1963)
Man's Nurse (Chariot, 1961)
Hot Blood (Chariot, 1961)
Diploma Dolls (Kozy, 1961)
Dark Passions (Kozy, 1961)

Twisted Lovers (Kozy, 1961)
Suburban Trap (Kozy, 1961)
Carnival Honey (Kozy, 1961)
Wild Lovers (Kozy, 1961)
Easy Women! (Novel, 1961; reprinted 1963 as Inflamed Dames,
    1964 as Love Seekers, 1965 as Jenkins' Lovers)
Shocking Mistress! (Novel, 1961)
Peeping Tom (Wisdom House, 1961)
Love Thief (Beacon, 1962)
Dial "M" for Man (Beacon, 1962)
Torrid Cheat (Chariot, 1962)
Twin Beds (Chariot, 1962)
Naked Model (Chariot, 1962)
Libby Sin (Chariot, 1962)
Passion Street (Chariot, 1962)
Bad Wife (Chariot, 1962)
Passion Hostess (Chariot, 1962)
Bold Affair (Kozy, 1962)
Campus Tramp (Kozy, 1962)
The Naked Flesh (Kozy, 1962)
Violent Sinners (Kozy, 1962)
Love Slave (Kozy, 1962)
Frustrated Females! (Novel, 1962; reprinted 1963 as I Need a Man!)
Warped Woman (Novel, 1962; reprinted 1963 as Taboo Thrills,
    1964 as Wilma's Wants)
Abnormal Norma (Novel, 1962)
Bed Crazy (Novel, 1962; reprinted 1964 as Perverted Doctors)
Man-Hungry Female (Novel, 1962; reprinted 1964 as More! More!
    More!)
Carnival Sin/Playpet (Vest-Pocket, 1962)
Torrid Wench (Kozy, 1963)
Strip Alley (Kozy, 1963)
Nude Doll (Kozy, 1963)
Loose Women (Lancer Domino, 1963)
An American Sodom (Novel, 1963)
Male Lover (Gaslight, 1964)
Passion Pool (Lancer Domino, 1964)
The Color of Lust (Lancer Domino, 1964)
The Passion Hunters (Lancer Domino, 1964; Domino, 1966 as This
    Wild Desire)
Lust Prowl (Lancer Domino, 1964)
The Love Seekers (Novel, 1964)
The Tavern (Softcover Library, 1966)
Woman's Ward (Softcover Library, 1966)
While the City Sins (Ember Library, 1967)

The Sex Pros (Beacon, 1968; Softcover Library UK as Cindy)
Panda Bear Passion (P.E.C., 1968)
Nude Model (MacFadden, 1970)

As by Kay Addams
Queer Patterns (Beacon, 1959)
Warped Desire (Beacon, 1960; Softcover Library UK as Night of
    Desire, 1975)
Lucy (Beacon, 1960; Softcover Library UK as Beautiful Tramp,
    1972)
Three Strange Women (Beacon, 1960)
The Strangest Sin (Beacon, 1961)
The Autobiography of Kay Addams (Novel, 1962; aka The Secret
    Perversions of Kay Addams, possible reprint as My Lesbian
    Loves, Novel, 1964)
My Secret Perversions (Novel, 1962; reprinted as Hidden Hungers)
My Wild Nights With Nine Nudists! (Novel, 1963; reprinted as
    Nocturnal Nudists)
My Two Strangest Lovers (Novel, 1963; reprinted 1964 as Beyond
    Love)
Cherry (Novel, 1963)

As by Joe Black (as told to Hitt)
Unnatural Urge (Midwood, 1962)

As by Roger Normandie (co-authored with Joe Weiss)
Run for Cover (Key HC, 1957; as Race With Lust, Kozy, 1959)
Web of Evil (Key HC, 1957)
The Lion's Den (Key HC, 1957; as Tormented Passions, Kozy,
    1959)

As by Charles Verne (co-authored with Joe Weiss)
Mr. Hot Rod (Key HC, 1957)
The Wheel of Passion (Key HC, 1957)

As by Nicky Weaver
Love, Blood and Tears (Kozy, 1963)
Love or Kill Them All (Kozy, 1963)

Short Stories
Nothing in My Way (*Smashing Detective Stories*, July 1955)